THE BETTING VOW

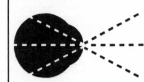

This Large Print Book carries the
Seal of Approval of N.A.V.H.

AN UNCONVENTIONAL BRIDES
ROMANCE

THE BETTING VOW

K.M. JACKSON

THORNDIKE PRESS
A part of Gale, a Cengage Company

Farmington Hills, Mich • San Francisco • New York • Waterville, Maine
Meriden, Conn • Mason, Ohio • Chicago

Copyright © 2017 by Kwana Jackson.
Thorndike Press, a part of Gale, a Cengage Company.

ALL RIGHTS RESERVED
Thorndike Press® Large Print African-American.
The text of this Large Print edition is unabridged.
Other aspects of the book may vary from the original edition.
Set in 16 pt. Plantin.

LIBRARY OF CONGRESS CIP DATA ON FILE.
CATALOGUING IN PUBLICATION FOR THIS BOOK
IS AVAILABLE FROM THE LIBRARY OF CONGRESS

ISBN-13: 978-1-4328-4570-4 (hardcover)

Published in 2018 by arrangement with Dafina Books, an imprint of
Kensington Publishing Corp.

Printed in the United States of America
1 2 3 4 5 6 7 22 21 20 19 18

To Will,
I'm so glad you bet on me.

ACKNOWLEDGMENTS

First and always, I want to thank God for all my blessings, those seen and unseen. The words "Thank you" could never be enough.

Writing the novels in the Unconventional Bride Series has been a true joy, and I'd like to give never-ending words of thanks and praise to my editor, Selena James, for the amazing opportunity. I'd also like to thank the entire team at Kensington Books for their care with the series. You all are a joy to work with.

Thank you once again to my dear husband, Will. You have been my constant strength and support. Your love has guided me forward all these years. I'm so grateful to have you in my life.

My gratitude also goes to my children, Kayla and William. You are and will always be my forever reason for striding on. Thank you for being the amazing young adults you are. I'm so proud of you both.

And I wish to express my gratitude to my family for never wavering in cheering me on. Thank you for always being there for me. I love you always.

To my dear writer buds who come to the page and grind it out in the most wonderfully creative ways, you all inspire me to do more and be better. Thank you for your magic.

And now to my readers. I'm always astounded and deeply humbled that someone has read my words. I'm so grateful for each and every one of you. Thank you from every part of my heart.

CHAPTER 1

Balancing on the hood of a sports car while slickly oiled up was a lot harder than most people imagined. Add to that doing it hands free, because you've got your hands wrapped around a fully loaded burger. Plus, you are in a bikini and are wearing six-inch stilettos. Well, then, you've got yourself a straight-up high-wire act.

Leila Darling tried her best to suck in her stomach, push out her behind, while simultaneously "making love" to the camera by puffing out her lips into a sultry, come-hither pout. She narrowed her eyes ever so slightly, as if extending a welcome invitation to wanton sex, while still appearing approachable with her version of the ever popular smize. Why it took this much sex to sell a hamburger still baffled her, but hers was not to reason why, since she was getting paid a small ransom to sit on the shiny car, be extra shiny herself, and make the

Barn Burger the most lusted-after burger in fast-food history.

"Give me more. Give me more!" yelled Matteo, the famed photographer, fighting to be heard over the blaring bass of the heart-thumping rock music in the studio. If you could call the rented garage space in a rather sketchy part of East LA a studio. The tips of Matteo's dark hair, what little he had left, were bleached and spiked so that they stood up at odd angles, and he wore an excessive amount of kohl around his eyes, making his deep under-eye bags all the more pronounced.

"That's right, Leila. Just like that. Oh, darling, you are selling it. Those eyes, those breasts . . . I'm getting hungry just watching you. You're a sexual beast, *darling!*"

Leila pushed back a sneer at the way the word *darling* rolled off his tongue. Though it was her last name, in her case the word could be used as a proper noun, an adjective, or sadly, as of late, a verb. "Pulling a darling" was, now thanks to social media, used for all sorts of things, and none of them good. Such as wild clubbing until the wee hours of the morning. Though, for the life of her, Leila didn't understand what was wrong with blowing off a bit of steam. Or it was used when one threw a fit. Though in

Leila's eyes, demanding respect, even if it was in a forceful tone, was essential in her business.

But worst, in her eyes, was that now — thanks to her ex, well, her third ex-fiancé, Miles G, and that crappy song of his, "Darling Leila" — "pulling a darling" was synonymous with being a man-eater who used men, made them fall in love, but never committed to them. Of course, it didn't matter that in all her terminal relationships, it was the guys who'd failed her, making promises they ultimately had no intentions of keeping. Giving her perfectly valid reasons to bail on the so-called relationships.

So today, with Leila's nerves already frayed, Matteo's use of the word *darling* slid over Leila in a way that was too slimy and too personal and had her questioning his usage altogether. In the end, the sneer won out, and Leila went with it, her top lip curling as she looked at the photographer. Besides, the "sexual beast" comment had got to her, too. Especially now, when Leila considered herself in a career transition. She couldn't just let a comment like that go unchecked.

Sure she knew she should be happy and feel accomplished as one of the few African American top models in the business, though her current position of burger eating slash car hood bikini balancing would bring one to question that fact. Still, most would think Leila had it all and was living on top, but in reality, she felt something was sorely lacking. Respect. Leila wanted so very much to be seen as more than a sexy body that could sell anything, be it fast food or French couture.

Leila inwardly sighed as she recalled, while balancing herself precariously, one leg cocked up, the other pushing hard into the hood of the sports car, that a little over a month ago she'd been in Cannes, being celebrated as a breakout star in a less than breakout movie. Sure, she might have had only a few actual lines in the movie, and yes, she'd been brought on for her looks. However, she'd taken that part and ran with it. Showing she had chops, and for that she'd been rewarded for something besides the way she filled out a bikini top. Leila wanted more of that.

But here she was, back home in the States and back to the same grind. *Stand. Sit. Turn this way. Tilt that way.* Was it any wonder she was on edge? Add to it the fact that taking an early flight back from Cannes had resulted in the demise of yet another high-profile relationship when she caught Miles in his words, "just doing what he do," horizontally with the skank du jour. Well Leila was officially done with her life as usual.

"Now take a bite. We want to see you eat it," Matteo said, his voice piercing Leila's musings and pinging her nerve endings with its raw excitement, so much so that Leila didn't quite know if he was talking about the burger or something else that she didn't want to touch.

Leila let out a low breath and went in for the burger, but then, as if on cue, the music in the studio changed and on came the familiar first thumps to the song Leila was fast growing to hate. "Darling Leila." Would she ever escape Miles or that damned song? And really *Darling Leila*? Talk about an unoriginal name. The jerk didn't have an original bone in his overly hyped body let alone thought in that little brain of his.

"Oh yeah!" Matteo yelled, now smiling wide and circling her with his camera as he clicked, clicked around her. Each click of the shutter felt like a tiny prick to her skin.

Leila shot Matteo a death stare but then forced her features to soften as she glanced over to the side of the room and saw the group of execs from Burger Barn huddled in the corner, looking at her expectantly.

Bills needed to be paid, and for that to happen, the customer was always right. Leila reminded herself of this tried-and-true mantra as she let out a sigh and further softened her features, going on automatic pilot as she mentally blocked out the song that mocked her and Miles's now failed relationship and, worse, all her relationships before that. She took a hungry bite of the burger, imagining for a moment that it was the head of the photographer.

Method acting. Zone it out, woman. Use that anger.

Just then her agent and longtime friend, Jasper Weston, stepped into her side view as he went over to glad-hand the Burger Barn folks. Leila took another bite of the burger. This time it was Jasper's head she was biting off, as she remembered it was he who had told her that taking this job would be a good idea.

"That's it, Leila," Matteo finally said. "Though, maybe next time you could go at it with just a little less enthusiasm?" He lowered his camera and turned toward his group of assistants. Leila noted that they were all young and all blond, whether male or female with slightly vacant eyes. It would seem Matteo had a type and stuck to it through and through.

"We're going to need another burger on set," he said to no one in particular before turning back to Leila. She hoped that the actual food handlers picked up on his query and that it wouldn't be one of the Stepford blonds who handed her the next burger. "How about we get ready for the next set and wardrobe change, but before that we'll do the rain sequence?"

Rain sequence? Since when was a rain sequence on the shoot list? Leila thought as she looked around for a rain machine. She saw none. It was then that another on set blond assistant came over and took the burger missing two bites from Leila's hands and scurried off into the background. Then another young blond came toward her with a large hose and a dubious look in her eyes. Instantly, Leila stiffened.

"No way, honey," Leila said with a sharp look at the young woman. "You come at me with that hose, you'd better be prepared to eat it." It was as if the whole garage had got put on mute, as all heads swiveled Leila's way. She saw Jasper smile uncomfortably at the Burger Barn people and take a step forward.

"Aw, come on now, Leila, darling," Matteo began. "We need a shot with you wet on top of the car. You moving around for me.

Doing a little dance. Selling those burgers as only you can." And with that, the damned near geriatric photographer standing in front of her, holding his camera at his side, mimed his version of sexy dance moves, rubbing his hands over his body, bringing them up and, to Leila's revulsion, licking his fingers.

Leila looked at him in horror and then blinked her way out of the shock of it all and leveled him with a hard glare. "Like I said, little Miss Assistant of the Corn here is not coming near me with some dirty-assed water hose. Now, if you want to try, you can, but I warn you, you won't like where the hose ends up in the end."

And with that, Leila slid her oiled body off the car as gracefully as she could and walked off set toward her makeshift dressing room, Jasper following quickly behind.

"You almost had a grand slam with this one, Walker. Almost."

Carter Bain watched Grayson Hill, the CFO of Hillibrand Inc., give his critique of their weeklong schmooze fest. All he could hear was the admonishment in the loaded word *almost*. Screw almost. He'd wanted to hit it out of the park. He hadn't come all the way out to California to take on the launch of Sphere, World Broadcasting's new nightly station programming, for an "almost."

Carter's boss and mentor, Everett Walker, shook Greyson's hand and nodded. "Don't worry. You just get your ads ready. By the time we're in place for pilot filming, all will be perfect and vendors will be clamoring for spots. You'll want to be in on the ground floor with this one."

Greyson raised a skeptical bushy gray brow. "I hope so, because I see a lot that we think may have potential, with the right players. Especially that *Brentwood* concept, but you have to get bang-up talent behind it. All that deep thinking programming may be fine for cable and those O channel guru–loving ladies, but we can't forget the males from eighteen to twenty-four while still capturing the thirty-five-plus moms. We want the kind of shows that are worth them streaming on their tablets, as well as getting the ladies checking in and tweeting live. The way we see it, the moms are the destination watchers, and they are harder to pull away from the shows they're already loyal to. So it's new viewers you're going to have to scramble for. And to get the young males, there is only one tried-and-true way, and that is to pull them in with sex. Give them something to come for, and keep them coming so they stay." With that statement, Greyson gave a pointed turn of the head toward Carter's assistant, Karen.

To keep his job in place and the potential ad revenue still in play, Carter chose to ignore the look, but still he stepped into Greyson's field of vision. "Thank you, Mr. Hill. Your insight is very much appreciated. But believe me, you don't have to worry about *Brentwood* or any of our upcoming shows. We have a long line of A-listers fighting for casting consideration." Carter feigned a humble look. "Unfortunately, due to some contractual obligations and the way the press works, we're not at liberty to share them yet. I'll just say, be prepared to be wowed at our next meeting." He gave Greyson a wink and a pat on his shoulder.

Greyson looked over at his brothers, the Hill Pack, and gave a short snort. "I sure hope so," he said before turning back to Everett. "You've got a real go-getter in this one," he said, indicating Carter. "He's hungry. I like that."

Everett looked Carter's way and gave a nod. "That he is. Carter is one of the best. When there is a job to be done, I can always count on him. Like he said, there's no need to worry. You all just get your ads lined up.

18

Let us handle the programming."

Carter shook Greyson's hand a final time. "I'll have my assistant e-mail yours with all the details of our meeting and the kits."

Carter then turned his attention toward Greyson's brother Waymon. Next to him were Bret and Cliff. It would seem the rumor about the Hills traveling in packs had officially been confirmed. At least when it came to getting off their property in Tennessee and coming out to California to do business with the so called "city folk". They all had thick accents, but Carter had no doubt it was more for show than anything else. You didn't run a multinational company with businesses in the food, media, and technology industries, not to mention exert political influence that went deep, or so the rumors said, while being country bumpkins. But, hey, Carter could play along. Anything to seal the deal. If he had to, he'd chew tobacco and don a pair of overalls to bring in their ad commitment.

Still, it was with relief that Carter stood beside Everett and Karen outside World Broadcasting's California studios and watched the limo take the Hill clan away, their expressions all nearly frozen in place as they waved their final good-byes. The next car to pull up was Everett's. No limo

19

this time. It was a not so understated Mercedes convertible. Everett turned to the duo and shook Karen's hand first.

"You did an outstanding job this week, Karen. I know a lot was thrown your way, but you stepped up to the plate. Carter's lucky to have you on his team."

Karen smiled as she returned the handshake. "Thank you, sir. Just doing my job."

"You do it well. Never sell yourself short."

He turned to Carter, sobering. "You both did very well. But Greyson is right, there is room for improvement. I want this account. If we get Hillibrand, then more vendors will follow suit. Don't make a liar out of me. I expect to have a short list of names ready by next week to consider for *Brentwood.*"

Carter fought to stay cool and keep from frowning. He had known this would come up with Everett, but he had thought he'd maybe get a five-minute congratulatory breather. Hell, who was he fooling? This was Everett Walker. He wasn't into pats on the back, and he definitely wasn't into giving breathers. It was part of the reason Carter admired him. Carter had always respected Everett's no-nonsense business manner and drive. It was so different from his upbringing, where his business sense and appreciation of capitalism were considered a fault.

Coming from a working class family, you'd think his accomplishments would be celebrated, but to his bohemian parents, they were more of an embarrassment.

Still, he couldn't complain all that much on the parental front. Though he'd been poor, Carter counted himself lucky having grown up with both a mother and a father in the home. His father, Malcolm, was an artist who was a jack-of-all-trades and a master of none, and his mother, Faye, was a woman with an obsession for helping those less fortunate, which only came second to her obsession with trying to manage her only son's life.

"Don't worry, sir," Carter said, "I have some ideas in the works. We'll discuss them next week."

Everett pulled off, leaving Carter and Karen standing together, once again with plastered-on smiles, as they mumbled behind clenched teeth and waved. Karen let out a grumble before she spoke aloud.

"I'm so glad this week is over. I've had enough California sunshine to last me awhile, thank you very much. And I swear, if that little perv, Cliff Hill took one more leering look at my boobs, I was going to gouge his eyes out. It wasn't only the older Hill who couldn't keep his eyes to himself."

Carter's smile wavered ony slightly as he gave Karen a quick glance and continued to wave at Everett's car. Part of him couldn't blame the Hills. His assistant, Karen Woodley, was a good-looking woman, he supposed. But it didn't matter, since Karen was a part of his staff, which put her in the off-limits category. And since she was his assistant, in a weird sort of way, Carter felt that put her under his protection. He knew it wasn't entirely true, and was clearly overstepping on his part, but still he wouldn't have her messed with or in any way disrespected.

Despite word on the street about his slick reputation, he did have a conscience. It was that same conscience that kept every woman on his staff off-limits in his book. Sex was one thing, but it didn't trump money in the bank.

"Thanks for not gouging his eyes out," Carter said, addressing Karen's comment about Cliff. "At least not just yet. Let's get all the signatures we need from them and seal this deal first, and then you can gouge away. Metaphorically, of course. Hell, I'll do it for you. Hey, at least you didn't have Waymon breathing down your neck. The man was looking at my package like I was fresh crab legs just put out at Caesar's buffet."

At that comment, Karen pulled a face, and he couldn't help laughing. The car turned out of sight, and they both put their hands down and shook their heads.

"You think his wife knows?" Carter asked.

Karen nodded. "Probably so. Believe me, even if she says she doesn't, she has a clue. The wife always knows . . . something."

Carter shrugged. Given that she was twice divorced, he figured Karen knew what she was talking about, so he just deferred to her on such subjects. Besides, he steered clear of romantic attachments. Nobody was ever on the up and up. At least not when it came to matters of the heart. His parents were the rare exceptions and he was sure last holdouts of a bygone era. And he wasn't swayed in the least by his best buds falling so hard that they both went the commitment route. Hell, part of him felt bad seeing them as whipped as they were.

Not him, though. No way. That was why he'd rather stick to business. At least across a boardroom table, a man looked you in the eye before stabbing you in the back. Not that he didn't love women and indulge in his fair share of them. It was just that he wasn't foolish enough to believe in the fallacy of true love, trust, soul mates, forever and all that bull. He'd had his fair share of women who'd been with him for what he could do for them and then hit the road when he'd taken them as far as his position would go. So yeah, he had learned his lessons about love and found it best to leave the fiction for what he was producing for the small screen.

Carter let out a breath and tugged at his collar before looking up at the blazing sun. "How can something so beautiful be so torturous? What is with this freaking heat?"

Karen shrugged. Her sleeveless white blouse and black skirt had remained unwrinkled. "Well, it would help if you dressed a little less for New York and a lot more for California. You could practically choke on that tie of yours. You look like you're ready for fall in London instead of spring in California." She arched a brow. "And is a bow tie necessary?"

Carter's brow rose. "Yeah. It is. Besides, it won over ole Greyson. We were matching."

Karen let out a snort. "Matching. Ah, now I get it. Knowing you, you did that on purpose."

Carter grinned, and Karen's eyes went skyward. "I swear, is there anything you won't do to make a deal?"

Carter put his finger to his temple and feigned thinking. "Not that I can come up with."

Karen shook her head. "That's what I'm afraid of."

Carter let out a snort. "Tell that to your holiday bonus."

With that, Karen held up a hand. "You win. The tie is a perfect touch." She pointed to her feet and looked down. "Somebody has to keep me in these fancy shoes."

Carter laughed, relieved to have the dog and pony show over, as they walked back inside the studio. The lights had been dimmed, and the stars — what few they had and what few they could call stars — had all left, as had the live studio audience from the last taping. Today they had tested a pilot for a family comedy with quintuplets that so far had received high test ratings. It was risky, but they were using actual quints to star in the key roles. Carter knew it was a big gamble, but each time he'd had *The Morning Show* broadcast an update on the "miracle babies," their ratings had gone through the roof. Why not try to re-create that magic in prime time?

So as not to be considered too far off his rocker, though, Carter had been smart enough to cast actual actors in the lead parental roles. This was much to the chagrin of the quints' mother, but the blow was softened by the fact that her sub was a very well-known blond beauty who in her heyday had turned quite a few heads by being the lead in a top lifeguard dramedy.

But that was just one of the shows they'd gotten settled. There was still plenty to do back in New York, where most of the productions would take place and where World Broadcasting was headquartered. Carter knew he'd be spending a little time in LA, but he was thankful that shooting was moving east and he wouldn't have to upend his life completely. California was nice, but all this sunshine could turn a guy's brain to mush. Hell, this week alone had put him halfway there. The Hills liked to party, and hard. They might be older, but they came with stamina to spare, both natural and, he suspected, in some cases pharmaceutical. Each night he and the rest of the network's team had taken them to a different hot spot, where they'd been wined and dined in the VIP lounge. Due to the company going liberal with the tipping and bottle service, and the Hills heavily greasing the right palms at the after parties, they had never been without arm candy as they made their way back to their hotel villas.

But the partying only got so hard for Carter. He knew that keeping a clear head at all times was paramount on this trip. He was there for the clients. His pleasure would come when the deal was inked. Getting a woman to warm his bed, well, that was easy. All he had to do was make a call, but he didn't need any distractions or possible entanglements. These next few months — hell, the next year — were too important. Everett had put a lot in his hands this time, and it was up to him to pass or fail this most important of tests.

And Carter was sure many were expecting him to fail. Maybe even wanting him to fail. Sure, he'd heard the watercooler talk of how he'd gotten as far as he had only because he'd been close friends with Everett's son, Aidan, all these years. And yes, being friends with Aidan had maybe gotten him in the door. But Everett didn't play when it came to his money or his business. It was Carter's hard work and determination that had kicked the door down, and it was that same determination that would take him to the very top.

If he'd learned anything from his parents, who worked hard on their respective endeavors but didn't have his same drive, it was that hope and a righteous cause didn't pay the rent. The lights got left on due to cold, hard cash. As a family, they had had their lean years of living hand to mouth and had even endured the embarrassment of living off the mercy of the system. Coming home from his fancy Upper East Side school, where he was on a scholarship, and being hit by a red eviction notice on his door had taught him early on that the streets were paved with promises and good intentions, but it was cash that made the world go around and kept a roof over one's head. Not that Carter had any animosity or regrets. He considered his past nothing but a supersize classroom, one that had taught him that when opportunity knocked, you hurried up and opened the damned door.

That was what he was doing with this new network, Sphere. It would be a hit if it killed him. Still, the wrinkle in this week's dog and pony show was *Brentwood Drive,* a sort of retro nod to *Three's Company,* but flipped, with two guys and one girl rooming together. So far the male leads, a couple of up-and-coming comedic actors, seemed solid, but the female leads that had been tested had left the focus groups with low feedback numbers. For the female spot, they needed someone with real star quality, but honestly, the network didn't have the budget or the cachet to warrant an actual star.

They couldn't even get any big names to come in and test during this off season. All the real stars were off vacationing, doing feature films, or taking up off-season DJing. Either way, no one was out to risk their career on a possible disaster of a pilot comedy on an obscure no name station. But Carter had to make this work. Getting these pilots off the ground could turn this germ of a side network into something, and possibly something big. He needed this. There was only so much hard news he could do and still compete with the other two networks. He'd taken mornings as far as he could.

Making a bit of a splash with his more reality-based pieces had awakened him to the fact that viral scripted content was the way to go. Everyone was leaning toward destination watching, and that was where the network needed to be, even if his old friend Aidan didn't agree. Let him handle the real life, and Carter would keep everyone suitably placated over in dreamland.

But for that to happen, he needed some certified hit shows. And there would be no hits without a few stars.

CHAPTER 2

Carter and Karen made their way into the back conference room to grab the last of their papers before heading back out to their waiting car and driver. Next stop: the hotel. Then, by this time tomorrow, he'd be back in New York, thankfully. The thought of going home made Carter infinitely happy. He was frankly over being driven everywhere, and this freeway traffic situation was no joke. Give him the subway any day. But the thought of his upcoming conversation with Everett Walker filled him with dread. With no real star draw pinned down for the *Brentwood* show, Carter knew this future conversation would be focused less on his wins and more on that glaring omission. He let out a low sigh as he put the last of his papers into his bag.

Karen's head turned his way. "What's with you?"

"Huh?" He looked at her with confused eyes.

"The sigh," Karen said. "What's with that? You should be about ready to dance out of here. Besides sighing is not your style, so what gives?"

Carter shook his head. "It's nothing. You must be hearing things."

Karen's eyes went skyward. "Yeah, okay. We'll go with that." She finished packing and started for the door, then turned back to him. Now he was frowning and staring at his phone, as if it contained all the answers to the world's problems. "How about you finish your not sighing and gnashing of your teeth as we make our way in Cali traffic? I'd like to get back to New York as soon as I can."

Carter's gaze shot up, and he nodded. "Let's go. And for the record, I'm not gnashing, either."

"Sure, Captain."

Once inside their car, both Carter and Karen allowed their thumbs to fly across their phones. They were just getting up to cruising speed on the freeway when suddenly their car jerked forward, then swerved left. As the car jerked, Karen's papers slid off the leather seat, and both she and Carter reached forward to retrieve them. Coming

31

up, Carter noticed the copy of *Variety* magazine in the driver's side back seat pocket. Distracted, he decided to grab it and flip through it. Only moments in, his eyes glazed over, as he was bored with the usual trade ads. That was until *her.*

Carter's eyes widened as his entire body sparked in response to the undeniable beauty that was Leila Darling. As he looked down at her, she looked back at him, dark eyes seeming to sparkle as she innocently licked at the ice cream running down her arm and stared into the camera's lens. *Oh, God, to be that arm. That ice cream!* Carter practically groaned out loud.

"You okay?" Karen asked from his right.

Damn. Did he really groan out loud? "I'm fine." Carter said, more sharply than he intended as he shifted in his seat. He could feel Karen's disapproval from over on her side of the car. He would not explain himself further. Done was done. Besides, he doubted he could find any convincing words, anyway. Carter looked back at the magazine. Leila Darling was gorgeous. Those deep, sparkling eyes; that wild mane of dark hair; that wide mouth, with full lips that always seemed to beckon for a kiss. But what was this ad all about? Carter's eyes scanned the page. He vaguely became aware of the pool, the hotel, the luxury car in the background. He didn't really know what was for sale in this ad, but whatever it was, he was ready to buy.

"Now, that one can move product," Karen said.

"Excuse me?" Carter replied.

"Well, you can't stop staring. And truth be told, neither can just about anyone else. Look." With that declaration, Karen jerked her head a bit, causing Carter to look out the window and up at a large billboard. There was Leila again. This time her gorgeous body was on display in a bikini, and her eyes twinkled down at them from at least fifty feet above as the ad touted her appearance this weekend at some sort of vodka launch party at a Las Vegas hotel and nightclub. Carter's mind did a quick flip back as he remembered something about that launch.

He heard Karen chuckle beside him. "And my point is proven."

Having his attention diverted from Leila, he looked back at Karen, annoyed. "Was there an actual point you were making?"

She raised a brow his way. "Well, you can't stop staring, and like I said, neither can anyone else." Karen paused there and stared at him for one beat, then another. Finally, she shook her head. "Jeez. What are they paying *you* the big bucks for? Maybe she's someone we should be considering for the *Brentwood* show."

Carter pulled a face to express his disbelief. "No way! She's a model, not an actress. Why should we consider her for the *Brentwood* show? Not to mention with her wild reputation, I'd be laughed out of the network if I went to the bigwigs with her."

Karen's shook her head again. "Wake up, boss. You're not running a newsroom anymore. You read the trades, and you've got to be more up on what's happening in pop culture. Haven't you heard that she wants to get into acting now? She had that little part in that weird sci-fi movie, and from what I hear, she wasn't half bad. People actually saw past the bikini and catsuit thingy, which were her primary costumes, and thought she delivered a decent line. Besides all that, she's white-fire hot. Her party girl rep is what makes her that way. I say you should be pursuing her before reality TV grabs her and sucks the lifeblood out of her."

Carter looked down at the magazine again. It was true. Leila wasn't half bad in that movie. Not that he wanted to admit to being one of the folks who contributed to the surprise opening weekend box office success of *Robot-x*. But he was a bit of a closet geek, and damn it, the truth was he'd been crushing on Leila Darling since she appeared on the modeling scene years ago. Despite what Karen said or thought, he was way up on his pop culture. Especially when it came to the gorgeous Ms. Darling.

Carter frowned. It was because he was up on pop culture and all things Leila Darling that he knew about Leila's party girl reputation and her revolving door of famous male suitors. The latest relationship, with rapper Miles G, had ended with her breaking off yet another engagement and him recording a hit song that delved into the way she'd done him wrong.

No, Leila was a bad idea. Carter had enough to worry about with launching this new network without trying to add reining in a wild starlet. Carter tilted his head, the image of Leila in her latex space suit coming to the forefront of his mind. On the other hand . . . maybe Karen had a point. Could Leila, or someone like Leila, be the answer that he'd been looking for? Hell, because of Leila, that crap song had shot to the top, and now Miles G's album sales were through the roof. The mostly auto-tuned rapper, who could barely be considered a talent, had been lucky to have hitched onto the star and gotten his heart broken by Leila. So the woman handed him a career along with his broken heart. Sounds like he got a pretty good deal.

Carter thought harder, tossing Karen's idea around in his head. Though he'd had quite a few wins while in California, Carter was still dreading going back to New York without a full house. Everett Walker was tough, and Carter knew that it didn't matter that he was like a second son to him. The truth was he already had a son, and Carter was just an employee. One who had to get the job done or risk losing it. When it came to business, Everett was a shark. It was what Carter admired about him and what he tried to emulate. He thought for a moment about what Everett would think of the idea of Leila Darling for the *Brentwood* show and smiled. His gut told him that Everett would consider it a win. What man wouldn't? She had the sex appeal that Greyson had earlier said they needed. The kind that men lusted after and women wanted to emulate. Carter grimaced. *Crap.* Karen had it right, and he wondered why he didn't think of it himself. But that was why he had her as an assistant: she was damn good at her job, and he valued that.

Suddenly, Carter knew why something was niggling in the back of his mind. "Wait a minute." He looked over at Karen. She was busy scrolling through her phone. She put up a quick finger to stop him from talking, and then she gave him an arched brow.

"I'm already on it," Karen said to Carter's unasked question. "Yes, you did get an invitation to that vodka launch party three weeks ago, from Jasper Weston, Leila's manager. I just pulled it up. Do you want me to send a note to Jasper's assistant, saying that you'll be there, after all? The opening is tonight, so if you go to the hotel and change, I can arrange for a flight to get you to Vegas within a few hours. I'll just have the rest of your flights diverted for New York."

Carter smiled. Yes, Karen was damned good. "Thanks. Please do that. And I'll send Jasper a text letting him know I'll be there. It's been a long while since I've seen him, but I think in this case, it's time for the personal touch."

Karen nodded and turned back to concentrate on her phone, ready to get to work. By now the traffic had eased up and they were moving steadily once again.

Carter gave her a nudge. "And thanks. That was really good thinking. I'm lucky to have you on my team."

Karen just tilted her head to the side. "Oh, I know you are. But thank you for saying it. Now, you just go to that party and come back with a win for the team so you can keep me in the shoes I like. And when my expense report for this trip comes in, just sign it and pay no attention to that extra massage I'm going to add on once I get back to the hotel this afternoon."

Carter grinned. "No problem. You definitely earned it."

CHAPTER 3

"Leila, over here, over here!"

"This way, Leila! This way!"

"Give us a big smile, Leila! Turn around! Come on and let us have a view of your best assets!"

And with that last insult and the myriad of flashes in her face, Leila Darling had officially had it. This already had been a most frustrating week, with the tabloids all over her about her breakup with Miles, not to mention that stupid song of his following her everywhere. And now she was stuck, obligated to stand and be shouted at by a bunch of no-manners photographers while holding up a ridiculously tacky, blinged-out bottle of overpriced, low-quality blue vodka. *Blue?* Who wanted to drink blue vodka? It wasn't like they were selling Kool-Aid, or hell, maybe they were.

Leila shot the offending photographer a glare and was this close to giving him a piece of her mind when she felt the gentle pressure of her manager, Jasper's hand on the small of her bare back.

"Don't do it, Leila," he said low in her ear. "You've done enough damage for one day by insulting Matteo and the Burger Barn people."

Leila knew he was smiling with his mouth since flashbulbs were still going off, so she heeded his words of warning and continued to smile too as she spoke through clenched teeth.

"Matteo is lucky I didn't shove a burger up his ass and have it come out through his mouth. A little reverse consumption." Leila grinned wider when, out of her peripheral, she saw Jasper's cool smile falter. "But seriously," she continued, "that line about turning around and showing my best assets deserves no less than me telling him off. I want that photographer gone."

Jasper let out a low breath. "You're right, of course, and jerks like him don't make my life any easier, but please can you just roll along tonight and try? I'll have him removed. You won't see him anymore tonight. Now just thirty more seconds, and then hand me the bottle, and you can go on ahead into the club. Have a few drinks, a good time, and this will all be over before you know it."

Leila turned and looked her longtime friend straight in the eye. "Promises. Promises." She gave him a smile, then got deadly serious. "I want him gone now. You know I'm not one to be treated like just a piece of ass. If somebody is going to treat me that way, then they'd better be prepared for the consequences." Leila handed Jasper the bottle and moved on to stand farther in front of the Double LL vodka logo sign, smiling wider when she caught a glimpse of one of the clubs' rather impressively large bouncers having a word with the offensive photographer. Her eyes then connected with Jasper's over the crowd, and she gave him a brief nod.

Leila pushed down on the twinge of guilt that threatened to rise inside her. She didn't mean to make Jasper's job any harder, but she had to stand her ground. She's been in the game long enough to know that being a pushover got you nowhere, and it was time to start thinking past her modeling career and about a more serious future. One where it wasn't just "stand, pose, smile, and turn around." She'd had it with these club openings, the cameos in videos, and the occasional print ads. Besides beauty was fleeting; it was time she was recognized as a talent that could do more, be more. Leila was ready to branch out, and Jasper, as well as the rest of the world, needed to get on board with her plan.

Leila arched her back and held back on a sigh as Jasper walked up to her again, ready to escort her into the club and the waiting party that she was due to host.

"Are you ready to go in and party it up?" he asked.

No, she wasn't ready to go in and definitely she was not in the mood to party. She'd much rather go back to her hotel room, order some room service, and relax by watching TV for a few hours after a hot bath. But no, she had to be on. The crowd was here to see Leila, the party girl, and all her fabulous party friends celebrate with Double LL vodka, so that was what she had to do. At this point, all she could only hope was that this would be one of the last times she did this type of gig — if she played her cards right and got her career going in the direction she wanted it to go. But for now, the smile, tease, and pop, shimmy dance was on.

Just then there was a small uproar. First, there were murmurings, which quickly turned into a few gasps, and as if on the same que, the photographers suddenly stilled, then shifted right in unison, all their attention focused on the party coming in to Leila's left.

"Chloe! Chloe Caraway! What are you doing in Vegas?" yelled one of the photographers.

Leila's back went ramrod straight as Chloe, flanked by her small entourage of hangers-on, her supposed squad, glided up the blue Double LL carpet. Leila turned and looked at Jasper. "Really?" she mouthed.

He gave her a slight tilt of the head by way of apology.

The photographer had it right. What was Little Miss Granola doing in Vegas? And better yet, what was she doing on Leila's carpet? Chloe pretended to be oblivious to the photographers as she simultaneously gave them all her best poses. She gave the "Not tonight, boys," line and the "I'm just here to chill with my friends," speech. Finally, she sidled up to Leila, who suddenly felt foolish for standing and posing in her minidress on the carpet, while holding a giant bottle of vodka no less, while Chloe, looking cool and unaffected, was a beatnik's wet dream. Chloe gave Leila a soft smile and kissed her on both cheeks, like they were in the south of France and not at some nouveau riche club in Vegas. Still, Leila smiled back.

"Great to see you again, Chloe."

"You too," the other woman said, twisting her artfully designed faux dreads through her thin fingers. "My friends and I were bored with Malibu, so we thought, why not try a little bit of fun out west?"

Leila bit back her retort. *Bored with Malibu?* Only those who had too much could get bored with the very best. But the cameras were flashing, so she kept her smile in place. "Well, then, please go in. Enjoy yourself." Leila turned that smile around and waved to the rest of the crowd waiting outside as she linked arms with Chloe.

Jasper gave her a wide grin and a wink as he leaned in close to her ear. "Nice going, hon."

Leila knew that this was the highest of praise and that she owed it to her ardent determination to turn over a new leaf. Because if she wasn't a full three quarters of the way into her new Leila mode, she would have gut punched Little Miss Granola for having the nerve to show up at one of her events, given that the last time Leila saw her, Chloe was ass up in front of Leila's ex—number two, the almost famous actor she had been engaged to and her costar in

Robot-x, Wade Shephard. Not that Wade was a big loss, but it was the principle of the thing. And, damn it, it was the breakup with Wade that had sent Leila into arms of the even more nefarious Miles, so the fact that Leila did not have the warmest feelings for Chloe freaking Caraway was perfectly warranted. The woman was a menace in every sense of the word.

Leila shot Jasper a quick side eye and muttered under her breath, "Let's get this night over with. I can't get back to New York fast enough."

Carter wasn't quite prepared for his first glimpse of Leila Darling, but he should've been. It wasn't like it was the first time he'd seen a beautiful woman. Hell, he'd seen plenty of beautiful ones, even been with plenty of beautiful women. Some would say even more beautiful than Leila. Though, that thought made Carter chuckle to himself. Who was he fooling? In his mind, no one he'd ever seen or been with was more beautiful, more exciting, or more captivating than Leila Darling.

It was already late by the time Carter arrived at the club in the newly built Swenson Hotel at the far end of the Strip. But the late hour didn't seem to matter, as it looked like the party was just getting into full swing. As usual, Karen had done her job well. Carter had no problem getting past the crowd vying to get inside the club, and once he made it to the door, he gave his name and was immediately found on the list and then personally ushered into the coveted VIP section by a sleek looking hostess. Gaining easy admittance to these types of things still floored him. Though it was his dream, he had never imagined being one of those on the other side of the velvet rope. And it wasn't something he took lightly. Being a have-not made hanging with the haves something he didn't take for granted, and he doubted he ever would.

Looking around and surveying his surroundings, Carter took a too large swig of the god-awful blue vodka given to him by a perky cocktail waitress with bright shining eyes. He coughed and choked on the vile liquid, at that moment saved by Jasper who came up behind him and gave him a rough pat on his shoulder.

"Hey, I'm so glad you made it," Jasper said as Carter turned around to greet him. "It's been too long. You just missed Chloe Caraway and her crew . . . well, squad, whatever. You know how they roll nowadays."

Carter nodded. "I do. That's too bad. I have meetings set up with her people in the not so distant future. It would have been good to connect."

He watched as Jasper raised a brow. "Do you now? Care to tell?"

Carter grinned. "Not just yet, man. Not just yet." Just then, another server in a black bodysuit walked by with a tray, and Carter passed her his leftover drink. He then shook Jasper's hand. "It has been too long, but it's good to see you again. You're always jetting off with your favorite client. What's it been? Two years? Or is it three years since I saw you and we got in a game?"

He and Jasper used to go to the same gym years back, and in all honesty, they both knew what was up — two guys getting in 6:00 a.m. workouts while shooting hoops and making contacts with the moneyed execs before the breakfast dealings. New York truly never did sleep, and a deal could be made just about anywhere. He and Jasper had hit it off because game recognized game.

Jasper laughed and ran a hand over his slim belly. "Man, it's been way too long. I'm feeling totally out of shape. Running on a treadmill does not compare to running up and down the court. Hopefully, I can get back to it soon."

"Hey, you don't look like you're doing too badly for yourself. Truth be told, it's been mostly the treadmill for me, too, when I can get to it. Life has gotten a little bit crazy."

Jasper laughed at that and shook his head. "Crazy? Is that what you call being made the head honcho for the start-up of the new network? Looks to me like the boy done made good." He frowned. "We need to make a toast, but you don't have anything to toast with."

Carter raised his brow. "I'm cool, man. That vodka is not for me."

Jasper laughed. "I got you." Jasper looked around and made eye contact with the server who had gone by before. She walked a little more slowly toward them this time, making direct eye contact with Jasper, her eyes wide and bright with invitation, as she licked her lips and gave him a smile. "Yes, Mr. Weston?"

"Two Jacks on the rocks please. It's Chevette, right?"

The young woman preened and her smile widened at Jasper remembering her name. "Why, yes, it is, Mr. Weston. How nice of you to remember."

Jasper tilted his head. "How could someone ever forget you, Chevette? If you'd put a little bit of your extra sweetness in my drink, that will be just fine." He flashed a smile. One that he probably flashed at each of the girls in the club, if Carter remembered his game correctly, but he knew the drinks would come along quickly, no doubt with the server's number attached to Jasper's.

"Good to see all your success hasn't gone to your head and nothing's changed with you," Carter said.

"Hey, if a guy can't work out on the court, a guy's gotta work out where he can. Get in where you fit in and all that. Am I right?"

Carter answered with nothing more than a head tilt as, just as he'd thought, Chevette returned with their drinks in practically no time. *Oh well.* He didn't have time to judge Jasper or his pickup tactics. He was there to play his own game of pickup, so to speak, and for that he needed to be on Jasper's good side.

Carter took his drink from Chevette as Jasper took his, along with what looked to be her number on a napkin. Carter just raised a brow. "If you say so," he said, answering Jasper's earlier question. He took a sip of his much better drink and let the beat of the music and the hard thumping bass vibrate through his body.

There was a slightly awkward silence as both men drank and seemed to be thinking about where they had come from compared to where they were now. A minute later, though, the silence was broken when Jasper spoke. "I hope you're prepared to party. We'll be down here only a little longer, and then it's up to my suite with the VIPs for cards, some more drinks, a little more reveling. There will be plenty more hostesses like sweet Chevette there and I'm sure a few of her friends."

Carter thought a moment about his answer. He'd been in this situation plenty of times — the parties, the drinks, the schmoozing — and yes, part of him wanted to let loose and have fun, but technically, he was still on the clock. He knew he had a job to do, and that job was to assess Leila Darling to see if there was any potential for her and *Brentwood.* But Carter also knew that in order to get to Leila, he had to go through Jasper Weston.

With that thought, he realized that the already loud, thumping music had somehow defied physics and had got even louder. His time out west was officially getting to him. The sound was vibrating against Carter's skull when he was bumped into by particularly enthusiastic booty shakers behind him, causing his drink to slosh over his hand. Jasper was quick to offer him a napkin, but when Carter looked down, he noticed Chevette's number on it. Carter laughed and waved him off, then retrieved the handkerchief he carried in his own pocket.

"I swear, you are the only dude I know who carries a handkerchief. That type of shit must have the girls swooning," Jasper commented.

Carter shook his head. "I don't know about that, but it comes in handy for spilled drinks. Now, tell me more about this game. Is it poker? Because if so, I can go for a round, but only if the limits aren't too high. A trust-fund baby I'm not."

Jasper laughed. "Hey, neither am I. But trust me, you'll be fine with this bunch, trust fund or not. I think you'll come out a winner."

Carter raised a skeptical brow. "We'll see." He looked around. "Speaking of winners, where is that famous client of yours? Isn't she the host of this party?"

Jasper frowned. "How did you miss her coming up the stairs when you walked in?" He then jutted out his chin, bringing Carter's attention to the dance floor below them. "She's right down there, holding court on the dance floor, blowing off some

51

of that energy of hers, doing what she does, captivating the crowd and getting the party turned up."

Carter looked over the balcony railing and down into the synchronized sea of people. They all seemed to swell, sway, and move as one to the thumping up-and-down bass of the music.

All except one spotlight-lit area.

Carter didn't know why he hadn't noticed it before. He must be truly tired and off his game. But there she was. Leila Darling, in the flesh. Of course, the spotlight would be on her. She was the type of person who should always be in the spotlight. And if there was no artificial light, well, no matter. She would still shine brighter than the rest just by her freaky inner glow, which radiated out and set her apart from the world's slightly dimmer, more normal humans. Carter watched as the rest of the humans below moved to the right and Leila did the opposite, swerving to the left, somehow making the crowd look off cue with her amazing moves instead of it being the other way around. Her hips swayed as her back arched. Her chest heaved up and down as she danced, with her arms spread wide and her eyes closed, to the beat of the song, letting the music take her over fully and completely.

Though the dance floor was practically jam-packed, the other dancers allowed just enough space around Leila so that she could do what she did and everyone could see every perfectly timed shimmy she shook in the barely there, low-front and somehow lower-back, sparkling minidress that she wore. How she got her long legs to move like they did in the death-defying stiletto heels she wore was beyond Carter. The way her hips went one way while the top of her body shimmied another way was almost jaw dropping, but what got Carter the most, what truly took his breath away, was how she seemed to be so lost in the beat of the music, how it seemed not to matter to her that there were hundreds of people all around her.

Leila's eyes were closed, and there was a tiny sheen of sweat across her perfectly hued, pale cocoa skin. Her long dark hair was a wild halo all around her shoulders and face. Carter knew then and there that it didn't matter if it was Leila dancing with the multitude or if it was her all alone on the dance floor. She was a woman who was one with herself, and for just a moment he imagined himself dancing with her. Coming up to her and putting an arm around that beautiful waist of hers; her eyes opening;

the music changing to something slow, mellow, and sexy as he pulled her in close; the dance turning from a dance for one to a dance for two.

Just then though, as if on cue, the music changed, Leila's eyes opened, and for a moment, it felt as if Carter had willed it so. But now her expression was not the one in his momentary daydream. Carter watched as all the calmness drained from her face and her brows drew together tightly. Her hips abruptly stopped moving, and she looked up and past where he was to behind him somewhere.

"Oh, shit," Jasper ground out from over Carter's shoulder.

Carter turned toward where Leila was looking. It was the DJ's booth. After turning back toward Leila, he saw her utter words. Deciphering the movement of her lips, he decided that those words had to be "What the fuck?" It was then that the crowd around her all started to cheer and dance at the same time, having noticed the song that was playing. "Darling Leila." The song that had quickly skyrocketed to the top of the charts after Miles and Leila's breakup and had, no doubt, been lining Miles's pockets. The song cast Leila as the femme fatale heartbreaker in a hip-hop love story of a woman who changed men with less thought than she changed her shoes. The lyrics not so subtly hinted at her past failed relationships — her fling with an actor, her costar in the mediocre sci-fi movie; her short dalliance with an NBA star; and of course, her relationship with Miles. Not that it mattered, but Carter couldn't help but wonder how much of the song was true and how much lyrical license Miles took.

He watched as Leila shook her head and looked as if she was about to stomp off the dance floor. But the crowd started cheering her name, egging her on to dance. Jasper was now leaning over the balcony, looking down at Leila. Carter saw Leila look up at him, and there was some sort of silent exchange between the two as Leila shook her head once again, then shrugged her shoulders. A cocktail waitress with a tray of shots of the blue vodka came over to where Leila stood on the dance floor. Carter thought he noticed a shift in Leila as she picked up two of the shots and raised them high. Suddenly, the DJ cut the music and there was silence. Leila twirled around, looking beautiful, regal, heads above the rest of the crowd. Everyone hushed and waited for her next words.

"Tonight we celebrate the launch of Double LL vodka and, for me, personal new beginnings. Ladies, if you got 'em, raise them high. Don't accept anything less than the very best in your life and for damn sure nothing less than the best in your mouth. Only the strongest and the smoothest. The rest can kick it to the curb!"

The crowd let out a roaring cheer as Leila raised her glasses even higher. "To new beginnings and letting go!"

"To letting go!" the crowd roared.

Leila downed one shot and then the next. She pointed to the DJ, and he once again queued up "Darling Leila," right on the beat where her name was being said on repeat. Leila started dancing hard and fast once again, this time with what looked like a renewed determination. Carter didn't see any of the serenity on her face that he'd seen just a few minutes before. This woman dancing now was a woman on a mission. Like she was out to prove to all the people watching her that she didn't care about the song being played, or about the man who was saying the words about how callously she had treated him, about how he had loved her, and how she'd left him.

Carter smiled to himself and raised his glass to her. Yes, Leila Darling was showing the world that she had moved on and she was ready to see who or what came next. Now, turning back in Jasper's direction, Carter hoped to grab his spot in line.

CHAPTER 4

Leila knew that Jasper would try to dodge her after the mess that was this launch party, but there was no way she was letting him off the hook. This thing had been a fiasco from the get-go, and she was going to let him know that she was officially and completely done.

As she walked into his suite, she noticed it was already packed with all the usual suspects: the VIPs wanting to see and be seen, a handful of execs from Double LL vodka, not to mention a liberal sprinkling of the hotel's most beautiful and, dare she guess, amiable servers, up for whatever. Checking the room, she was sure the female staff outweighed the male staff almost two to one at this gathering, and the implications of that made her want to clench her back teeth. This was something else to take a bite out of Jasper about.

People were milling around in tight

bunches, and few looked like they were already deep into intense card games at the small tables set up toward the back of the suite. Leila spied Jasper back there at a corner table and told herself to calm down as she made her way through the room, greeting people along the way. *Just play it cool,* she told herself. She was still on the client's dime, a fact that was punctuated by Jasper currently playing cards with one of the head guys from Double LL. He was no doubt securing the final payment on her gig — and, knowing Jasper, a fat bonus for himself — with the game. She didn't mind, though, as long as he wasn't offering her up for any more club openings like this one.

Leila might not always agree with Jasper's methods, but he'd always been there for her. They had come up together, and ever since junior high, he had never let her down. He'd had her back like a brother, but it was time for him, along with everyone else in her life, to realize that she was her own woman now and not just a commodity to be shuffled about.

Leila was about to make a beeline for the corner when Nia Henton, Jasper's assistant and, not so coincidently, one of her best friends since they were kids, stepped into her path. "How about a drink, Leila?" Nia said, giving Leila a wide but cautious smile.

Leila looked down at Nia. In the mood she was in, she wanted so badly to bite someone's head off, but for the life of her, she couldn't do it to Nia.

Damn it, Jasper was cagey. He had hired Nia, and now he had put her in the path of someone like Leila. Nia had worked with Jasper for the past three years, ever since Leila had gotten big and Jasper had become an in demand industry name. He had capitalized on that and had started taking on more clients, which wasn't a problem, but it meant that in order to keep up with the demands of managing Leila, he needed real help for his growing operation.

Nia was petite and curvy, with wide eyes and chocolate-brown skin and an almost unflappable sunny disposition, that was until you crossed her, and then every bit of her born-and-raised New York heritage came out. She took none of Jasper's bullshit and always told it like it was.

"Don't smile at me like that, Nia. You know this thing was a total shit show. First, that shoot, and then this party and that awful DJ."

Nia gave a slight nod and spoke in a low tone. "Yes, I know. And so does he. But you handled it beautifully, as you always do.

Don't worry. That jerk photographer is gonna pay. And Double LL vodka is in love with you, so I'm sure they would love more meet and greets, and they would give you the world right now. Jasper is probably negotiating another print ad as we speak."

Leila felt her lips tighten.

"Lighten up," Nia said. "You've got to let things roll off. I know you've had it rough lately, but come on. It's just a song. And if you let that jerk see he's getting to you with it, then you are letting him win."

Leila shot Nia a harsh look. "Just a song? How can you say that when daily he's taking my name through the mud over the airwaves?"

Nia shook her head and patted Leila's arm. If it was anyone else, Leila might have jerked away. "What he's doing is making you a legend. And raising your stock every time it gets played. All you have to do is let it go. Let the song do its job, and you will reap the benefits. Be the opposite. Prove him wrong. Keep the folks guessing as to who is the real and true Leila Darling. You will be more famous than ever!"

Leila looked over at the little huddle Jasper was in with the Double LL guys and squelched a sigh. "Yeah, but the problem is, I'm not sure that's the type of fame I want anymore."

Nia's brows drew together before she smiled once again. "Then you create the kind of fame you want. This is your time, Leila. You call the shots. Don't let a bastard like Miles have the last auto-tuned word." Her grin went wider now. "How's about that drink?"

Feeling a little more bolstered, Leila smiled back. "Anything but that damned vodka."

Nia nodded. "Of course. I'll get you a ginger ale."

"Thanks. I really appreciate it."

"It's my job. No problem."

"Well, really, it's not. So thank you."

After Leila got her ginger ale, she attempted again to make her way across the room through the crowd toward Jasper.

"And there's my star!" Jasper said by way of greeting when she reached him. He stood, along with the rest of the men at the table, and they all folded their cards into their palms.

Leila smiled a smile that she knew only Jasper would be able to tell held dissatisfaction. "I wouldn't go that far, but thank you, J."

She then turned to Bradley Wright from Double LL, who already had his hand extended to take hers. Leila wasn't in the mood for pleasantries, but pleasantries were what she was being paid for — and paid handsomely, no less — by this man and the company he worked for. So she kept her smile in place and let him take her hand in his to give it a shake, but when she went to move away, he held on to her hand for more than a moment or three too long. She looked him straight in the eye with her usual measure of steel, her smile still firmly where it was.

"You going to return that to me? It got enough of a workout tonight from holding up your bottles. Those things are heavy as hell," she said.

Bradley coughed and looked suitably chastised as he pulled his hand back. "Of course, you're right. I'm sorry about that, Leila. But I'm sure you're used to it by now. You must have men starstruck by you all the time."

Leila waved a dismissive hand in front of her face. "No, I wouldn't say that. Besides, we've met each other plenty of times before, so I wouldn't imagine you'd be one for getting starstruck. And you've got a beautiful wife at home to go to. Now, there is someone to get starstruck over." With that, Leila raised a brow ever so slightly and watched

Bradley lower his blue gaze and run his hands through his already unruly blond hair.

She almost laughed, but there really wasn't anything to laugh about. She knew that he and probably half of these married execs at this party would somehow find their way back to their rooms with one of the available cocktail servers, given half the chance. It was a sad reality of the business and made Leila quietly sick. It was just another reason why she was ready to get out of the business or at least transition to something that focused a little less on her looks and more on her talent. Just then someone else joined the fray, or had he been there all along? The fact that Leila wasn't quite sure gave her pause and let her know, tired or not, she needed to get on her game.

"While we're talking about being starstruck, it seems you have another admirer here that I'd like for you to meet." It was Jasper who was talking now, and though Leila knew that this was what this night was about — pressing the flesh, smiling, and meeting the clients — once again she wished more than anything that she had begged off, claimed she had a headache or something, and stayed in her own room, with room service and a burger.

After this afternoon, maybe not a burger.

Focus, Leila.

Leila swallowed a sigh and turned toward the man whom she'd barely noticed up to that point and whom Jasper was indicating. She licked her lips and smiled wide, going into work mode, as she arched her back and put her chest out. The man extended his hand.

"Don't worry. I'm not starstruck," the man said, his deep, no-nonsense tone just the cool splash of water Leila needed to zap her right out of her stupor. "He's just exaggerating. We both know Jasper lays it on a little bit thick. Well, of course, it is very nice to meet you, Ms. Darling. I just don't want to go and oversell the moment."

Exaggerating? Not starstruck? Oversell? Leila was so caught off guard by the guy's dismissive answer, not to mention the smooth tenor of his voice, that she almost didn't notice the sparkle that resonated in his deep-set, dark brown eyes. *Almost.* Still, she was shaken. Leila wasn't used to being brushed off. Especially when she was immediately attracted to someone.

This feeling was foreign to her. So much so that it put her on edge and set her off kilter when he stuck his hand out for her to shake.

Hesitantly, while looking into those dark

eyes to see if he was just trying to play her, Leila took his hand and then immediately recoiled, as she was zapped by an electric shock. The kind of zap you used to get as a kid by running in place on the carpet and then touching your best friend. "Ouch!" she gasped, jumping back, bumping into the server behind her with a full tray of drinks, sending it crashing to the floor and creating a cacophony of clanging glass and shocked gasps.

"Oh, my God, Mr. Weston. I'm so sorry! Ms. Darling, your shoes. I'm such a klutz. Please step back. I don't want any glass to get on you. This is all my fault. I'm really sorry," said the server.

Leila jumped out of the way, then turned toward the server and immediately bent down and helped her retrieve her tray. "It's okay. It wasn't your fault." She looked up to give a sharp glare to the man who had surprised her with his distracting and frankly dismissive answer. Who the hell did he think he was, with his talk of exaggeration? Hell, this was her party. "You ought to holster that thing," she said, nodding her head toward his hand, but her tone implied she could be referring to anything. For her trouble, she watched as Mr. Unaffected looked suitably chastised and lowered his lashes. A certain shyness came to his cheeks, and the look was way too swoony for his own good.

Damn it. He really should holster all of it, she thought. Too much more of this, and she'd start thinking about fiancé number four, and that was the very last thing she needed.

Leila decided to refocus her energy on the problem at hand, the trembling server by her side. "As I said, it's not your fault. It was me," Leila said. "I was distracted."

"No. I should have been paying more attention. Please, you go on. I don't need to get into any more trouble. I've already been reprimanded enough about being clumsy," the server replied.

Leila placed her hand on the younger woman's forearm to still her. "It's just a little broken glass. I've broken plenty in my day. And, trust me, you won't get into any trouble." She looked up and over at Jasper, who was probably calculating the cost of the glasses and wondering if it would be charged to his suite.

Jasper cleared his throat. "Of course you won't. It's not a problem at all." Jasper looked past Leila now. "And here come reinforcements." He leaned down to help Leila up as a couple of other servers came over with rags to help clean up the mess. With a pull on her hands, he brought Leila eye to eye with the unimpressed stranger once again.

But just that look, in just that moment, had her practically faltering. She was met by a completely too handsome man. He was tall and lanky, but she could tell that he had a muscular build by the way he filled out his immaculately cut suit. His hair was cropped low, his nose was strong and angular, and he had ridiculously full and probably thoroughly kissable lips, but the kicker was his way too-sharp eyes, which looked at her and at the same time seemed to look right through her. Those deep-set dark eyes, surrounded by sooty, ultra-full lashes, were the stuff that a makeup artist's dreams were made of. Leila didn't know what it was, but there was something in this guy's eyes.

He held out his hand again and then grinned sheepishly and pulled it back. "Carter Bain," he said. "I'm a friend of Jasper's and work at WBC. It's really nice to meet you. Sorry about the mess. Despite all that I said before, I am a fan."

Leila was just about to wave a hand and brush him off when she paused. *Carter Bain? Wait a minute and hold the phone. Carter flipping Bain?* Leila fought not to take a misstep again as her mind went into a mental tailspin.

Jasper looked at Leila now with concern in his eyes and gently steered her over to the left a bit so that they were closer to the large screened-in balcony area, which offered an amazing view of the lit Vegas Strip and the mountains beyond. "Are you okay? I know this has been a long day."

"I'm fine," she told Jasper by way of placating him. "But Carter Bain?" she whispered. "As in WBC's Carter Bain? The one with the new network?"

Jasper raised a brow as he shook his head slightly.

Leila leveled him with a hard stare. "I'm fine, Jasper. Now work your magic and please introduce me to your friend properly."

Jasper's eyes narrowed more as his gaze shifted from Leila to Carter. He let out a sigh and led Leila back to the group with a smile. "Leila, now that we've all spilled drinks together, let me properly introduce you to Carter Bain. Carter and I've been friends for a couple of years, and I'm glad you two are finally getting to meet in person."

Leila watched as Mr. Cool and Unaffected stuck out his hand once again, this time testing it by tapping on Jasper's sleeve first. It was Leila's turn to play it cool, though, as she looked at his hand briefly and then rubbed her two hands together and gave a shrug. "I think I need a towel or something for my hands. I don't want to get you wet, Mr. Bain," Leila said suggestively, just to see how cool Mr. Unaffected could stay.

She watched as his fist slowly closed and he pulled his hand back, giving her a slight smile. "No problem. I understand." He then reached into his breast pocket and pulled out a snowy white handkerchief and handed it to her.

"Seriously, dude, how many of those do you have? You're like Houdini," Jasper said.

Carter only shrugged by way of answering, then turned back to Leila and looked at her straight on as she wiped her hands. "I'm sorry if I rattled you back there." His lips spread into a grin, and he looked at her slightly sheepishly. "Can't say I've ever had that effect on a supermodel."

It was Jasper's turn to laugh then. "Laying it on a bit thick there, are you, man?"

Leila watched as Carter slid Jasper a look, letting him know that he wasn't doing himself any favors at the moment. The whole thing was slightly cute, for what reason, she didn't know why. Leila was used to guys coming on too strong and trying to play it cool around her. But what Leila wasn't used to was them having any sort of real "knock her off her feet" effect. That part was new, and she supposed, exciting. Leila refolded the handkerchief, noting the initials *CB* monogrammed on it, and went to hand it back to Carter.

He shook his head. "You can keep it."

Leila felt her cheeks heat up and pushed away the emotion, which came almost out of left field, as she pulled her hand back and let it tighten around the handkerchief. She had to play it cool. She knew who Carter Bain was. She had read about him in the trades and knew he was the head of World Broadcasting's newest startup network, the same one that was looking to cast actors in upcoming shows. Meeting Carter had to be a sign. This could be her big chance. All her dabbling in acting classes and then her little role in *Robot-x* . . . Maybe this was the break she was waiting for. Besides, she'd done her homework, and she knew WBC had some particularly interesting shows they were producing, ones with gritty leads for women of color.

Leila needed to pull Jasper aside and let him know that she was interested in finding out what it would take to get her on Carter

Bain's good side, and to get him to think of her as more of an actor than a model. Leila smiled inwardly. Hell, maybe Carter Bain was already on board. There had to be a reason he was here at the party, right?

Leila looked Carter straight in the eye, then gave him a smile. "Rattled? Oh, Mr. Bain, it takes a lot more than that to get me rattled. But if you think you're up for the challenge, you're welcome to give it a try."

Carter gave a slight cough, then looked embarrassed. The way his gaze wavered, and those lovely lashes of his lowered, and the way he did this little lip bite thing were positively disarming. "I'm sorry," he said. "I didn't mean *rattled*. I think I meant, well, *startled*. You know, with the glasses breaking and all." He shook his head. "I'm probably stepping off on the wrong foot. Can I start again? And please call me Carter. Of course, why would someone like me be able to stir anything in someone as stunning as you? As you can clearly see, I'm the one who's stumbling over here, Ms. Darling."

Leila waved a hand, and for the first time, her smile was genuine. Strangely, she started to feel relaxed. More on solid footing. Yeah, he was interested, and it was in more than her looks. This guy was here for a reason.

"Looks like we're both a little off our

game. It's been a long night. And I'll call you Carter if you call me Leila." She looked around the room and noticed the pockets of people in conversation, though many of them were not really talking but rather training their eyes on her. The breaking of the glasses had no doubt shifted their attention. No one seemed more interested than Jasper, who was positively mesmerized. Leila gave him a frown.

Time to get things back on track.

"I'm sorry to have interrupted your game, gentlemen. Please go back to it. I'll hang back and watch," she said.

"You don't play?" Carter asked.

"I do, but you have a full table." She gave him a sly look up through her lashes before turning to the rest of the group. "Besides, I don't think any of you want any part of my game. I may be too much for you."

With that statement, Leo Hartley, another executive with Double LL, gave a laugh and held up his hands. "You know what, Leila? I'm going to let you take my spot." He gave his collar a little tug then looked around playfully at the other men. "These guys are trying to do me out of my hard-won bonus, anyway, and I'm not about to let that happen." He held up his empty glass and gave the ice a shake. This brought a particularly busty server bounding over, ready to give him a refill. He looked her up and down and licked his lips as he gave Bradley a quick wink. "Yeah, I can think of much better ways to spend my money."

Leila watched with thinly veiled displeasure as Leo walked away, his hands trailing down from the server's back to her ample behind. When they stopped so that she could pour his drink, she leaned over sharply, showing all her special assets. Then he signaled to another girl, one in a short fuchsia dress, to come and sit beside him on a corner settee. Leila turned away from the scene and back to the company at hand. She raised a brow at Jasper as he gave her a look that clearly told her to keep calm, as these men were the clients and the clients were king. She decided then and there that Double LL was officially off her client list.

Still, Leila smiled as she eyed the cards and hoped their checks cleared quickly. She then looked at Carter Bain. "So, what's your pleasure, gentlemen?"

CHAPTER 5

Jasper gave a slight nod to one of the club's hired game makers for the night. The mess Leila had helped make had been cleaned up and the tables had been righted. Everything was back as it should be.

Leila looked Carter's way. "Are you still game?" she asked. She stared at him intently for the brief moment in which he considered his answer. She was surprised that she hoped he was still in, and it wasn't just because of the potential career implications. Sure, maybe she should be somewhere pining over the breakup with Miles, but crying over past relationships was not her style. She was not one to beg for affection. Either you were all in or you were out. That was how Leila lived, and that was how she loved.

Finally, he spoke, giving the answer she wanted. "Sure. I'm always game."

Her smile came from somewhere deep, and she felt rejuvenated as she took the seat opposite him, while Jasper and Bradley took the remaining two. They quickly got into a spirited game of poker, and Leila was glad to lose herself in the cards and the company as she let the rest of the party fall to the background.

As if anticipating Leila's hunger, Nia had some snacks sent over, knowing Leila would be starving after an evening of standing, smiling, and twirling, not to mention expending all that energy while dancing. Leila noticed the jaw-dropping looks on all the men's faces, save Jasper's, when she was the first to dive into the tray of tapas, forgoing the vegetables and going for the pulled pork tacos.

"What? Am I not supposed to eat?" she said to a gawking Bradley.

"Of course you are. And it's not that you don't look utterly delectable doing it," Bradley began. "I'm just shocked you can keep your figure and put it away like that. I thought the burger commercials that touted your appetite were just for show."

Leila licked the sauce from the corner of her mouth and noticed, with some satisfaction, a slight squirm from Mr. Unimpressed on the other side of the table before turning back to Bradley. "I enjoy my food. And I'm not one to apologize for it or make myself an emaciated stick figure for my career."

Bradley gave her a slight leer and looked her up and down. "Well, we at Double LL are not complaining. Whatever you're eating, it's landing in all the right spots, so enjoy."

Leila was holding back on rolling her eyes when she heard a snort from Carter's end of the table. Just that quickly she forgot that she needed him at that point more than he needed her, and she allowed her mouth to jump ahead of her head. "Please, don't tell me you have something to add to the conversation about my eating habits, having just met me and knowing nothing about me."

But Carter shook his head. "Not at all. My sigh —"

"It was a snort," Leila interrupted, correcting him.

Carter nodded. "My snort was more a comment on Mr. Wright's interjection. It's not like you were asking for or needed permission for your eating habits." He then turned to Bradley. "No offense, of course. But you are lucky enough to have such a sought-after spokesperson. I'd think she, and her talents, should be more respected."

Leila blinked and swallowed down on the sudden lump, which she'd labeled the pork taco, in her throat. *Well, damn.* Where did he and that come from? Then her eyes narrowed on Carter as she took in the exchange between him and Bradley Wright. Carter didn't know her from Adam and had no reason to stand up for her on such a trivial thing. As a matter of fact, she was doing fine on her own and would rather not have him stand up for her. So what was he getting out of it? Was this a play for her or a way to rattle Bradley?

So far in the card playing, Bradley had been beating them two hands to one, and she could tell Carter had had enough. She'd been looking for a way to get him out of the game, to throw him off and now she wondered if Carter Bain was doing the same. If not, was he merely trying to a) get to her to do some business deal, b) work his way into her pants, or c) both?

Leila decided to finish her taco and hold her thoughts and her cards close to her chest. No need to let any of the men at the table know what was going on in her head. At least not at that moment. The stakes were too high, and this was her game to win.

It wasn't long before she was able to see what Carter was up to. It would seem his tactic of calling out Bradley Wright had indeed thrown the man off and he wasn't thinking as clearly as he had been earlier.

Add to that the distraction of the pretty cocktail waitress he couldn't keep his eyes off of, and the fact that he couldn't keep his thin lips off the rim of his constantly refilled glass, and Bradley was bound to make careless mistakes. He kept asking for cards when he shouldn't, calling with low pairs, ridiculous things like that. And now Leila and Carter, or so she suspected, were able to discern Bradley's not so subtle tell of tapping his knee when he actually did have a hand worth fighting for. He had proven to be an adversary who was not worthy of much.

After losing out to Carter with a pair of nines and jacks to his queens, Bradley threw his cards down in frustration. "That's it for me," he declared. He looked over at Leila and gave her a bleary half smile. "Lovely lady, I'm going to take my leave before I embarrass myself further."

Leila nodded. "I understand. Please give your wife my best. I hope to see her on my next trip out this way."

But Bradley Wright was already looking past her in search of his prey for the night, since the party was clearly starting to wind down, most of the revelers having made their exits over an hour before. It wasn't lost on Leila that his partner had already gone, along with the girl in the fuchsia dress. Wright cleared his throat and turned back Leila's way. "Of course." Bradley exited as Nia was walking over to the table. He passed his most attentive server a key card, leaving no doubt that he wouldn't be alone tonight.

Leila looked Jasper's way and let out a weary sigh. "I think I'm done with them. Not that it matters, but that dude is an ass. An ass with a wife at home, an ass who is right now going to meet some cocktail waitress. Not to mention his vodka sucks. That was not the formula we agreed to when signing the contract. I'm done with these types of deals."

She heard what she thought was another snort from Carter's side of the table and shot a look his way. "You have something else to add, suit? Care to use your words?"

With that, Jasper put a warning hand on Leila's forearm.

She turned to him. "Yes, J, I get it. Business is business." She then turned back to Carter and pasted on her working girl smile. "I'm sorry. I tend to get a little, well, passionate about certain things."

Carter stared at her for a moment. Longer than she found entirely comfortable, though it wasn't unwelcome. Then he finally shook his head. "Not at all. Your business is your business. That is, unless it happens to be my business." Leila raised a brow, and he shrugged. "And you're right. That vodka is awful. Any sales they get, I'm sure they can contribute to your spokesmanship."

"See there, Leila? The man has a point. You are the hot commodity here. The rest doesn't matter. Now, don't go making rash decisions when you're tired," Jasper said.

Leila shot him a hard look. "You know me, J. Do I ever make rash decisions?"

Just then, as if on cue, the music changed and "Darling Leila" came on. Leila suspected the DJ was doing his swan song for the night. Both Nia and Jasper started to laugh, and Leila shook her head at Jasper, then turned to her friend.

"You too? You're supposed to be my girl," she told Nia.

Nia held up a hand. "Of course I am, but you have to admit, the timing was too perfect. Now, if you want me to go find Miles and break some kneecaps, I've got your back. But Jasper's got the right of it with you and rash decisions."

It was then that Leila couldn't help but laugh. She needed that. She needed this. Just a moment to let go. She looked over at Carter and stilled. She had forgotten he was there for a moment, but his quiet, assessing stare brought her quickly back to the reality that she was still on display and had not just gathered with her friends to play cards.

Jasper put his hands over hers gently. "It's okay, hon. Carter is cool."

Leila raised her perfectly arched brows as she continued to stare at the stranger. "Is he? Or is he just like the rest of these suits working in entertainment? Full of false promises, out to see what or who they can score with, and willing to do it by any means necessary, no matter who gets hurt in the process."

She watched Carter's eyes narrow as a spark of fire ignited. "I'm sorry, but I think you must have me confused with the jackass who just left. Or perhaps it's one of the *many* men you've dealt with in the past," he said.

His emphasis of the word *many* was not lost on Leila, and she felt her temper start to rise. "I'm afraid you've been giving too much credence to the gossip rags, Mr. Bain. That or listening to the wrong kind of music. Because really, you don't know anything about me."

"I'd say the same about you," Carter fired back, looking her straight in the eye.

Jasper chose then too jump in the fray. "Well, there now, children. Isn't it cute how it went from zero to a hundred just like that?" He turned to Nia. "Maybe it would be best to change that damned song. Seems to bring out the beast in the best of people." Jasper then turned to Leila. "My guy here is right. And he's totally cool. I invited him in hopes that you two would get along. He's got great things happening, and the fact that you're two workaholics with commitment issues, hell, I don't see why you two can't be the best of friends."

Carter's smile faltered at the same time Leila frowned as they both looked Jasper's way in confusion.

"Carter is just about as afraid of the altar as you are," Jasper said, directing his line to Leila.

She balked. "I am in no way afraid of the altar."

Jasper rolled his eyes. "Really? Tell that to your three ex-fiancés."

"How's about the fact that each of them is an ex for a reason? When I find one that can at least be as loyal as my damned dog, maybe I'll make it to the altar. At this point, none can stand up to their word for shit."

Jasper nodded. "Okay, you have a point there. But still, all those broken engagements and your, shall we say, temper have not done you any good."

Carter cleared his throat before speaking up. "Can I ask what any of this has to do with me?"

Jasper nodded his way. "You see, just like Leila, you, too, would benefit from having a more settled and stable image."

Carter pulled a face, then looked from Jasper to Leila, then back to Jasper again. "Wait? How did we get here, and what does my being married have to do with my job or my family?" Carter said, his voice hilariously high.

"Yes, how? What?" Leila chimed in. "And how much of that damned vodka did you drink tonight?" Suddenly she wanted to kick Jasper. Why was he pursuing this line of talk? He was her friend and agent, and as her agent, he was supposed to be engaging Carter in a talk about his new network. Not bashing her in front of the man. "What the hell are you talking about?" Leila added. "And what does my relationship status have to do with anything? Why should I settle down? You're the one who has told me all these years that I shouldn't attach myself to anyone. That being single is better for my image. And if you haven't noticed by my contracts and tonight's turnout, you were absolutely right."

Jasper calmly took a sip of his drink and

proceeded to shuffle the cards before he spoke again. "To answer your second question, Leila, I've hardly had any of that blue swill. And as for your other questions, yes, you're doing great, but by your own admission, is this where you want to be? You yourself have been on me about sending your career in another direction."

Leila swallowed. *Bingo.* Damn, he was good. She gave Jasper a steely gaze before turning back to Carter, her mind now swirling in an entirely different way. "Oh, he's full of it." She waved a hand. "Pay him no mind. He's just trying to get us riled up and get into our heads. He probably slipped a message to the DJ to play that stupid song, too. Jasper hates to lose, and so far, he's lost one too many hands. You don't see no rings on his fingers, either. So what does he know from commitments or relationships? He's just as screwed up as the rest of us."

Upon hearing that comment, Nia snorted and raised her glass to salute those particular facts.

Leila continued. "Don't let him ruin your night, our night. Let this be the start of a beautiful new friendship. One which we'll both benefit from." Leila raised her glass to Carter. She hoped she was on the right track, following where Jasper was going with all this.

But she was wrong. As Jasper finished dealing, he pitched wild with yet another curve. "Yes, to new beginnings. Though, now that I think about it more, your recent string of public breakups and tabloid headlines really have done us more harm than good."

Leila almost let out an audible sigh. How was this agenting? She wished he'd just drop it, but no, he continued.

"If you want to break up with clients, like the randy men of Double LL, and get out of suites like this and go over to the more manicured side of the tracks, then I think it's time for an image makeover. The public needs to see you doing something different. View you as somehow more stable. Maybe it's time to say good-bye to America's party girl and hello to Miss Apple Pie."

A look was exchanged between Jasper and Leila that gave her more than a slight chill. She picked up her cards, then put them back down, looking between the two men. "What are you getting at? Have you two had conversations that I should be privy to?" She looked at Jasper and got his usual look of innocence, and then she looked at Carter and got what she could only suspect was confusion, though who knew? She sure didn't know the man.

"I have no idea what you and he are talking about." Carter then leveled Jasper with a hard look, one that on a lesser man, Leila thought, might cause a quiver. "And, bro, I'd appreciate you keeping my business from the table. Really, my relationship status has nothing to do with this."

Jasper had the good sense to look sheepish. "My bad, and excuse me, but I think it does. I was just hinting that I noticed all the stable pairings at your corporate level. Must be hard being the bachelor at those corporate dinners. Aren't all the other VPs married, with children or with one on the way? White picket fence and all that? And don't worry about Leila or Nia here. Nia's ride or die. That's why she's on my team. She'd never give up a state secret. Consider this the cube of silence."

Carter looked at Nia, and she gave him a cool look back. "To the grave," was all she said.

Still, Carter looked leery. "How about we just finish our game? It is getting late."

It *was* getting late, and Leila was feeling like she'd have to come about this network thing another way and at another time. Jasper with his singles, image crap had thrown her off and shot it all to hell. *Nice going,*

J. Thanks for blowing my chance. If the guy didn't think of me as a risk before, he sure as hell does now.

Leila looked at her cards, then kept her expression neutral. A straight. Not bad, but it was a low one. Definitely not a surefire winner. *Perfect.* This night was going downhill faster than anticipated. But her eyes popped open and new hope bloomed at Carter Bain's next words.

"I'm sorry it's so late," he began. "However, since Jasper brought it up, I'd love it if you have some time — if not tonight, then back in New York — to get together to discuss a project the new network is putting together."

Hello! Give that man a prize.

He'd said it all so nonchalantly, so smoothly that Leila was sure it was his intention for being there all along. Smooth. Game recognized game. Part of Leila wanted to stand and give him a high five. Instead, she waved her hand with the cards. "We have nothing but time now. Tell me what you're working on." She looked at her hand again, this time holding back a smile. "Oh, and I'll raise five hundred."

Both men looked at their cards quickly, then looked at each other and promptly folded.

Shit, Leila thought. *Is everything tonight going to be like pulling teeth?*

Leila began to shuffle the cards as Carter started to talk. "First of all, I wanted to tell you how impressed I was with your performance in *Robot-x.*"

Leila steeled herself and waited for the other shoe to drop. She anticipated a comment about her wardrobe, her makeup, or questions about how she had balanced so well in the platform boots she had to wear. But none came. No, Carter Bain proceeded to rock her world by talking about her comedic timing, despite the lackluster script, and the vulnerability she brought to the role. He even mentioned her favorite scene with her young costar. Damn, the man was good.

So good that he ended up taking the next two hands. Then the third went to Jasper. Nia gave her a kick under the table, which caused Leila to jump.

"You okay?" she mouthed when Leila turned her way.

Leila nodded. She must be tired. Back home, she never lost to the guys. Her brothers had taught her well, and by the age of twelve, she'd been a champ at taking lunch money off even the most hardened juniors and seniors in school. "I'm good. Though, I think I could use another drink. It's getting late."

Nia got up to get her another soda. She brought it over, then left to dismiss the rest of the staff. The party had dwindled down to nil. Leila was so into Carter Bain that she'd hardly noticed the people who'd wandered in and out of their conversation, saying their good-byes.

"Should I go?" Carter asked, seeing that he was the last in attendance.

"Nah, let's finish this game first. You were saying?" Jasper replied, not ready to let go of potential business.

Leila took a sip of her drink. She was ready to get on a better footing and finally hear Carter out.

"Well, we're developing an exciting comedy with the Swoop brothers called *Brentwood Drive.* It's a modern flip on a roommates' story, with a couple of guys and a girl living together, and we'd love someone like you, Leila, for the lead." His eyes were bright now as he went into his sales pitch. "You're, of course, beautiful, but you're more than that. You've proven you have comedic timing, and you're sexy. You'd definitely bring in the demo we want."

Leila frowned. "And what demo is that?"

She saw something in Carter's jaw tick.

"Well, young men from eighteen to thirty-four."

Leila nodded, then looked at her freshly dealt hand. She shrugged. "I'm not sure if it's for me."

"Oh, hell," she heard Jasper say from her side.

"What's the 'Oh, hell' for?" she asked as Nia returned to their little party.

"Yes, what does that mean?" Carter inquired.

Jasper sighed. "It means she's shutting you down. And I don't know why. Leila, you're being unreasonable. This could be a good opportunity. How about you read the script? You said you wanted to branch out into acting."

Leila shot Jasper a look. "This doesn't sound like acting. This sounds like T and A modeling with a laugh track. And, sorry, but knowing the work of the Swoop brothers, they don't have the best rep when it comes to female characters. No offense."

Carter raised a brow. "Offense taken."

Leila snorted at that. She liked that he pushed back. She rarely got push back. Though now wasn't the best of times for it, still it was refreshing.

"Why? Am I wrong about the Swoop brothers?" Leila asked.

Carter looked at her hard. "Well, no, not entirely, but you're prejudging this project, rejecting it without even giving it a thought or a read."

"And you're not prejudging me and my abilities by thinking I'd be a perfect fit, the type that would fit the Swoops' mold?"

There was a brief standoff while she and Carter stared at each other across the table, and for a moment Leila thought she could feel the air practically crackle between them. She didn't know if it came from the twinge of animosity she felt or from something else entirely. Maybe it was a bit of both.

"How about we just finish this hand?" she finally said, hoping her voice came out cooler than she felt. "All in? While we're at it, you can tell me about the projects you're not considering someone like me for, like the *Shadowed Dreams* one I've heard about, with the kick-ass woman of color attorney lead." She watched as Carter's nostrils flared a bit, and had to admit this was infinitely sexy. This man was hot when he was riled up. Leila smiled sweetly. "Tell me, has that part been cast?"

He swallowed before he spoke. "No, it has not, but we, uh, were considering more seasoned actors for that series."

Unblinking, Leila looked him straight in

the eye. "Oh really? And just how seasoned is seasoned? Care to give me an example?"

She watched as the wheels quickly turned in Carter's brain. She had to admit he was cool with it, though. He barely flinched when he nonchalantly uttered the name she somehow knew she would hear. "Oh, someone like, say, Chloe Caraway."

Leila was cool. Or at least she hoped she was. Was Chloe Caraway now officially stalking her? She'd shown up at her opening, and now here she was, jacking the part Leila wanted. And no, it didn't matter if she was already up for the role. Leila was over the perfect Ms. Caraway. Besides, Chloe was one year older than her, but she officially claimed that her acting age was two years younger. How that counted as seasoned, Leila didn't quite know. But Chloe had been acting for years, having lucked out by being cast as a petulant teen when she just so happened to be a petulant teen by her director father in his breakout indie film. Leila had never understood the appeal of Chloe Caraway, but for some reason, the woman's bohemian "live and let live" attitude and nouveau riche lifestyle appealed to the masses.

Leila gave Carter a nod. "Good choice. Chloe is a definite draw, if you're going for that sort of thing."

She caught a slight spark in Carter's eyes. "Of course, nothing is set in stone yet, but like you said, no offense, we were just looking for a different type," he retorted.

It was Leila's turn to swallow now. "And like you said, offense taken."

They were both stunned once again when laughter came from Jasper's end of the table. "Kittens, sheath those claws. How about we end this game, this night, with a proposed solution that could be beneficial to us all?"

Leila let out a long sigh, while Carter let out a growl, and they stared at each other.

"Why do I feel like we're both about to be shafted?" Carter asked her.

Leila raised her brow. "Because we are. And he won't even buy us dinner first, knowing his ass."

CHAPTER 6

What had they gotten themselves into? More importantly, what had he gotten himself into? Carter looked at his hand and willed his body not to sweat as he fought the urge to tug at his collar. It wouldn't do any good. His collar was open, anyway. And it wasn't like it was hot in the suite, but still, he was burning up. Currently, he was holding a full house, jacks over tens. Solid, but not solid enough when the stakes were as high as they were on this night. How had he so quickly let Jasper tangle him in such a web? Damn, he should have anticipated this move, since Jasper was such a fast talker.

But most of the time it was Carter who was used to being the player and fast talker when it came to negotiations. And now here he was, the playa being played, and his whole career was now on the line with a lousy hand of jacks over tens. If it was merely money, he wouldn't care so much.

Money he could get back, but this was his reputation. Worse yet, his freedom, at least for the next six months.

Carter grinned, baring his teeth with a false bravado he definitely didn't feel. He looked over at Leila. What could she possibly be holding in those lovely hands of hers? She looked up at him. Those dark eyes with a cool glaze gave away nothing and promised everything. Carter swore his heart did a little skip-flip thing the likes of which he hadn't felt since sixth grade. She smiled back, not much, barely a hint of a movement, as her full, sensuous lips spread ever so slightly.

"Hmm," she murmured, then moved her gaze from him to Jasper and then back to him again. "Who's playing who? Suddenly, this night has gotten real, and I'm loving it."

Carter couldn't tell if she was being honest or sarcastic. She was a variable that he couldn't pin down, and it excited him as much as it infuriated him. For a while there, he had thought he had the upper hand with her. He'd won quite a few hands, and it had got him feeling pretty good, but then she had flipped the script on him and had started making unexpected calls. And the way she had dismissed his proposal for the

Brentwood project out of hand, he had to admit it had shaken him. Hell, maybe that was what had taken him out of his game, but worse, or equally as bad, was Jasper and his ridiculous bet/proposition disguised as a win for all of them. It had him thinking that maybe the two of them had been in cahoots from the start.

"So let me get this straight," Leila began again, pointing a blinged-out diamond embellished nail Carter's way. "If Carter here wins, then I will read for his *Brentwood* part, and if they like me, I have to take their offer, pending your approval of contractual stipulations, of course." The end part she directed toward Jasper. "But," she continued, "if I win, I get to read for both shows, and I get my pick of shows, and if the part in *Shadowed Dreams* is what I want, then that's the part I get." She leveled Carter with a stare, and he fought not to swallow against the lump in his throat.

It was then that Jasper chimed in. "But if I win, you both get married here now, tonight, and start in on Operation Image Makeover. You both have to stay married for six months' time. The original stipulations are in place. If one of you bails before the six-month period is over, then the other gets their pick of show." He turned to Carter then. "We have time, yes? These are all only in the talk stage for next summer. Filming is not due to start for at least six months, am I right?"

Carter gave him a tight nod. "Yes, but we'd like a commitment sooner."

Jasper let out a sigh. "And they'd like ice water in hell, too. This is the deal. Leila is highly sought after. I can pick up the phone right now and have her booked clear through the next year. Either you're in or you're out."

Carter stared at Jasper for a long beat. "And what if we both last the six months."

Leila and Nia's in unison chuckles almost unmanned him. He shot them both a hard glance which only made them laugh harder. Carter shook his head.

"If you both last," Jasper started, "Leila reads for both and gets her pick, with my guidance of course. She is my client and I have all faith in her abilities. She is an amazing talent."

Carter nodded. He too had all faith in Leila. He wouldn't be here putting his career in her hands if he didn't, but still, it didn't stop the fear from churning in his gut. What would his boss say to such a crazy scheme? When he'd made his arrangements to come out to Vegas, he'd called Everett and hinted about Leila. Everett had practically jumped through the phone with excitement. Carter knew there was no way he could go back to New York if she wasn't still an option on the table. But putting the future of another show in the balance? It was crazy. It was too much of a gamble.

Finally, Carter turned Leila's way, and their eyes locked. In that moment he was thankful he was seated, because if not, surely he would have fallen. *Shit.* She was dangerous. No matter where or how, the woman was pure gold. When she turned it on, she really was a force to be reckoned with. Carter let out a gruff sigh, partially to ease the pressure on his brain and partially to clear his throat. "I'm in."

Leila let out a harsh laugh at that. "Good. For a minute, I thought you were going to get cold feet and cut and run on me."

Carter shook his head. "One thing you should know about me, Ms. Darling, is when I say I'm in, I'm in."

Jasper grinned, then looked at Leila. She shook her head and for just the slightest moment, Carter thought she looked tired. The slight dropping of her guard had him wanting to throw his cards in and call the whole thing off. But then she sucked in a breath and looked up at Jasper and smiled.

Suddenly, the spark was back in her eyes. She grinned wide at Jasper and grabbed his face, smushed his cheeks together, and pulled him to her for a kiss.

"You really are a smart one," she said. She pushed him back into his chair, then looked at Carter. "I'm in, too. This is Vegas, baby!" She took out one card and asked for another. "All in!"

Nia shook her head. "You all have lost it."

Jasper grinned wide. "No cards for me. Shall I call?"

Leila shrugged, and Carter nodded.

"It's your game. You call it," Carter said.

"I'll defer to the lady," Jasper said.

Leila snorted. Then put down her cards. Lifted, then dropped her shoulders. "What's life without a little chance?" She dropped two pairs. And not even a good two pair. Eights and fours.

Carter frowned in confusion. A hand that should have made him happy brought a strange hollowness. "Sorry, Leila." He spread his full house, and waited for Jasper.

The man was quiet, too quiet, as he looked over at Nia and gave her a slight nod. "Pick up the phone, my dear, and see how quickly we can get a preacher." Jasper looked from Carter to Leila and spread his cards. "A straight flush. All hearts, queen high. We're going to have a fantastic next six months."

Leila sucked in a breath, and Carter looked at her in shock.

Her eyes softened then, and her smile was gentle and sweet. "Feel free to run now. It was only a silly game."

Carter shook his head. "The second thing you should know about me, my dear fiancée, is I never go back on my word or a bet."

Leila nodded, then turned to Nia. "Can I get a drink? I think it's time to break out something a little stronger than ginger ale."

CHAPTER 7

What the hell was she doing? Leila thought as she paced back and forth in the immaculately appointed penthouse bridal suite of the hotel. It didn't matter that it was the middle of the night, the hotel, living up to its newly acquired five-star reputation, had pulled out all the stops and in under an hour had gathered all they would need for her wedding to Carter Bain.

Carter Bain? Leila let the name roll around in her head a few times, and then she said it out loud. "Carter Bain. Carter Bain?" The next time she added a British accent. "Carter Bain." And then "Mrs. Carter Bain. Mrs. Leila Bain. Ugh." Leila shook her head and made a face.

Was she really going to go through with marrying a man she had known for under four hours? A man whose name still sounded strange and foreign on her lips? Sure, she had a crazy reputation for jumping in and out of relationships, but how was this really supposed to solve anything? How was she supposed to be able to stick it out for six months with a complete and total stranger?

Leila paused when the image of him looking at her with those soft but somehow challenging eyes came to the forefront of her mind, and she had the ridiculously juxtaposed feelings of both panic and calm. Panic over the fact that she was about to be legally bound to a total stranger. The legal part gave her more than a little trepidation, enough so that she rang up her lawyer, who was now currently in full panic mode, since she had had him draft a quickie pre-nup stating that what was hers was hers and what was his was his, and in the event of a shit storm, never the two shall meet.

And, yes, calm over the fact that for some odd reason, when she had looked at him from across that table and had made the crazy all-in bet, she'd never felt so sure or right about anything in her whole life. Not when she'd said yes to Miles G or yes to Wade, and not even when she'd run off with that dancer in Dubai. Sure, she was a girl who loved love, but the good thing was this wasn't about love.

She hardly knew Carter Bain. Sure, she

felt an initial ping of sexual attraction, but that she could get past. Because the thing she really connected with him on was about so much more. This was about something more solid than sex and, judging by her past experiences, even love. It was about business, and he seemed like the type of guy whom you could count on when it came to business.

Leila looked at herself now in the silver-plated wall mirror and tried to see herself through her soon-to-be husband's eyes. Did he look at her and see only what just about everyone else saw? The thought gave her pause and an unexpected lump in her throat. She blinked quickly as an unwanted glassy sheen of tears came to her eyes. *Not now. Please not now.* Now was not the time for emotions. *Save that for a real wedding.* One where actual feelings were involved.

She took stock of herself, standing in her strapless bra and thong, her hair now pinned up in a tousled chignon to create some semblance of elegance to fit some idea she had of what a wedding should be. Would he really see her or only pieces of her? Leila shook her head. What did it matter? She had made her choice when she went all in on that tired hand. She'd known she didn't have a chance of winning. Not a chance in hell. She'd also known what Jasper was holding. She'd made her choice in her heart when Carter said yes to the bet that she was going all in and was taking a chance on this guy, no matter what.

There was a soft knock, and then Nia walked into the room with a large garment bag over her arm. "What are you smirking about?" Nia asked.

"Oh, nothing much. Just the irony of me finally walking down the aisle, so to speak, and it's nothing like the media spectacle I had expected my wedding to be."

Nia paused before putting the garment bag on the bed. "So . . . what? Are you disappointed? Trust me when I say all I have to do is mention this to Jasper and he'll have no fewer than ten media outlets camped outside the door quicker than you can shimmy into your dress."

"Oh, God, no! The last thing I need to add to this drama is the press. They would eat me alive after the string of relationship disasters that I've had. Besides, we're doing this to revamp my image, though I'm starting to think the quickness of this may be counterproductive. Could this all be that damned Double LL talking? I can practically see the headlines already. 'Impulsive Leila is at it again!' and 'How long will this one last?' "

Nia shook her head. "Well, if that's how you feel about it, and you're so convinced that this will go wrong with the press, then why are you going through with it? Not to mention how your family will react."

Leila sucked in a quick breath. The image of her father's impending meltdown, not to mention her brothers', was something she was trying hard to keep in a lockbox in a far corner in the back of her mind. "Don't remind me. I'm trying my best not to think of them right now and to consider only how important this is for my career. Besides, my father would be thrilled to see me going in another direction. Acting rather than posing on the hood of a car. I say he'll probably consider it a step in the right direction."

Nia shot her a look. "You keep telling yourself that. Though he may not be overly thrilled when your photos end up in the lockers of some of his coworkers, he's always indulged you and supported you. But this . . ." Nia shook her head. "I don't know."

Leila bit at her bottom lip. Nia was right. Her father would be beyond hurt over her taking a huge step like this without him being here, whether it was fake or not.

Finally, Nia threw up her hands. "That's

it. You're wavering. I'm going to go out there and have Jasper call this whole thing off." Determined, she turned on her pumps and started for the door, but she wasn't quick enough and was caught when Leila lunged, snaked out her hand and grabbed Nia by the forearm. Nia turned around, and this time she didn't look anything like Jasper's sweet, patient assistant. No, this young woman was very much the Nia whom Leila had grown up with. Strong, fierce, and determined.

"What is it? Why you stopping me?" Nia asked. "I knew this whole thing was ridiculous back up in Jasper's suite, and there is no way I'm going to let you throw your life away on a silly bet."

Leila looked at her friend long and hard. She knew Nia was just looking out for her, trying to save her from what, yes, could be a horrendous mistake. But for some reason, Leila couldn't just let her go. Something in Leila wanted this. Told her that this was the right thing to do — though everything else in her life was strongly pointing in the opposite direction.

Leila swallowed before speaking. "I don't know, Nia. I made so many stupid mistakes in the past, especially when it comes to men. And who knows? This very well may be another one. But at least this one is not based on a crazy emotion. This time it's based on business. I look at this guy, and I can read him. I know exactly what he wants from me, and he knows exactly what I want from him. There are no misplaced emotions or lies wrapped up in promises of forever. Here we just have the promise of what we can do for each other in the very near future."

Nia looked down at Leila's hand, the one that was still grasping her arm tightly. "If this is so emotionless for you and you have no feelings about the matter, then why in the hell are you still gripping me so damned hard?"

Leila let her go suddenly, as if she had caught fire. "I'm sorry. I just didn't want you to go out there and set things in motion, giving Carter any doubts about the arrangement we are getting into." She then tried to put on a smile, but she knew instantly by the narrowing of her friend's gaze that Nia didn't believe it for one moment.

Leila turned away from Nia and focused her attention on the garment bag on the bed. "Now, come on and show me what you've got here. I might as well see what fabulousness I'm tying the knot in."

Though Leila expected another protest, Nia knew she was beat. So all she did was shake her head slightly and lean down and unzip the bag. Out of it she pulled two beautiful dresses. The first was a simple, long, bias-cut satin slip dress that was held up by the thinnest of straps that tied around the back of the neck in a halter style. The back of the dress dipped low, and Leila saw it had a lovely little train that was accented with little seed pearls. It was gorgeous in an old Hollywood way and something in which she could imagine walking toward her intended on a beach at sunset. Leila blinked, quickly guarding herself once again against potential glassy eyes, as Nia put the dress back down on the bed.

Leila let out a long sigh and was happy to find there was another choice of dresses in the garment bag. This one was also beautiful, but it was a lot more fun and flirty, being that it was a simple short dress that was strapless and had white lace and beautiful beading to accentuate the bust and waist area. The dress was lovely and definitely more suited for a Vegas wedding than the satin dress.

Leila gave a nod. "This is the one."

"Are you sure?" Nia asked. "I was so sure you would choose the other one. It seems more your style. A little more elegant and a little less flirty."

"Ah, but I surprised you once again, didn't I?" She gave a longing glance at the elegant satin dress before turning away and smiling toward the other dress. "No, this one is it. I think it's definitely more fitting for the occasion."

Nia nodded. "I agree. And you'll look beautiful in it."

Leila stepped forward and gave her friend a hug. "And I'm lucky I'm going to have you by my side when I wear it. Thank you so much for finding these for me. And for, well . . . you know, everything else."

Nia waved a hand. "Oh, hush. It's what I get paid for."

Leila shook her head. "Once again, no. It's not what you get paid for, and you know it. It's what you're my friend for. And I love you for it."

Nia tilted her head and arched a brow. "I'm going to hold on to that real tight, because we're both going to need that strength when you get home, married, and have to face your father and brothers."

Leila winced. "Like I said, don't remind me. And I thought the paparazzi would be the biggest challenge. That's going to be a total nightmare."

■ ■ ■ ■

On the opposite side of the suite, Carter Bain paced in his room. Noticing what he was doing and becoming quickly annoyed with himself, he abruptly stopped, jogged in place, and rolled his shoulders. "Get it together, man," he said to himself by way of a pep talk. But the motivational words weren't doing much motivating at all. Carter shook out his tingling hands, then rubbed his sweaty palms along the thighs of his pants. He let out a long breath.

What had he gotten himself into? Who in the hell took such a stupid bet? Worse than that, who took such a bet and had the nerve to lose? He, more than anyone, knew you didn't gamble when it came to business. Sure, when it came to love, but that was an entirely different thing. A person could play fast and loose with their heart. All you had to lose there was a few tears. Perhaps your dignity, when you looked like a fool on Facebook. But this was his name that was at stake. His legacy, his career, his goddamned money!

Carter flopped down onto the settee at the end of the bed, put his elbows on his knees, and clasped his hands together on the back of his head. He fought against the overwhelming desire to hyperventilate. He wasn't one to do the hyperventilating thing. Hell, he wasn't one to even panic. But right now he was sure ready.

He sucked in a breath and tried to look at things objectively as he thought back. In the moment when he'd made that bet, though he knew it was madness, it felt like the right thing to do. Like what Jasper was proposing was a win all around. Either way, he was coming out of the deal with Leila Darling, and that was a potential boon for the network. Getting her signed on with *Brentwood* would surely cement his standing at WBC for the next year or two at least. And Carter needed that. Despite his longtime relationship with the Walker family, he still knew that you were only as good as your latest conquest. And he also knew that being set up with this new network deal was a big test for him. So why was he so afraid?

Because you're crazy for her, you idiot.

Carter doubled over even more as the answer jumped to the forefront of his mind, along with the visual of Leila looking at him with those challenging eyes from across the table. Her. Why did it have to be her? Anyone else and he gladly would have made the bet, signed the papers, and walked down

112

the aisle without a care knowing he had a firm handle on his feelings. But with Leila? Carter knew he was setting himself up for pain that was far worse than financial loss.

Carter let out a low moan. That was it: he was an out and out fool. If anyone ever found out that he had lost — worse yet, had thrown everything away on a hand he knew he'd lose — for this totally unknown territory, why, he'd be kicked out of every professional club he belonged to. But when he looked at Leila, what he saw was, not the financial gain, not the big pat on the back from his boss, or the fact that with her, he could cement his legacy. What he saw in her eyes was a very real setup for the heartbreak that he'd been guarding himself against for so long, pushed up against the chance of a happiness he knew was near unobtainable. And still Carter couldn't let it slip through his fingers. He had to take his chance.

But, he was nervous. He was finally about to have his turn at bat and what if he struck out in the most epic way possible?

Carter reached for his phone and flipped it over a few times in his hand. More than anything, he wanted to text one or both of his boys, Aidan and Vin, to let them know what a colossal mess he was about to venture into. Hell, if he was lucky, Aidan just might talk him out of it. He'd at least give him a little reasoning to go against his father by saying that no deal for the company was worth putting his heart out on the line. If anything, Aidan could always be counted on to go against his father. However, Vincent might be another story: as wrapped up as he was in his newly inked monogamy, it seemed he wanted nothing more than the whole world to join him in the institution. Carter's fingers hovered over his keyboard, but then he put the device back to his side and shook his head as thoughts of his friends and then his own parents threatened to seep into his mind. His father, as usual, would be terribly disappointed. Marry for a business deal? Unheard of. And his mother, well, just the thought of marrying without her approval, he didn't even want to go there. But what did it matter? The ceremony was taking place here and now, and there was no one, besides himself, who would be able to stop this train from leaving the station and right now his instincts were telling him this was a move he needed to make.

There was suddenly a knock on the door, which jolted him, causing Carter to stand quicker than he thought was dignified. He coughed and cleared his throat before beckoning the person to enter.

"You all right here?" Jasper said, peeking his head around the door. "Mind if I come in?"

Carter nodded. "Yeah, man, I'm fine. Sure, come on in."

Jasper walked in, balancing a small bag and two tumblers of brown liquid. "Thought you might be in need of this, considering the circumstances of the evening."

Carter shook his head. "You know what? I think I've had enough for the night. Best I keep a level head before going about saying my 'I dos.' "

Jasper looked at him for a moment with hard eyes and then gave a shrug before putting one glass down and then taking a long pull from the other one. "No problem. I get that. But, listen, are you sure this is something you want to go through with? I mean, it was just a silly bet. Just something I thought up on the fly. There really is no need for you to go through with it. I can head over to the other side of the suite and talk Leila out of it. And, hey, given a little time, trust me, I'm sure Leila will be happy to read your script. Though as I said earlier, you should give her a chance at the other show. She's extremely talented. She may surprise you. And this is not just her agent talking."

Carter looked at Jasper seriously now. The man had a point, and besides, he knew his client very well. If anyone could convince Leila to read for *Brentwood,* he should be able to. He knew that they were more than just agent and client. They had been friends for a long time, and their roots went very deep. But he also knew that though he had confidence that Leila would be adequate for the other part, he had no faith that he could sell her to the network. Her experience and her reputation just didn't fit. No, she was good for *Brentwood.* And he had to do what he could in order to convince her of it. Besides, though it was the wackiest idea he'd heard in a long time, Jasper had a point. Leila did need an image makeover if she wanted to make it anywhere in Hollywood and be more than just a fly-by-night girl. She needed to be cleaned up. And maybe, just maybe, her settling down in some farce of a marriage would be the thing that did the trick. If it wasn't with him, Carter had a feeling it would definitely be with someone else, and then where would he and his show be? Better the devil he knew. At least that was the reasoning he was going with.

"Nah, man, I made the bet, and I lost it.

So I'm prepared to deal with that. And like you said, it's not really a loss at all. If Leila and I play this right, we can both come out on top. She with a more refined reputation, and I get the new star that my network needs."

Jasper snorted. "Yeah, and it doesn't hurt that you will be coming out of the deal married to one of the most beautiful women in the world." Jasper raised a brow.

Carter paused as he thought for a moment, his mind going to all his past dreams of Leila, and now here she was, just a moment away from becoming his reality. But was any of this really real? No. He looked at Jasper and gave what he hoped was an emotionless smile. "Listen, I may be crazy, but I'm no fool. That woman is looking at me as a means to an end and vice versa. Even if I were attracted to her, I know where I stand."

Jasper laughed at that. "Well, I'm glad to hear you know where you stand." Suddenly, his voice got deadly serious. "Because, as you know, she's my friend before my client, and I don't want to see her hurt. You make sure she's not, otherwise this business arrangement we have will turn sour real quick."

Carter looked at him straight on. "You

don't have to worry about me."

Jasper stared a beat longer, then suddenly relaxed his tense stance and grinned, handing Carter a small bag with the hotel's logo. "That's great, because you're about to embark on quite an adventure, my friend, and let me tell you, with Leila, it won't be easy, and it definitely won't be dull. Now here. You guys are going to need some rings to make this thing official. The hotel was kind enough to send up a couple of selections. Let's pick out something worthy of your soon-to-be bride."

Feeling like some reality show sham, Carter did his best to hold back his nerves as he went over the selection of platinum rings that the hotel had sent up. In the end, he went with his gut and chose a simple diamond infinity band that he knew was probably not the most impressive for a woman of her status but had an elegance he thought suited her and well, she could always stack more diamonds on top of this . . . whatever this might be . . . got past the six-month point. Jasper was surprisingly quiet after the ring was picked out, and then he headed out to check on Leila's final preparations.

As Carter slipped on his suit jacket once more and straightened his tie, he looked out the window and saw, far on the horizon, the first flickers of the sun as it hinted at rising. It was getting close to 5:00 in the morning. They'd been up all night. It was almost time for the ceremony. Just about time for him to become part of a "them." Part of the sensation, really. Carter Bain, bachelor producer, would be no more, and the world would be introduced to Mr. Leila Darling. Carter grimaced as he thought of that awful name, which would no doubt get picked up by the press. It was either that or some awful moniker that would be a fusion of their two names. He made a mental note to get in touch with Karen first thing so that she could get ahead of the stories once they were back in New York. Branding was everything when it came to this deal.

Carter let out a deep breath and headed toward the bedroom door and out into the open living area, where they would have their ceremony, but then turned back feeling more secure when he wrapped his hand around his almost forgotten cell and placed it in his breast pocket. When he reached for the door handle, he realized he had forgotten something else, then turned once again, striding over to pick up the beautiful diamond ring. He held it up to the light watching the diamonds sparkle on all sides. Would she think it was beautiful? What would she feel like as he put it on her finger and made a pledge of love, and what about her pledge of fidelity and trust to a man she'd just met? Would she believe him when he said his vows, or would she laugh it off as just another publicity stunt? Carter frowned. What did it matter as long as they both lived up to their ends of the deal for the next six months? After that, all contractual promises were null and void.

Carter put the ring in his pocket, where it clinked against the glass of his phone as he headed toward the door and his impending destiny.

Chapter 8

Do you take this man to be your lawfully wedded husband? To have and to hold from this day forward as long as you both shall live?

Carter groaned as he stretched out in the hotel bed and the words from the evening before — well, the morning before — washed over him. Was it real? Did that all really just happen? He opened his eyes cautiously and noted the harsh sunlight coming through the sliver of an opening in the curtains in the hotel room. So he wasn't home, safe in his own bed in New York. And he wasn't still in California. No, this was an entirely different room. Carter raised his left hand, gave it a glimpse, and winced against vision of the platinum band mocking him.

"Fuck." Upon hearing his word vibrate against his eardrums, Carter pushed himself up and looked around the room, suddenly worried. Did she hear that? No, the room was empty. No one to hear his word of regret or witness his sudden panic except himself. He let out a long breath of relief as he pulled the covers back to get up and noted his nakedness. *Naked?* So when the hell did that happen? Carter frowned as he cautiously got up and found his boxers where they'd been discarded on the side of the bed. He yanked them on, and tried to pull a visual rewind of the missing hours into his mind.

Still slightly groggy and confused, Carter padded over to the bedroom door and listened for any outside voices. All seemed quiet in the outer section of the suite, so Carter cautiously peeked out, ventured forth, and found five bottles and four champagne glasses, all empty, but no sign of his new wife. He picked up an almost empty bottle and held it up to the light. The image of Leila as she'd looked up at him with those sparkling eyes and given him her hand in marriage danced in his mind. But then she'd blinked and gave a cheeky little smile and turned to the officiant in answer to his "Do you take this man . . . ?" question.

"Basically. That's what we're all here for, isn't it?" she'd said.

Carter had stifled a groan, but a grunt had escaped.

She'd turned his way with a slight frown. "Oh, don't be so serious. You're not my husband yet." No need for those types of looks. She'd patted him on his hand and cleared her throat as she turned back to the officiant, a quite reserved older gentleman who seemed to be taking his duties a tad too seriously, given the fact that they were in Vegas in the wee hours of the morning. The man had looked upon Leila in a reprimanding way, leaving no opening for quips or jokes.

Leila looked back at him, this time a bit more solemnly, "I do," she said, her voice so clear, it practically echoed off the walls. She looked back Carter's way and gave him a nod that seemed more of a challenge than a promise.

Carter gave her a nod back. He noted this wasn't the most whimsical or the most romantic way to go into a marriage, but since this was more of a business arrangement, he'd rather keep things on the up and up and totally aboveboard.

With the exchanging of rings, Carter was glad to see that Leila had also picked out something simple for him, a simple thin platinum band, nothing gaudy or intrusive, and it fit his finger perfectly, though maybe it was a bit snug for his liking. So she had to push a little to get it passed his knuckle. The tightness made him wonder what he'd have to do to get it off when the time came.

But when he pulled out her ring to slip it on her finger, he steeled himself, preparing for her condemnation of the ring. Carter didn't expect the relief he felt when, instead of expressing dismay, she looked up at him and gave him a smile. Once again she'd done it, made his heart flat-out stop. And for a second, he almost believed that this whole thing wasn't calculated, that she liked what he'd chosen for her.

The ring slid on her finger more easily than his had, and the simple diamonds looked surprisingly at home on her elegant finger. He was still looking at it when the officiant's next words echoed in his ears and reached his brain. "And I now pronounce you husband and wife. You may kiss the bride."

The words came so fast and were so sudden, Carter felt like he'd been smacked across the face with a very large, very wet hand. *Husband and wife? Kiss the bride?* Why in the hell didn't he think of that one? Carter's head jerked up, and he looked at Leila wide-eyed and was tongue-tied for the first time in a very long time. He was hyper-aware of the judgmental officiant and the eyes of their two witnesses, Jasper and Nia, as they watched his every move, Nia with her cell phone out, capturing the moments. How was he supposed to handle this? Carter sucked in a breath and leaned in, going for the side of Leila's cheek, not wanting to be too forceful or to embarrass her. This was the time to set the tone for what they were about to embark on.

But just as he was going in, Leila turned. Her head twisted toward his, and her cool, full lips touched his for the first time, causing his whole body to flame from the inside out.

The interaction probably lasted no more than three seconds, but in that span of time Carter surmised he was a dead man walking. It was as if a rocket had gone off, transferring energy from her lips to his and sending it throughout his entire body. As if everything that was once dead inside him had suddenly flared to life. His eyes had closed on their own, and when she pulled back and he opened them again, the whole world was new and he didn't know how to navigate it. Shit. When had he turned into such a melodramatic wuss?

Carter heard a distinct buzzing coming from his bedroom and realized that he'd been standing there, staring at the empty bottle like an idiot, for quite a while. He put it down and ran into the bedroom to grab his cell, but just missed the call. Scrolling through his phone, he noticed that he'd already missed at least ten calls. How in the hell had he slept through all that? Once again, his mind did a quick reversal, and he looked toward the doorway.

He recalled all the toasts with the drinks. Jasper and his goddamned liberal pouring. The four of them laughing over how they were going to play their next moves. If only he had been smart enough to take notes, he'd be okay. But he hadn't, and now he felt like he was just drifting. Listing in the middle of the ocean without any way back to shore. Carter leaned against the desk in the room, scrolled through his messages again, and took note that Karen had called him at least three times, his boss twice, and that there were texts from Aidan, Vin, and Karen. Even his mother had reached out four times. This was not going to be fun. He went over to his text messages and clicked open the first from Karen.

So what happens in Vegas doesn't stay in Vegas, or does it? Call me. Did you really just do what Page Six is saying you did? Of course you didn't. K

He clicked open Karen's second text. Okay, seriously, you really should give me a call. K

He read her third text. Call me. You have now blown my high from my massage. There are fires and then there are fires. This one looks like an inferno. We need to do damage control. K

Then there was the one from Aidan.

What have you let this job get you into now? I sure hope she's worth it. See you when you get back.

From Vin, a man of few words, there was just an LOL. The worst was from his mother, for whom he should've never gotten a smartphone.

Carter Reginald Bain, if you did what they are saying you did, you had better start praying. Are you seriously trying to kill your mother? Call me.

Carter shook his head. Damn it. This was really happening. He let out a breath. But how could he have done this without at least giving Karen a heads-up? If his phone was blowing up then his poor assistant was probably being pummeled. And how could he have not intercepted his mother? If he'd been thinking clearly at all he'd have proposed, he and Leila would have dated or fake dated for a while to see if this fake marriage deal was something they both wanted, if it was even worth the media spectacle that would ensue. They had been married for less than half a day, and already the word had gotten out.

Carter frowned. *Wait a minute.* How had word gotten out? They'd paid the hotel a good sum of money to be discreet. The officiant, Reverend Stern, had been given more than triple his usual fee. So who had let it slip? Carter felt a burning start low in his belly. Had Jasper screwed him already? This early in the deal? They'd agree to handle it quietly and let the news slip out via a perfectly timed interview. But now here it was, all out there without any media management. What sort of people had he gotten in bed with this time?

Carter looked over at the disheveled bed, now noticing that it was only his side that was messed up. *Way to go, newlywed.* He looked down at his phone again and shook his head in frustration. And where the hell was his wife? On instinct, Carter went to scroll through the numbers on his phone and then stopped, laughing wryly to himself.

"Hello, dummy," he mumbled. Then went to his contacts and found Jasper's number.

He got a pickup on the second ring. "Hey there." Jasper's voice was way too bright for the bricks in his head but Carter stayed silent, not wanting to show weakness this early on. "I feel like I should practically call you brother-in-law. You know, since Leila and I are so close. I almost feel like we're family," Jasper said.

Carter fought back a growl. Family? Now that was seriously pushing it. "That's okay. Carter will do fine," he said. "But speaking of family, you have any idea where my dear wife is today?"

"You don't remember?"

Carter didn't have the patience for playing "You don't remember?" type games with Jasper. If he remembered, he wouldn't be calling. "If I remembered, would I be calling you?" he said, letting his words uncharacteristically give away his thoughts.

"All righty, then," Jasper replied. "No need to get in a tizzy. Damn it. You'd think a man on his honeymoon would be in a better mood."

"You're pushing it, Jasper," Carter warned. The fact that his marriage was unconsummated, and would likely stay that way, was not a subject he felt in the mood to joke about.

"Okay, okay. She's at the shoot right now and then on the red-eye home to New York."

"Great. Thank you. I'll arrange to fly back to New York with her."

"Okay, that sounds good. I just have a few loose threads to clean up here —"

"Ya think?" Carter said, cutting him off.

But Jasper didn't take the bait and just continued. "But I'll see you back in the city once I get in. We already need to do some damage control."

"Ya think?" Carter spit out again.

Suddenly, Jasper changed his tone and turned softer, less jovial. "And, Carter, loosen up a bit. Don't be so serious when you talk with Leila. I'd take a softer tack. Remember, this is something you wanted, too."

Carter cleared his throat. Jasper was right. He hadn't been pushed into this, and he hadn't been sidelined in any way. He'd come to Vegas for the sole purpose of getting Leila Darling to agree to be on his show. He'd told himself he'd get the job done by any means necessary, and that was what he did or was doing. It didn't do him any good to play the victim card or the remorse card now. If it were someone else, he'd call them out as a whiner, eating sour grapes. "I'm fine," he told Jasper. "Just a little groggy from all the celebrating last night. I'll see you in New York. Right now I need to get myself settled so that I can make arrangements to fly back with Leila. We cool?"

"Absolutely," Jasper replied. "I'll talk to you soon."

"Wait!" Carter yelled, suddenly embarrassed. "Um, can you, uh, please give me my wife's number?"

Carter hung up after getting the number. Shaking his head, he headed toward the bathroom, the champagne of the night before now catching up with him. He swore Jasper's laughter would follow him for the next fifty years.

But in the bathroom doorway, Carter was stopped short by a glaring message in red lipstick across the bathroom mirror. He groaned. Still, he couldn't help the upturning of the corners of his lips as he read her message.

We'll always have Vegas.

xxx,
Wifey

Leila didn't want to answer the phone. She was sitting in hair and makeup, feeling

131

every bit like death warmed over but doing her best to hide it. She knew if she answered the phone and let the real world in, her hiding days would be done. After last night, her mind was doing a wraparound Tilt-A-Whirl thing, and for the life of her, she couldn't make it stop.

The wedding ceremony had been more emotional than she dared dream it could be. Who would've thought that attaching herself to a perfect stranger, even if it was in name only, could feel so real? But it did. Worse yet, what was with her going all wild Leila and turning her head at just the wrong moment and kissing him? Why had she gone and done that? And why had that kiss rocked her to her toes?

Was that what married kissing felt like?

Was it some big secret that the marrieds were keeping from all the singletons to keep them out of the toe-curl club?

Not to mention that even though she had tried to make light of the ceremony and the vows, still when she had looked into Carter Bain's eyes and had said that she would take him, to have and to hold from that day forward, something in her had felt like it was a true and solemn vow. A vow she should keep as if she had been in church and had promised to God. But they hadn't been in church, and the ceremony had been nondenominational for a reason. Did God even go to Vegas?

Leila squelched back a sigh over her stupid thought. *Damn it.* Now she had gone and done it. She'd made the vow and known immediately that she didn't want to break it. God or not. She was screwed, utterly and completely. Besides, this probably wasn't God at all, but the devil laughing his ass off.

Part of her told herself to take solace in the fact that ridiculous decisions like this were what divorces were made for. But just thinking that, even for a second, put a lump in her throat and made tears threaten her eyes. Her mother and father had been through so much together, including her mother's cancer, and her father had stuck by her mother's side, faithful to their love up until the very end and beyond. They'd shown her what love and commitment meant. How could she do something so horrible like make a mockery of it? All for just another rung up the ladder of so-called success. She knew her father was going to be so disappointed in her. How could he not be if she was already disappointed herself?

"You okay, Leila?" the makeup artist asked. "I'm going to need you to stop blinking so that I can get these lashes straight."

"Sorry. I'm fine." Oh, hell, she had to get herself together, and she had to do it quick. She was on a job; there was no room for emotions. Today she was being paid to look beautiful, almost ethereal, as she sweltered in the Vegas desert, hawking five-dollar-a-bottle water. She let out a long breath and told herself to think beautiful, calm thoughts.

But calm was short lived. Leila knew the exact moment when word had got out. When she first arrived on set with Nia, everything had been normal. Leila was smart to have remembered to take her ring off and place it in the change compartment of her wallet before stepping onto the set. She hadn't expected to have any emotions while doing that small act, and yet she felt something as she tugged at the band of diamonds and let it slip from her finger. She was exhausted, as was Nia, though Nia was handling the all-nighter bounce back quite a bit better than Leila was. She was up and coherent, well caffeinated and pinging away on her cell as fast as her thumbs would take her. The woman was a marvel.

For what it was worth, Leila was grateful that at least the night before didn't show on her face, thanks to her going old school and dipping her face in an ice bath to keep down the puffiness. Also, the little dabs of hemorrhoid cream under her eyes had helped. Gross, yes, but when it came to the unforgiving eye of the camera's lens, a girl would do anything to bury the previous night's sins. It was okay, though; she just had to get through this, then she, Jasper, Nia, and Carter could put their heads together without the influence of cards, music, or bad vodka and would come up with a plan to handle this potential PR nightmare before it got further than the four of them.

Who knew? Maybe she could convince Carter to cut his "wifey" a break while still giving her the read she wanted. She'd sleep on her red-eye flight home tonight, gather her thoughts, and hit New York ready to rock. But it was on that thought, as she was getting into her next outfit, her phone, as well as Nia's, started buzzing like mad. At the same time it seemed as if everyone else's phones started pinging, too. Nia looked at her phone, then gave Leila a wide-eyed look and a slight head shake of warning.

Just then her dresser looked up at Leila with her mouth agape, pausing as she was slipping a pair of red stilettos on Leila's feet. "Leila, darling, tell me this is a joke. You can't really be married, can you? Don't tell me some guy finally found a way to tie you down."

Leila's eyes went wide as she looked over at Nia, who gave her a quick warning glance that told her to steel her features. Quickly, Leila let out a little laugh as she adjusted the cups of her black bra. "Oh, please. What sort of mess are the fake news outlets writing about me now?"

The dresser laughed at her little joke.

"I swear, I should start asking for royalties off all the papers they sell due to me. Now come on. Let's get this shoot done before this sun goes from scorching to frying," Leila declared.

Without a backward glance, Leila snatched her phone and headed for the back of the trailer, toward the bathroom area. Blinking quickly, she looked at her phone and swiped the screen open to reveal the calls and texts she had been avoiding all day. As she feared, there were messages from all three of her brothers and her father. From Jasper she'd received a short note that had gone to both her and Nia, and there was one from an unknown number, which she would've normally ignored, but for some reason, her finger couldn't help but swipe it over.

Got your number from Jasper. Thought it might be something we should share. Hoping we could make arrangements to travel home together tonight. Apparently, what happens in Vegas doesn't stay there for long.

CB
Hubby

Shit. And then the blinking started again. Leila fought back against the potential emotional onslaught and the little wobble of a smile that teased at the corners of her lips. *Hubby.* She didn't expect that hint of playfulness from him, and it pierced her like a flaming arrow to her heart. Leila let out a long breath. No. She couldn't let him get to her like that. She couldn't start to think of him that way. Sure, she'd written "Wifey" on the mirror, but that was a joke. That was her fooling around. It was her thing. He needed to know off the bat that they both had to stay in their lanes if this business arrangement was going to work out for the two of them.

There was no room for cute texts or sweet emotions.

Oh, well, now he had her number. At least that bit of ice was broken. And she had his. No biggie. If they were like any real couple and, say, had dated for a week or two, they would have shared more than phone numbers by now.

Leila shook her head, trying to force in some clarity and block the carnal image of Carter that popped up in her mind, just as Nia walked over. "Are you all right?" Nia inquired on a low hiss so as not to alert the rest of the crew.

"I'm fine," Leila said but held up her phone for her friend to see the text. "But do you think we should ride back with him or perhaps book a detour? Say, two weeks in Maui? Honestly, I don't know if I'm ready to face the music quite yet."

Nia tilted her head. "*We?* This is your deal. I don't see an invite for me in that text." Nia seemed to sense Leila's panic and looked at her friend with soft eyes. "I don't know, hon. It's up to you. But I guess you could use the time to have a sensible talk with him and come up with a really good game plan. I say go for it. I can still fly back as planned with Jasper. I think it would be for the best."

Leila's eyes went wide. The thought of flying back to New York with Carter alone without the buffer of her little crew seemed suddenly overwhelming. But she knew she had to face the music sometime. She might as well not put off the inevitable. And more than anything, she had to get a game plan in place for dealing with her family. The press would be one thing, but her father and brothers were something entirely different. She might as well start by getting to know and getting comfortable with her new husband, one on one.

"Fine. I'll meet him. It's probably for the best, anyway. And he seems to be the sensible type. The quicker we both approach this head-on, with no baggage, the better we'll both be."

Nia smiled. "That's the way to go about it. Face those problems head-on. Now, as for baggage, I suggest you bring cash, because you're surely going over the weight limit."

"What the hell is that supposed to mean?" Leila asked, suddenly defensive.

Nia shrugged. "I'm just saying that you're bringing a lot to the table and the situation."

"What situation? Why does it have to be a situation? It was just a stupid idea after a silly night of fun. And like Jasper pointed out, really, it's no more than a business transaction."

"A business transaction? Oh, come on. A business transaction was what went on between those party starters, the cocktail waitresses, and the executives from Double LL vodka. What you had last night with Carter Bain was way more than the business transaction. At least on your part, it was."

Leila folded her arms across her chest and peered at Nia. "Oh, come on now. It was no more than what I said it was. And it could still be exactly like we planned it, as long as we play our cards right."

"You mean as long as you don't let your emotions get in the way, which, I suspect, they already are."

Leila felt the heat rising from her belly up to her chest. "There are no emotions involved in this at all."

"Darling, that bull might work with some other assistant, but you know it is not going to work with me. You were so hopped up on emotion last night that the littlest thing set you off. I know you say it was for the job, and maybe that was part of it, but I know you truly went for that arrangement only because you are so angry over Miles and that damn song. Not to mention the fact that he pinned this whole relationship situation on you, and you're too kind to fight back and let the world know that he was the one who screwed you over, and not the other way around."

Leila blinked quickly. "Why should I let anyone know how he humiliated me? Bringing not one, but two women into our bed and then having the nerve to ask me to join in? No. Better to be painted as an insatiable man-eater than one who can't keep a man satisfied."

Nia reached out and took Leila in her arms. "Oh, hon, you know that's not how it is. Miles is an ass. Plain, simple, and being a horny ass is no excuse for his behavior, nor does it have any reflection on you."

Leila sniffled loudly, pushing down on a tear, as she pulled away from Nia. "Really? Then why does this keep happening to me?"

Nia shook her head. "Hon, I don't know. If I did, I'd write the book on it and be rich. Take me a cut of that big-time self-help guru money. But one thing I do know is if it can happen to you, it can happen to any of us. Men are just stupid. The end." Nia paused, pulling back, as if thinking hard. "That's it. Maybe that's my book title. I'll put you on the cover and put the air quotes around the word *stupid,* making it ironic to entice stupid men to buy the book. And *bam*! There you have it. My million-dollar idea."

Leila's low chuckle didn't quite make it to

her soul. Finally, she let out a sigh. "Well, whether stupid or not, I can't get all crazy about it now. Despite what you think, I was thinking about business last night. I want to start changing my image, and I think this hook up with Carter Bain, if handled correctly, might do the trick. Lord knows, I've hooked up with worse guys. This will be in name only, no emotions involved, and we'll both come out with what we want in the end. Who knows? We may have inadvertently invented the perfect marriage."

Nia shook her head. "Well, if you did, then you'll write the book and be the one rolling in dough when this is all said and done." Nia reached around the counter and handed Leila another expensive bottle of water. "Now, let's get out there and finish baking in the sun so we can head back to New York and civilization and get started on project image overhaul."

CHAPTER 9

Leila was not used to being ignored.

She had successfully avoided Carter for as long as she could by declining his offer to swing by and pick her up on the way to the airport. Instead, she took her own hired town car, leaving herself little time before the flight. She took a back route, which, thankfully, allowed her to avoid both the paparazzi who were camped in front of the hotel and the huge swarm at the airport. And by the time she'd made it to the area in the airport where she was to meet Carter, they were almost due to head out to the plane.

She saw him first, and though the sun had long set, she was glad that she still had on her shades to hide any hint of the expression in her eyes when she caught her first glimpse of him. Over the course of the day, she had let his image dull a bit in the back of her mind. But now that she was seeing him up close and in person, once again she couldn't deny his quiet magnetism. There was something strangely intriguing about him, Leila noted as she spied him talking on his cell. There were people around, but he seemed to be singularly focused on whatever business had him preoccupied on his phone. Once again, it hit her how he was nothing like any of the men she'd ever been with before. Tall and slim, he carried himself with an almost overly polished air, which on anyone else would probably bug her to no end, but on him it seemed to be a natural fit.

Whereas everyone else around him in the terminal looked somehow slightly disheveled in their jeans, track pants, and board shorts, Carter Bain had not a hair or a thread out of place. He was wearing perfectly pressed khakis, a finely checkered shirt with a striped tie, and a navy blue blazer. He was also wearing glasses, which was surprising, but she had to admit they suited him. They were dark tortoise-colored thick frames and added an even more serious air to his already serious appearance. Not that he needed the topper. Leila guessed that his idea of going casual was the fact that his pants and jacket didn't match. His whole effect made her smile while it had her hands itching to reach out and muss him up a little bit. She really should be reassured by the fact that she was currently tied to this man, who was so very opposite everything she'd been attracted to in her life. Leila told herself she could do this.

Piece of cake.

Finally, Carter finished his call and seemed to notice her presence for the first time. He paused as his deep brown eyes at first showed a small measure of shock as they went slightly wide and had her wondering if he was surprised to see that she had actually shown up. He recovered quickly though, pulling himself to his full height as his lips spread into a wide smile, which for some reason, Leila got the feeling was a well-practiced one. Still whether it was practiced or not didn't make it any less devastating.

"You came," he said, coming toward her and relieving her of her carry-on bag. He leaned slightly forward, as if he might come in for a kiss or a hug, but then thought better of it. Leila was suddenly hyperaware of the eyes of the people around them. Surely, at least a few had been on the Internet and had seen the breaking news rumors of her marriage. Better to get ahead of it.

"Is that any way to greet your wife?" Leila said and watched Carter's eyes go wide.

"I don't know, is it?" he asked cautiously.

She cut him with a challenging stare. "You tell me —"

Before all her words were totally out, Carter's lips were on hers. Full and surprisingly warm. He covered her mouth with his at the same time he wrapped an arm around her waist and pulled her in close to his body. The fluid motion shocked her and left her breathless, but she melted into him and closed her eyes, enjoying the warmth as it spread throughout her body. The steady firmness of his body juxtaposed with the softness of his lips was both erotic and intriguing, but the encounter was way too short lived for her taste. Carter abruptly let her go, leaving her momentarily swaying on her feet.

She blinked as his handsome face came into focus again.

"Better?" he asked.

In that moment, all Leila could do was nod as she coughed to clear her throat and her head. "Uh, sure." She looked around.

Carter raised a brow. "Since the story is out, I figure it's better we get ahead of it."

Leila narrowed her eyes. She wanted to wipe the smugness from his face. This was just what she didn't want to happen, and here it was . . . happening. He was getting the upper hand. She let out a sigh and was just about to give him an earful for pulling her in and kissing her like he did without permission when a pretty blonde in a blue uniform came over.

"Mr. Bain, Ms. Darling, we're ready to board your party now. If you both just follow me." The woman nodded Leila's way and gave her a polite smile. Then she ushered them over to a separate kiosk, where she quickly checked them in, took a last glance over their credentials, and then escorted them to the plane.

Their pilot and copilot met them, along with the flight attendant, Cindy, an almost mirror image of the same blond who'd helped them moments before. The plane was a luxurious ten-passenger Gulfstream made for cross-country business travel. All the bleached wood and beige leather throughout the luxurious cabin had Leila sufficiently impressed as she took her seat and placed her handbag on the seat next to her. But it was then she noticed the shadow over the seat.

So five and a half hours trapped in a speeding box with the man who just so happens to be your new stranger husband. What could go wrong?

Leila looked up. "I'm sorry. Did you want to sit here?" she asked, indicating the seat being taken by her purse.

Carter shook his head and leaned over toward the opposite side of the aisle. He placed his bag on the seat across the aisle before looking back at her. "No, I just wanted to make sure you settled in fine." He proceeded to tug at his jacket and remove it from his shoulders. The action brought to Leila's mind how he'd looked as he made his way to his hotel bed the night before. Halfway sloshed but cute as hell, discarding clothes as he rambled on about being the "luckiest son of a bitch" on both coasts. Jasper had put him to bed, but Leila had looked in on him before she'd gone back to her own room in the hotel. She'd left him a note and taken in his sexy, muscular form as he slept.

He was about to lay his jacket in the seat next to him, but in a flash Cindy was by his side. "I can take that for you, Mr. Bain. I'll just hang it in the front closet up by me."

Leila was once again glad she still had her shades on, this time so that Carter couldn't see the narrowing of her eyes as he handed his jacket to the eager flight attendant. She knew she was being silly. She'd spent too

148

much time on wasted relationships with the type of men who would probably already be making moves on a cute little piece like Cindy, hatching a plan for clandestine meetings in the narrow bathroom. And just the fact that she thought this had Leila wanting to kick herself. Was this her fate? Not yet thirty and already a paranoid shrew? Jealous over a man she barely knew and still wasn't sure she even liked? Honestly, even though he was her husband, whom he passed his jacket to — or anything else, for that matter — was none of her business.

Leila removed her shades and slipped them into her handbag. She gave herself credit for doing a damn good job at being nonchalant as Carter loosened his tie and unbuttoned the top button of his shirt before rolling up his shirtsleeves. She cleared her throat. "Cindy, when you get a chance, would you mind bringing me a bottle of water?" she asked.

Cindy gave her a nod. "Of course, Ms. Darling. Anything you like."

Leila noticed Carter's lips curl a bit. *What, requesting water is a problem?*

"If you just give me a couple moments," Cindy continued then turned Carter's way, "and for you, Mr. Bain?"

Carter grumbled something about a beer

and Leila decided to chime in with a request for a white wine. Suddenly this long flight felt like it was going to be a lot longer. Cindy nodded then informed them that they had runway clearance and she would be back with refreshments as soon as they were underway.

Leila gave the woman a tight smile. What she would like was not to have to be in this mess in the first place. But wishes were a waste of time, so she'd just settle for the drink and then maybe a chance to shut her eyes for the next few hours before hitting it hard in New York.

But, of course, that was not meant to be. No sooner were they seated than Leila could feel the burn of Carter's eyes on her. She turned his way. "So you really want to start in now?" Leila asked, already hating the sound of her voice. *Cool down,* she told herself. She needed to be careful how she went about things. She knew that no one forced her into this situation and either way, it was supposed to be something that was mutually beneficial, for both of them. Leila let out a breath. "I'm sorry," she continued. "It's just that we had a really long night, and then there was the shoot today. I'm just tired."

His look turned from one of cautious

questioning to one of concern. "Of course. I totally understand. Why don't you just rest? We have plenty of time to hash things out. Like how we're going to handle the already quickly spreading rumors, our respective friends and families, schedules, our living arrangements." It wasn't lost on Leila that Carter's voice went up with each item he added to the list. Could it be that it was starting to hit him, too, what a truly harebrained idea this was?

"Well, yes," she said, forcing calm into her voice. "It would seem we have a lot to figure out. And I'm sure we will. Don't worry. It doesn't take much to outsmart the paps or the gossip hounds. As long as we stay one step ahead of everyone, we'll be fine."

Carter snorted. "And you think our PDA back there was one step ahead?"

Leila felt heat rush to her cheeks. "Excuse me, but it was you who went full in, if I recall. I just said, 'Is that any way to greet your wife?' "

Carter's brows pulled in tight. "Wasn't that what you were asking for with that comment? I was just following your lead."

Leila shifted back in her seat. "And I was just talking about a little hug or something. Anything more than the awkwardness you were displaying. You didn't have to go full on snog with it."

Carter's eyes were suddenly downcast, and then he looked up at her again and coughed. "Well, uh . . . I'm sorry. I think we'd better get some ground rules in place. I wouldn't want to do anything to offend you or put you in a situation that you don't like."

Leila felt torn as the heat and the remembrance of their kiss still flourished on her lips. "It's not, well . . . it's just . . ." She paused. "It's not that I didn't like the kiss. The kiss was fine. I just think it's best if we take this slow. And maybe you were right about your original way of dealing. I have a reputation for putting it all out there for the media, and if any of this rebranding that Jasper wants to happen is going to work, I have to appear more reserved, so as far as PDAs are concerned, I guess we should go low key with those. I'll channel my inner royal and act like a wannabe duchess or something."

At that Carter grinned. "Lucky me."

Leila raised a brow. "Funny, that didn't come off as quite convincing."

He shook his head. "It's just that I have a few friends that would laugh their asses off at my predicament right now."

Leila's brows drew together. "Wow. Just

that quick I've become a predicament?"

Carter was quick cover. "No, of course not. How could you ever be? It's just funny . . . well, really not . . . that I'm the one chosen to somehow clean up your act. An act, mind you, that has taken you to megastardom."

Leila pulled a face. "Yeah, but on the wrong side of the universe."

Carter nodded at that. "I get that. But you have to know that where you are is not bad at all. Either way you're a star and folks have to look up to see you."

Leila looked at him hard. "So tell me, why are you feeling like you're in a predicament with me? The rebrand not withstanding?"

Carter let out his breath, then licked his lips before looking at her straight on with those deep eyes of his. "Because one would think I won the grand prize, getting to spend the next six months with you on my arm. Carter Bain, married to the world's most desirable woman. Lucky me. But all I can think is I won the award for being the world's top dullard."

With that comment, Leila once again looked into his eyes and then down at those, as it turned out, surprisingly talented lips. *Dullard. I'd think not.* Not that she'd be sharing that with him, though. Still, she was trying to think of the right placating words when the plane jerked to life and Carter tensed up completely. His fists were tightly clenched, and his body went ramrod straight.

"Are you all right?" Leila asked. Her hand suddenly darting across the aisle and latching on to his forearm, as if by instinct, as they taxied toward the runway.

Carter blinked and looked down at her hand. She noticed the slightest sheen of sweat starting to form on his brow. "I'm fine," he said, now looking back up at her. "I just get a little stiff during take-offs and landings. Something about them throws me." He swallowed down hard, she guessed against the pressure in his throat. "Honestly, I don't like flying at all, but I hate the takeoffs and the landings the most. And truth be told, I'd have liked a larger commercial jet or, hell, even to drive, if I'd had my way."

Leila's eyes went wide, and she gave him a hard tap on his arm. "Well driving back to New York is really not an option but come on, what are we doing flying in this little tin can?"

"Ouch!" Carter yelled dramatically against her tap. "Really? Less than twenty-four hours and already you're going in with hitting me? Maybe I wanted to impress you."

Leila gave him another arm smack. "Ugh. Seriously, do I really seem that shallow? And don't complain about that little smack. If I wanted to really hurt you, you'd know it."

He raised a brow at her then. "Is that a fact?"

Leila gave him a wink. "No, dear husband, it's a promise."

Carter's eyes took on a deep seriousness that was totally disarming. "Is it really?"

Leila's brows came together. "Is what?"

"This?" he said. "What sort of promise have we made to each other? I don't know about you, but I don't want to make you miserable, and I'm not here to trap you, anyway."

Oh, God, what was he doing? Was this what fear of dying did to a man? Made him all deep and philosophical? Have him go and get all confessional like to his stranger wife. "I don't know if you know this, but I have a bit of a reputation for being a relentless ass when it comes to getting what I want in business."

Leila smiled. "Trust me, Mr. Bain. There is more to me than what you see on the outside. I know about your business reputation. And you should know, I'm just as relentless. Despite my reputation, I don't step into business deals lightly or recklessly." She took a breath then let it out before continuing. "Listen, when it comes to love, I may be a total disaster, but with business, I'm on point. I think if we both keep our wits and our heads about us, we'll be just fine."

Leila looked around, suddenly feeling the intimacy of the cabin even more so. She patted his forearm lightly before moving her hand back to her side of the aisle. Relieved she watched as Cindy made her way toward them, wine and beer balanced expertly on a little tray. She placed each of their drinks on the tables before them before heading back to her little area up front. "Speaking of wits, see there?" Leila said with a wide grin. "Just like that, we're already up in the air and on our way."

Carter smiled slightly and shot her a side look. "Pretty slick of you to distract me like you did. Thanks."

Leila waved a hand. "No thanks necessary. It's the least I can do for my new mate." With that, she raised her glass and Carter leaned over to clink his bottle with hers, having declined the pour from Cindy. Their eyes met for a moment as Leila told herself it was the altitude and her lack of sleep that had her seeing the remnants of sparks and fireworks behind his eyes. She blinked and took a long pull of her glass before putting it down and to the side and stretching languidly. "I'm beat. Do you mind if I close my eyes for a while?"

"Not at all. I have plenty of work to do, anyway. We can talk real game plans once we're back in New York."

Leila gave him a small smile, then closed her eyes. She needed to think. That kiss was more than she'd bargained for. As was the fact that he was still wearing his ring from the night before, while she wasn't. She wondered if he had noticed. Probably so. He didn't seem like the type to miss much. What did it matter? Ring or no ring, she was married. They were married. Surely, she should be wearing her wedding band.

Leila shifted in her seat. Willing sleep that eluded her to come. "I see you're still wearing your ring," she said.

"And I thought you were sleeping," came his deep and quick reply from the other side of the aisle.

"Well, why didn't you ask me about why I'm not wearing mine?" She opened her eyes and looked at him. He already had papers spread out on the pullout table in front of him, along with an open laptop. But he was looking at her and he looked slightly annoyed by the intrusion. Leila wasn't used to that.

He shrugged. "I assumed you had a reason. You did have a shoot today, I figured that was it. I guess this is just another thing on our list of things we have to work out."

Leila stared at him before turning back around. "I guess."

"And?"

She turned back around. "And what?"

Carter let out an exasperated sigh. "And was I right? Were you not wearing it because of your shoot? And do you plan to wear it in the future?"

"I guess."

Carter's brows shot up as his nostrils flared while his lips thinned. Okay, so she was pissing him off a bit. Why should this cause her any glee? "Darling," he began with a low drawl, "you're going to have to come at me with something a little better than 'I guess.' "

It was Leila's turn to flare her nostrils. She didn't like the way that "darling" had flowed from his lips. Once again, it had been flipped from a proper name to a term of not quite endearment. "Fine. I'll wear it when out and not shooting. It's what's best for the remake."

Carter gave a small head shake. "Now, was

that so hard?"

Leila let out a snort wanting for some reason to tell him just how hard it really was. Thankfully she caught herself. "I'm going to get some sleep. Wake me when we're over New Jersey."

CHAPTER 10

Carter could kick himself for being so woefully unprepared. They'd stepped out of the baggage claim and into a wall of blinding flashbulbs. How could he not have expected that? With the early arrival time of the flight, Carter had thought that there would be one or two photographers at the most camped out after hearing the buzz of their marriage rumors over the wires. But so many? This crowd was insane. On the one hand, the producer in him was thrilled over how much press Leila Darling could pull. But, on the other hand, he was horrified over the fact that he was now smack in the middle of this media firestorm.

Carter suddenly thought of all the people he owed apologies to, and a knot formed in his stomach. God, now he really owed a big one to his friend Aidan and Aidan's girl, Eva. He should at least send Eva flowers after what he had put her through with that whole #insertgroomhere, get-married-quick scheme. Having her date one loser after the other on camera, sharing each cringeworthy moment with the world. Yeah, he owed her big time. Not that he regretted for one moment the segment or the through-the-roof ratings it got. And really, when he really thought it over, it should be Aidan sending him a gift, since if it wasn't for the whole bachelorette of the moment setup, the two of them would never have gotten together. Even so, he'd really put Eva through it that summer, with cameras constantly in her face, and for that he was sorry.

"Leila, over here, over here! This way, this way! Is it true? Is it true? Come on now. Show us your ring!"

The paparazzi was relentless, hounding them for that one shot. That magic shot that would make the rounds and fetch the big bucks as it got traded over the AP wires. They were being led to a waiting car by the driver who'd been sent by WBC. But it was hard to get through the throng of people, and though Leila had once again put her wide-rimmed shades on, Carter could tell by the tight set of her full lips that she was not happy with all the attention.

Carter didn't know quite what to do, but the question was answered for him when suddenly there was pushing and a scuffle between two photographers jockeying for position. They sent one poor traveler in their direction, and he knocked into Leila's shoulder. Instinctively, Carter's arm reached out to balance her as she teetered toward his side. She looked up at him, and he could tell she was wide eyed even through the glasses. Her body fit almost perfectly against his, her full breasts swaying against his chest for the first time. It was only for a moment, but in that moment everything in his body went on high alert as he righted her on the concrete once again.

Frowning, Carter took Leila's hand in his, all too aware of the feel of the circle of diamonds that she had once again placed on her finger. He gave her hand a slight squeeze as he put his other hand up to clear a pathway toward the waiting car. "A little room please, guys, a little room," he said as he ushered her toward the car and then quickly got in behind her, leaving the paparazzi without a comment. There were disappointed groans as more flashbulbs went off.

Letting out a sigh, he turned to Leila. "Well, that was a bit much for five thirty in the morning."

Leila removed her glasses, ran a hand over

her eyes, and then stretched, letting out a long yawn. The gesture was one that was done by countless people every day, but Carter was sure it had never done quite as beautifully or quite as sexily as Leila had just done it. "It sure was," she finally said, her voice soft and slightly gravelly due to the fact that she had slept for a few hours on the flight. He was supposed to have gotten work done during that time, but like a total nutter, he'd spent half the time just watching her, marveling at her beauty and wondering how in the hell he was going to put up a damned professional front for six months. "Talk about trial by fire. Now do you see what we're in for?"

Carter nodded. "I do."

"Excuse me, sir, ma'am. Where shall I drop you?" the driver asked from the front seat.

Shit. Once again Carter was out of his depth. Knocked over by what should be an easy question. It was Monday morning, he was with his new bride, and he didn't know where or, better yet, to whose home he was going. Carter looked at Leila sheepishly. "Care to let your husband know where you're living?"

Leila smiled, then leaned over and gave the driver an address in SoHo that was quite a way from his old place, but not too far from where he'd recently moved to in Midtown in order to be closer to the office.

On the plane they had decided that during this stint together they would, of course, keep both their apartments and would enter into some sort of shared living deal. They had agreed to check out each other's spaces and see which would be the easiest for overnights and wouldn't end up being too awkward. Though Carter had what was legally listed as a two-bedroom, Leila was confident that her space would end up being the winner, since she had a loft, though she hadn't explained her square footage situation.

Honestly, Carter didn't care. Most people thought upon looking at him that he was a man of luxury, and in a way, yes, he was. He liked things just so, but that wasn't always the case. He could make do just about anywhere, and if it meant sleeping on a pallet on the floor somewhere for the next six months, he would do that and whatever else he had to do in order to land Leila for this role. And his boss was willing to pull out all the stops to nab Leila, so if she wanted to rent a townhome off Park Avenue for these six months, he was pretty sure WBC would pay for it.

But it seemed Leila wouldn't be making those types of demands. Sure the woman he had married operated on impulse; that went along with her impulsive party girl image. But the reflective, more reserved, a lot more calculating, no-nonsense woman he had met on the flight didn't seem to line up with the public person he'd come to expect. Carter had to admit that this different Leila intrigued him. Made him want to look deeper than the package she presented on the outside. He felt his brows pull together as they sailed through parkway traffic and the Manhattan skyline came into view. Not that she really wanted to get to know him. Leila had made it clear that this was a relationship in name only, and that like him, she was out for the prize at the end.

And it wasn't that she was combative about it, just straightforward. Carter could respect that. She wanted things spelled out, cut and dried, so that she would get no surprises. If truth be told, he wouldn't mind the same. The only rub was the fact that at the end of this, they were both working toward opposite goals. How could this thing turn out and be a win for them both when truly only one of them could be the ultimate winner?

The driver pulled up to the curb on Leila's

block, and Carter instantly spied two photographers in front of her building and
groaned.

"Make a left up here and then circle
around, if you don't mind," Leila said. "On
your right you'll see a driveway that leads to
an underground garage. We can go in
through there."

Carter nodded when the car smoothly
slipped by the photographers and around to
the side entrance that Leila had indicated.
They were quickly headed underground,
and when they got to the security gate, Leila
gave a smile to the guard on duty and
flashed her ID which seemed unnecessary
given the huge grin she got in return from
the guard. But the no nonsense guard
quickly sobered and their driver had to
show his also, and when Carter showed his,
the guard, Joey, according to his name tag,
raised a brow.

Leila spoke up. "Joey, if you don't mind
making a copy of Mr. Bain's ID. I'll call
management, but can you please let the
other guys know that he'll be allowed access
until further notice?"

Carter's mind couldn't help pausing over
Leila's loaded "until further notice" and
Joey gave Carter a long once-over, which
should've annoyed Carter, but for some

reason, it was kind of reassuring. Finally, Joey gave a nod and smiled in Leila's direction. "Of course, Ms. Darling. Consider it done. And it's great to have you back. You know the building is not the same without you."

Leila laughed. "You're just saying that. You all will be tired of me in less than a week, and Mrs. Pembroke will be complaining about Ollie and my music by tomorrow afternoon."

Joey shook his head. "It wouldn't be a weekday if Mrs. Pembroke wasn't being Mrs. Pembroke, now would it?"

They headed deeper into the garage, and Leila let the driver know where to pull up by the elevators.

"I like the security you have in your building," Carter said. "Are all the guards as protective of you as Joey is?"

Leila smiled. "Pretty much. They kind of have to be. Being that they work for my father's company."

Carter's eyes went wide. "You didn't tell me your father ran a security company. Guess I'll have to stay on my toes."

Leila shrugged. "It wouldn't matter if he did or if he didn't. With me, you have to stay on your toes either way. But just so we get this out of the way, yes, he runs a small company that employs doormen and security agents across the city. He used to work for the company, but when the owner was retiring and talking about giving everyone their pink slips, he did some thinking. By that time, I had started making enough with my contracts to have a good nest egg, so my dad bought his boss out, and now he runs the company, along with my brothers. It's a win-win, actually, because even though they're a little nosy about my comings and goings, I never have to worry about whether my apartment is safe when I'm out of town."

The driver unloaded their bags, and Carter tipped him and let him go on his way. Then Carter took the bags and headed for the elevator. He figured he'd get Leila settled upstairs and then just get a cab to the office to start in on his work. After being on the west coast for the past week he was sure there was quite a pile up. He'd be able to make it back to his place that night, but for now, there was plenty to be done, and he'd already been away from the office for long enough.

On the elevator Leila swiped a key card and then pressed the button indicating her floor. They were heading up to seventeen.

Carter fought to push down any feelings of trepidation that he was having. "Well, I have to say with the level of security, so far this building is winning the apartment showdown between the two of us."

Leila gave him a smile. "Of course it is. And this is just round one. I have no doubt that I will win all the rounds in this competition."

"You're not lacking in confidence, are you?" Carter said as the elevator came to a smooth stop.

Leila looked serious for a moment before smiling once again. "You'd be surprised."

The elevator doors opened up to a small hallway with a tasteful console table with a telephone on it. Very hotel like. There was a mirror above the table, and two apartment doors flanked it. Leila turned to the right and slipped a key in the door to apartment 17B. Briefly, Carter thought about who could be behind the door of 17A, and as if guessing his thoughts, Leila leaned in toward him and whispered conspiratorially, "Mrs. Pembroke," before letting out a low giggle that brought light to her eyes and a soft glow to her cheeks. Carter looked down at her lips and took a half step back.

He was tired and hungry and in desperate need of coffee. The way he was feeling, he didn't trust himself not to lean down and once again take her lips with his own, especially when she was looking up at him like that. Leila opened the door, and thankfully, in that moment, thoughts of kisses, tiredness, and even coffee evaporated from Carter's head as he was met with a large space full of bright white walls and pale wood. The space was like a beach oasis high up in the Manhattan skyline.

Carter let out a low whistle. "And so it would seem that round two goes to you also."

Leila looked up at him, brightness shining in her clear eyes, as she led him into the space. "Now, don't go throwing in the towel. I haven't seen your apartment yet. I'm sure it's wonderful."

Carter shook his head. "It's all right, but unfortunately, I have seen it, and compared to this, it doesn't make the grade. Not even close."

Leila shrugged. "Well, I'll be the judge of that one. In the meantime, come on in and have a look around, though there's not all that much to see."

Carter raised a brow. "You can pull off a lot, but false modestly is not one of those things, Ms. Darling."

Leila blushed, indicating the truth of his statement and Carter followed her into the wide space, which seemed to defy the norms of New York real estate. The large, open floor plan was divided by pillars that a man could barely get his arms around. Her state-of-the-art kitchen was off to the right, and he could tell, it was made for a chef, though who knew if she ever spent any time in there? By the look of it, Carter wouldn't mind getting behind the large six-burner stove top and seeing what he could do. The counters were warm white marble, and the cabinets were a gorgeous blond wood. There were pendant lights that ran above the island that separated her kitchen from the dining area, which held a large farmhouse table that looked like it could easily seat twelve. It gave Carter pause. Just how many brothers did she have?

But having no real time to contemplate it, he allowed his eyes to rove over to what he assumed was her living area. In it was a cushiony couch flanked by two love seats. In between them were two leather ottomans that had been put together to form a coffee table. A large marble fireplace — Carter didn't know if it worked or not — created a beautiful effect, and above it was a large television. On either side of the fireplace were floor-to-ceiling windows that show-cased spectacular views of downtown Man-hattan. *Damn.* Carter could look at that view all day and was immediately drawn to the windows. He walked over and looked down at the city coming to life below him. For a moment, he was speechless.

This was living the dream. He looked over at Leila. Though it was early morning and she had just come off a long flight, she was still gorgeous in her casual tee and jeans tucked into her low boots. Her hair was slightly tousled. If this marriage were in any way real, then all his dreams really would have come true. But they had not. He let out a long breath and turned back to the view.

"It's an amazing view, isn't it?" Leila said, coming up behind him and putting an easy hand on his shoulder. It was light as a feather, but in that moment, Carter felt like it was the weight of the world.

He turned quickly and stepped back slightly, out of her reach. He was surprised to find her so near and so comfortable with him in her space.

Leila frowned. "Are you okay?"

"I'm fine," he said. "Why do you ask?"

Her brows furrowed together even more. "It's just that you seem a little jumpy." She gave him a narrowed side eye. "If I didn't know any better, I might think you are a little afraid of me all of a sudden." She looked at him hard. "Or is it something else? You being here is not keeping you from anyone else, is it? I'm not going to have to contend with an angry girlfriend or, heck, boyfriend coming at me for man stealing, am I? We did go into this at breakneck speed."

Carter chuckled at her outrageous questions. As if he would have gotten hitched to her if he'd had that type of connection going on. As if she'd go into it if she knew how over the top attracted he was to her and had been for so long. But when he looked back at Leila, he didn't see her smiling back at him, as expected. No, she was deadly serious. "Are you serious?"

She folded her arms across her chest. "Don't I look it?"

Carter frowned. "Surprisingly, yes, you do," he said, looking at her straight in the eyes. "And no, you're not keeping me from anyone else. No angry jilted lovers, either female or male, hiding in my closets. Though, for the record, I'm a strictly female kind of guy. But just to keep everything out in the open, this is not to say that I haven't been out there and dating." Carter paused when Leila's back went straighter. Which he thought was both funny and odd, being that she'd been attached to some of the most high-profile eligible men in the industry. "Strictly dating," he added. "I've made no promises to anyone." And with that, he gave her a look. "Out of the two of us, I have to say that I win that round."

Leila's lips thinned, and her eyes practically smoldered with simmering rage. "I'd watch it there, husband, or we just might have our first real fight, and we're not even forty-eight hours in. Despite what you may have heard or read or danced to, I have never broken a promise. To anyone." There was a slight tremble in her voice but she raised her tenor and spoke over it. "So if you think you just made an easy challenge and I'm going to bail at the first sign of trouble, you're wrong. When I'm in I'm in for the long haul."

Carter stared at her. Could what she was saying be true? Judging by her dead serious expression, it sure looked like it. Part of Carter wanted to run away and cry uncle, while the other part wanted to grab her and hold her, stroke her softly until all that hurt and pain that was so clear behind her eyes faded away. He wondered who had screwed her over so bad and why. Whoever it had been was a damned fool. Didn't they know what a treasure they had in Leila?

Carter relaxed his stance. "Listen, the only

woman you have to worry about is my mother, and she's my problem, since when she sees me, she's more than likely going to pretty much kick my ass for getting married without her knowledge or consent. No matter if it was a love match or a business arrangement. Besides that, up until this point, I've pretty much been married to my job, and I don't see any change happening there."

With that, Leila seemed to get pensive. Possibly thinking over what she'd entered into. What sort of man she'd formed an alliance with. Carter now worried that he'd come up short, at the same time that he felt the need to defend himself.

"Trust me. I'm no fool. Any smart man should be afraid of you. You are a formidable woman." He looked around. "And this is all beautiful. I mean really . . . the apartment, this weekend, the wedding. Everything is amazing. But I'm under no illusion as to what we're both out for here. Just as you should not be under any illusion from me."

Carter's heart started to beat a little bit faster. Was he a fool for putting it all out on the table? He probably was. This was not how his usual game was played. This was not how one went about sealing the deal and grabbing a new client. A new client was to be wooed, flattered, and smoothed over. But for some reason, he didn't feel like that was the game he should play with Leila; for some reason, he felt she needed more from him, demanded more from him. But as she stared at him straight in the eye, unmoving, unflinching, not giving a hint of acquiescence, he felt maybe he had played it all wrong.

Not able to take the silence, Carter finally opened his mouth once again. "So tell me, have I blown it? Should I take my bag and head back uptown, get started on low-key divorce proceedings?"

After what seemed like forever but was only a few moments, Leila smiled, and Carter couldn't help the infectious upturning of his lips. "Of course not, dear hubby. I like your style," she said as she reached out and straightened his already straight collar, then ran a soft index finger along his jaw, the small gesture sending a sizzle of excitement right down to his groin.

She went on. "Besides we haven't been married long enough or done anything to warrant more than an annulment. Now, follow me and let me show you where you'll be sleeping when you stay overnight. I hate to say it, but most of my time is spent on the road, going from job to job, so I don't spend as much time here as I'd like. But as I'm sure you heard when I was talking to Jasper, I'd like to change my career more than a bit, which is where you come in. Do fewer events, get more high-profile permanent contracts and, of course, get into acting. I've cleared quite a bit of my schedule for the next few months, after the fashion week shows, to really hone my craft and study. I've signed up to take classes with Shelley Atwood, and I'm really excited about seeing how I can grow with her. Who knows? She and I have even talked about something on the stage, though the idea scares the hell out of me."

"Well, it shouldn't," Carter said. "I have a feeling there is nothing you can't do once you set your mind to it."

Leila turned to him and smiled. "Well, I'm glad to hear it, especially from you. Now let's hope that when this is all over, the rest of the people on your team think the same thing." She then clapped her hands together as they made it to the guest bedroom. Like the rest of the apartment, it was perfect, and though he wanted to kick himself, Carter couldn't stop his mind from wandering to all sorts of carnal thoughts when he got a look at the large, masculine double bed.

"I hope you'll find sleeping here a pleasure," Leila remarked.

Well that comment didn't help. Carter fought not to let out a groan. *Sleeping?* As if he'd be getting any sleep in this apartment, and the word *pleasure* should never again be uttered by that woman in his company if she didn't want to risk being kissed senseless.

"Like I said, I don't spend as much time here as I would like. This room gets used by my brothers if they get stuck in town and don't want to head back to the outer boroughs or want to hang in the city if I'm gone for an extended stay. I'm sure you'll be comfortable," Leila said as she showed him the well-appointed guest room, which was across the hall from her bedroom.

Her brothers, huh? Less than two days in and he'd already been given brotherly status. It was not what he called progress, but he'd take it. Leila continued her tour. After pointing out the en suite bathroom, she led him back out toward the living area, giving only a passing wave to the closed door of her bedroom, he noted, as she headed back to the kitchen.

"Coffee?" she asked.

Carter nodded at the magic word, which

sounded like Leila throwing him a lifeline. "Please."

"It's still early. Did you want to head to your apartment now or go straight from here to your office, like you had planned? Sadly, I don't have any food, but I can order up some breakfast. I'm starving."

Carter was hungry, and he knew there would be no time to eat once he got to the office. The mention of food had his stomach instantly feeling like an empty cavern. "I could eat something, if you don't mind placing the order."

Leila smiled and nodded. "Great! I'll just call the deli down the street. They have everything and are open twenty-four hours. FYI."

Leila got out her cell and swiped a number. For herself, shocking Carter once again, she ordered bacon, egg, and cheese on a roll, then looked to him for his order.

"I'll take an egg-white omelet with turkey sausage," he told her.

Leila pulled a face as she gave the order and hung up.

Carter shook his head. "Really? I get that face with my order after you are doing cholesterol, fat, and carbs?"

"Don't start now," Leila said. "You heard me when I gave it to the Double LL dude.

179

Don't make me jump on you."

"Oh, I heard you, and you were right. I'm just saying you don't have to give me the judging face for eating healthy."

Leila rolled her eyes but nodded. "Okay, fine. You got me on that one. We'll just agree to disagree on our breakfast orders." Then she slapped the counter hard. "Damn it!"

"What is it?" Carter said, worried suddenly.

"Fries. I should've ordered fries."

Carter pulled a face, giving her a shocked look. "Seriously? Where do you put it, woman?"

Leila laughed. And turned to put coffee in the maker. "I'm just messing with you," she said. "But you really are too easy. You've got to loosen up. Now, why don't you go and take a seat on the couch, get comfortable, while we wait for the food? I'll let you know when the coffee is ready."

Carter shook his head as he headed over to her plush couch, which looked like a person could sink into it, never to be seen again. It was a far cry from his stiff black leather one back home, so he tried to get comfortable and sit for a minute. Her entire space was so different from the modern, minimalistic decor he preferred, but he had to admit, the laid-back coziness of her place did suit her. Carter sank into the couch. Hopefully, breakfast would come soon, and then he would be on his way to the office. The faster he got there and started facing the music, the better. He might as well start getting the ribbing about his impromptu wedding to Leila out of the way now so that he could get back to his day to day and the network launch.

Carter leaned back. The couch wasn't half bad, and he had to admit you couldn't beat the view he had of Leila from here. He looked back at her in the kitchen, and she gave him a short wave as she pulled out two mugs. Carter thought for a moment. No, you definitely couldn't beat this view. . . .

Carter woke to the smell of fresh brewed coffee, eggs, and bacon in the air and a wet tongue in his ear. "Lei?"

"Since when do you call me Lei?" came her voice from somewhere far off.

Suddenly, his eyes sprang open and his senses went on full alert as he swiped at his ear and jumped back to the far corner of the couch. Leila's musical laughter was now tinkling in the background.

"Ollie, cut it out. That is not how you greet our guest."

Carter's eyes went wide as he tried to slow his breathing, still anchored, as he was, to

his end of the couch. *Ollie? Who? What?*
He stared, but he was having a hard time
focusing, and then he groped around for his
missing glasses and finally found them on
the coffee table before him. He heard a low
growl, and there he was, now face-to-face
with his assailant. The pug was looking at
him with a less than impressed expression
from the other end of the couch.

"Ollie?" Carter asked, turning to Leila.

She grinned. "Yes, Ollie. The other man
in my life. Sorry he was so rude. He's just
not used to strange men sleeping on my
couch."

Carter bit back a retort, as he had a feeling it would both get him kicked out by
Leila and not do anything for his standing
with Ollie. He wasn't a fan of dogs. Especially ear lickers that were looking at him
like a mid-morning snack. "He's adorable,"
he said to Leila through clenched teeth.

"Don't lie," Leila said from over his
shoulder. "It doesn't look good on you. He's
a little ugly, and I know it. But he's loyal, so
I keep him around."

There seemed to be a lesson in that statement and while Carter mulled it over for
one beat, then another and then another,
neither he nor Ollie moved but only eyed
each other. Until finally Ollie let out a snort

and then stuck his long tongue out once again so that it touched his nose and then darted back into his mouth, as if he was saying, "I'll catch you later." What the hell had he got himself into? Carter thought.

It was then that Leila came around into his field of vision. She was carrying a tray with two plates and two mugs, but it wasn't the tray that captured his attention. It was her, with her hair pulled back in a high ponytail. Her hair looked slightly wet, as if she'd just come from the shower. Her face was freshly scrubbed, she was wearing a pair of white gym shorts with a white tank top, and her feet were bare. The whole effect was enough to make Carter thankful that he was already sitting down.

"Sorry about your wake-up call there. But my dog sitter brought him by, and he goes a little crazy when he meets someone new. Besides, I'm kind of glad he woke you up, since breakfast has already been here for half an hour. And the eggs will go bad if they wait any longer."

Carter ran a hand across his face and pushed himself up so he was seated normally and not looking like a total slouch while she placed the tray on the table in front of him and sat down on the opposite end of the couch. "Now, it's me who should be apologizing," he said "I'm so sorry that I fell asleep on your couch." He looked at his watch; it was already late morning. He had hoped to be in the office by now, but he couldn't very well jet out the door. As it was, she had gone to all these lengths, letting him sleep, making sure he was comfortable, and then saving breakfast for him. "I guess I was just a little more tired than I expected."

She nodded. "I'm thinking you were. Calling me Lei and all."

He looked at her, eyes narrowed. "Huh?"

"You called me Lei. Or at least I'm assuming it was me. You were coming out of your sleep. It's cute. Maybe we can work it into our deal. Make it our endearing thing."

Carter grinned. "As opposed to wifey?"

Leila snorted. "Yeah, as opposed to that or in addition to, whatever."

They were quiet for a moment, each lost in their own thoughts, until Leila spoke up. "Are you sure you have to go into work today? You couldn't just go home and rest?"

Carter shook his head, reaching for his coffee. He added a touch of creamer, then took a sip. "No. Though part of me wishes I could, there's no way. I just have too much on my plate, and spending a week in California has left me with enough time away from the office. Besides, I'm sure they'll be plenty of people who can't wait to hear the story of Leila and Carter."

Leila shook her head. "Yes, there will be, especially after our run in with the press when leaving the airport. We're already hitting the blogs."

Leila pulled her phone out and pulled up a site. She showed a series of pictures to Carter with the headlines DARLING CAUGHT. They were taken when Leila had almost fallen, and one showed Carter putting a protective arm around her. The circle around his ring finger was clearly visible in that photo. And another photo was of when she held his hand. Their entwined hands were blown up in a side caption, the small circle of diamonds on her finger clear for all to see.

"I guess there is no denying things now. Operation Image Makeover is out of this station and fully on the tracks. I say we still reveal as little as possible, save it for a big interview. Maybe something you can arrange? Are you okay with that?" she said, then took a bite of her sandwich. Carter was reminded of her popular hamburger campaign. God, no one could sell a product like Leila Darling. How could he not be okay with that?

"Sure," he said and took a bite of his omelet, which he knew didn't taste half as good as what she was serving up. "We'll go with love at first sight and leave it at that. Cool?"

Leila smiled and gave him a nod. "That sounds perfect. Besides, everybody loves a fairy tale."

Chapter 11

"I can't believe you did it, my boy." Everett Walker was positively beaming as he got up from his large leather chair and came around his desk to shake Carter's hand.

Carter really didn't know how to accept this praise. Never one to be humble, he was normally happy to bask in the glow of any props bestowed on him, but with this deal, with Leila, basking just didn't quite feel right. As a matter of fact, it felt downright slimy.

But still Carter shook Everett's hand. "Thank you, sir, though I don't know if there should be any actual congratulations going on just yet." He took in Everett's slight frown as Everett indicated for him to take a seat opposite his at his wide mahogany desk. "You see, Leila is open to the idea of coming on board with the network —"

"So what's the problem?" Everett asked, cutting him off. "Like I said, fantastic! With her onboard for *Brentwood,* we'll have the Hillibrand account locked up and signed in no time. After them, the rest of the endorsements will come flowing in."

"The problem is she's not so on board with the *Brentwood* show." Carter took a seat and dusted off an invisible speck of dirt on his pants before looking back at his boss. "The thing is, she's heard about our show *Shadowed Dreams* and how groundbreaking it is, and she wants to be considered for that."

Everett looked at Carter as if he'd suddenly started speaking another language. Not a man ever to be at a loss for words, he blinked for a good three seconds before bursting out laughing. "Good God, man. What have you gotten yourself into? Worse yet, who have you married? Is the girl delusional?"

Carter felt an instant and not quite understandable heat burn in his chest as he immediately felt the need to come to Leila's defense. "Now, hold on. It's not all that farfetched. She did a great job in *Robot-x.* The critics called her a breakout star."

Everett looked at Carter for another moment and then burst out laughing once again. "Oh, jeez, Carter, are you listening to yourself? Did you spend too much time in the desert? You know *Shadowed Dreams* is our high-profile vehicle. We have Simone Brently directing. Our star will be Chloe Caraway."

"Well, sir, Chloe is not yet signed. So that deal is not yet done," Carter said by way of explaining.

Suddenly Everett got deadly serious. "Well, you'd better good and well get it done. Chloe would be perfect for that part. Her image is stellar. She's got the talent, as well as the fan base. Chloe is our star."

Carter started to count in his head. He had to stay cool and play this right. When he spoke, it was with no emotion. "I understand that, sir, but as per the terms of our bet, if Leila wins, she gets her pick of shows."

Everett once again leveled Carter with a hard stare. "Well, then, you'd better good and positively make sure that that gorgeous, though temporary, wife of yours does not win the challenge over you. Because if she does, you'll surely be the loser in this deal. Are we clear?"

Carter bit back a rebuttal. "Crystal."

And just like that, Everett was smiling again. "Wonderful! Now, we're throwing you two a reception. I can't have my VP and soon-to-be newly signed star just slipping under the radar. My wife and I will throw you a dinner party."

"Really, sir, you don't have to." Growing up with Aidan as a friend, he'd been to enough awkward dinners at the Walkers to last him a lifetime; he surely didn't need one in his honor.

"Nonsense," Everett said. "I insist. You can even invite your parents. It's been years since I've seen them."

Carter suddenly felt ill when an image of the Walkers in their Park Avenue penthouse commingling with the Bains from the Bronx flashed through his mind. This should be, well, if not fun, then eventful.

Carter entered his office, glad to have slipped past Karen's empty desk, only to find Aidan waiting for him in his office. "Oh, great. From one Walker to another," Carter muttered.

Aidan turned from his spot at the window, where he'd been viewing Lower Manhattan, and gave his friend a raised brow. Carter noted that once again Aidan's hair had grown long and his jawline was shadowed. He'd obviously fallen back into his old ways of looking more like a wayward pirate than the heir to a national broadcasting station. Nevertheless, his bright eyes and easygoing smile suggested that he was entirely happy with his current circumstances, and Carter knew that it was due less to his work and more to his fiancée, Eva, with whom he'd been practically attached to the hip ever since she was featured on the air with them the year before.

"Always a smooth talker, but your flattery won't get you anywhere," Aidan said, coming forward to greet Carter. "Tell me it's not true. It can't be. There is no way you went to Vegas to get Leila Darling signed to a show and came back with a wife."

Carter ran a hand over his scalp, then frowned at his friend and went to close his office door. He turned back to Aidan. "So what if I did?"

Before he finished the question, Aidan burst out laughing.

"How is that funny?" Carter asked, going to take a seat in his desk chair.

Aidan sat opposite him. "It isn't, or it wouldn't be if you looked like you hit the marital jackpot, instead of looking like you just lost your best friend. What's up? Why are you not dancing a jig? I know you are the last one I'd ever imagine married, but you snagged Leila Darling. Now talk. How did you do it?"

Carter narrowed his eyes at his friend.

"What? You don't think a woman like her would just fall for a guy like me?"

By way of an answer, Aidan raised a brow.

"Screw you! I've had plenty of beautiful women in my day."

Aidan raised a hand. "All right, don't go getting your pocket square in a bunch."

Carter shot Aidan a look. "And don't you let the square fool you. I can still take you if need be."

"As if you ever could," Aidan said by way of a retort.

"It's been a while, but do you care to find out?" It had been a while since he and his old friend had really got in a scrap, but Carter's nerves were frayed, and the past few days — hell, the past week — had just about done him in. He needed to blow off some steam.

But once again Aidan laughed, and this time he shook his head. "So I guess the rumors are true. This so-called marriage of yours is nothing but a sham."

Carter continued to glare. "I promise you, it's good and fully legal."

"But I'm guessing by the way you're biting my head off and coming at me, it has not quite been consummated."

Carter let out a low growl at his comment.

"What's a little sex between business partners?"

Aidan shook his head. "Man, you're worse
off than I thought. Have you not learned
anything from me? There are some things
that are more important than work or the
next deal."

Carter looked at his old friend and shook
his head. He loved Aidan like a brother, but
in some ways Carter knew he'd never quite
understand him. "Spoken like someone with
the luxury to play fast and loose with their
privilege."

Aidan grew serious. "You know that's not
true, and it's not fair."

For a moment, Carter felt bad painting
Aidan falsely with a brush he truly had no
control over. What did he expect? For Aidan
to denounce all his worldly possessions and
live like some pauper, work from the ground
up just to fit in with his lower-class friends?

"It doesn't matter," Carter finally said. "I
did what I had to do."

"And tell me, what does your new wife
think of all of this?" Aidan's voice had now
taken on a self-righteousness, which Carter
was used to. Aidan had a thing for going for
the underdog, and though he was Carter's
friend, he clearly had decided that Leila was
the underdog in this fight. As if a woman as

accomplished as Leila could ever be any-one's underdog. The thought had Carter steaming.

"Don't get all high and mighty with me. Lei . . ." Carter frowned then as the new nickname suddenly slipped easily from his lips. "My new wife knew just what she was getting into, and if anyone is getting one over, it's her. She married me in order to get a part on *Shadowed Dreams.*"

With that, Aidan's brows drew together in confusion.

Carter nodded. "See, that was my re-action. I had her pegged for *Brentwood,* and here she goes, talking *Shadowed Dreams.* There were cards, then a bet. I don't know. What was I supposed to do?"

Aidan blinked. "I don't get how this all led to you getting married."

Carter banged a hand down on his desk just when his phone rang. "Damn it, bro. Neither do I. Not really, at least. Now that I say it out loud, I hear what an idiot I sound like."

The phone rang again, and this time there was also a knock on his door. Carter and Aidan both looked over and saw Karen through the glass, pointing at the phone.

"I guess that's my cue to let you go," Aidan said.

Karen came in. "Carter, it's your mother, and I don't think I can hold her off any longer. If you don't take her call, I think the next place you may find her is on our live news set."

Once again Aidan burst out laughing as he rose from the chair and headed toward the door. "Yeah, that's definitely my cue to go. But, hey, look on the bright side. We now owe you a bachelor party. Next round of drinks is on me. Tell Mama Faye I said hey."

Carter shot Aidan a look as he sucked in a deep breath and picked up the phone.

CHAPTER 12

Each time Carter saw Leila it felt like the first time. Though they were married, he'd laid eyes on his wife only a handful of times, so yeah, maybe he was being a bit dramatic. And maybe it was the model in her. Who knew?

She could very well be a natural-born actress, but to him the woman was also a chameleon. Carter had just gotten off the phone, having been only partially successful in placating his mother, so his nerves were frayed to the quick when he looked up to find Leila, or at least another version of her, standing in his office. Gone was the scrubbed-clean, laid-bare, sexy woman he'd left at her apartment, and standing before him now, a smile on her face, was every teenage boy's dream of the hot girl next door.

She was wearing a simple black cotton sundress, topped with a jean jacket, and sandals. Her hair was pulled into a loose ponytail, and once again she had on her large shades, but this time they were perched on top of her head to reveal her effortless make-up and her natural beauty. "So are you going to sit there and stare, or are you going to greet your wife properly?" she said, her voice a low, exaggerated whisper.

He raised a brow as he got up. Then automatically stuck his hand out in the most awkward way for a man to greet his forty-eight-hour wife.

Leila looked down at his hand, then back up at his face, letting out a low breath. "Jeez, hubby, we really have our work cut out for us. Could we be any more transparent?"

"Remember the last time you asked me that? I'm just respecting your boundaries."

Leila shook her head, then leaned in and pressed a soft hand on his forearm and kissed him softly on the lips. And, as it were, everything went on full and complete alert. All his nerve endings zinging at once, sending him into a state of sensory overload and a weird sort of fuzziness taking over his brain.

Carter suddenly found it hard to breathe. He gave himself silent commands, telling his body to carry out the simplest functions. *Breathe. In. Out. Inhale. Exhale. Now smile. That's it, fool. People are watching.* And they were. When he did become aware of his surroundings once again, it seemed all of WBC had converged on his little corner and everyone was, if not within earshot, then at least within eyeball range to take in the interaction between Carter and his new bride. He looked down at her and smiled a smile that he hoped was convincing. "So we're on?"

She gave him a smile in return. "Absolutely."

Oh, what a smile. It did him in every time. When she spread those full lips, she got the cutest little dimple on the side of her cheek, which, honestly, didn't appear all the time. Only, he suspected, when she was feeling especially mischievous. Like showing up at his office and surprising the hell out of him. Carter paused a moment with that thought and wondered if her appearance here was a way to knock him off balance and get him off track and off his game. Could it possibly be part of her plot to make him lose the bet? Just then Everett's words from earlier in the day came back to him. *Well, then, you'd better not lose.* No, he'd better not.

Carter looked at Leila and returned her

smile, taking a half step forward. Out of the corner of his eye, he saw Connie, Everett's assistant, rise from her desk on the other side of the office and head in his direction. She looked his way as she joined the crowd of spectators.

"You, my darling, are so right," Carter said in a low voice, but not so low that it wasn't heard by some of the nearby staff, as he wrapped an arm around Leila and pulled her in flush with his body. Once again it hit him like a stone how perfect she felt. However, the slight stiffness in her spine wasn't lost on Carter. She was expecting him to do this, or was she expecting it when he tilted his head and captured her lips with his own?

Sweetness. Her lips were sweet and somehow deliciously smoky. It was the subtle taste of her. Like there was some ingredient you couldn't quite place, but you wanted to keep on eating until you got it right. And he did. Continued to caress her lips with his until that rigid back went slightly soft under his palms and those sweet lips softened against his own so much so that he felt brave enough to extend his tongue ever so slightly against her crease.

But she pulled back then and looked at him wide eyed. He grinned and leaned in close to her ear. "Remember, as you said, we were on."

Leila gave a low growl and then walked around Carter, bypassing the chairs across from his desk and the little seating area he had for impromptu production meetings. She went around all that and then made the briefest of stops to glance out his window and take in his stellar view of Lower Manhattan and the Hudson River before taking a seat in his large leather desk chair.

Carter grinned. So his wife had come to show him who was boss. He was about to ask what had brought her there when Karen appeared at his door.

"I'm about to order lunch," she said, sounding more on autopilot than anything else. "You want me to order for you or —" Her words were cut off when she caught sight of Leila. Karen smiled wide and looked from Carter to Leila. "I guess not. I didn't know you had plans." She frowned, taking in Carter's silence, and gave him a look. Finally, she shook her head and walked around him toward Leila with an outstretched hand. "Hello. I'm Karen, Mr. Bain's, well, Carter's assistant. It's very nice to meet you, Mrs. Ba . . . , um, Ms. Darling."

Carter watched as Leila rose and took Karen's hand. "Leila will be fine. You see,

Carter and I were such a 'love at first sight' whirlwind thing, we haven't quite gotten around to the name thing yet. I was thinking we'd bat around a few things and see what floats. I've been Darling for so long, I can't imagine anything else. So who knows? Maybe I can convince Carter to go with a hybrid. Darling-Bain or maybe just Mr. Darling. I'd hate to think my new husband is anything if not enlightened." And with that, Carter groaned, and his groan might or might not have been heard.

Either way he blinked quickly, astounded by the scene in front of him and over-whelmed by all he had on his plate for the day. Although she looked and tasted totally delicious, he was at work and didn't have time for Leila at the moment or for having it out right now about names. It wasn't the time or the place. He had to go over all that had gone on in Cali the week prior and then devise a game plan for his next month's meetings. Not to mention he was still a consultant on the a.m. shows and needed to see what was going on there. There were meetings. Lots of meetings.

"Is there a meaning behind your arrival here today?" he asked Leila.

With that question, Leila and Karen turned to Carter in unison. Had they been talking? In that moment his mind had wandered and he'd been lost in thought, so he wasn't sure.

"Of course," Leila said to him. Her tone had taken on the syrupy sweetness of a public persona, and it was placating and patient, like she was talking to a five-year-old. "I came to see where you work and to say hello. I had a meeting this way and thought I'd kill two birds and all. See if you'd like a quick lunch."

Lunch? Carter looked at her and tilted his head. Had the woman gone nuts? Was the woman nuts? *Jesus.* What had he done, and how was he going to get out of it? Sure, this was all fine and good when she was a fantasy in his head and on a page, but here she was, live and in real life, and already she wanted more. *Wait.* She, Leila Darling, wanted more from him, Carter Bain? So he was nuts? But still, who just skipped off to lunch in the middle of the day? He had a schedule to protect.

"That sounds like a wonderful idea!"

Oh, holy hell! Everett. So word must have spread that their prey was in the building, and Everett had come slumming to his side of the tracks to check up on him. Carter hoped he hadn't got his shoes dirty. But then he let out a low breath and silently admonished himself. He owed everything to Everett and shouldn't be uncharitable. The only thing that annoyed him about Aidan was the fact that at times he was so privileged that he didn't seem as grateful as he could be for all he'd grown up with.

Carter smiled broadly and went to put an arm around Leila. "Everett Walker, let me introduce you to Leila Darling."

Leila came forward and gave Everett what Carter was coming to know as her more practiced smile. Only this time it was more demure. There was not a hint of her usual sex appeal, but the sparkle was still there in her eyes. "So nice to meet you. Carter tells me you all are doing wonderful things with the network. You all are really making great strides forward."

Everett looked at her with his typical calculating eyes, and Carter wondered for a moment what he was thinking. Was he as perplexed as Carter was by the persona Leila was presenting, or was he not fooled? "We're doing just fine, but we will be doing a lot better with people like you on board." Everett waved a hand. "But I'll leave that for another day. Right now we're all just getting to know each other. You'll find we're one big happy family here at WBC and Carter's like a son to me. Which is why I just told him this morning that my wife and I are throwing you both a dinner to celebrate your happy event."

Observing Leila's slight frown at this news, Carter interjected, "Well, we hadn't quite decided on that yet. Leila and I still need to work out our formal announcement."

Everett tilted his head Leila's way. "Of course. You want to do it in the best possible way. One has to be strategic about these things." He turned to Carter. "I'll leave that to you and Leila's management. You're always a wiz at these things. Keep them guessing, and then *wham!* Hit them at the perfect time, when they least expect it but right when they needed it."

Everett turned to Leila again. "You've got a good one here, Leila. Carter is the best." He looked Carter up and down, taking in his usual perfectly pressed suit, though today even Carter would admit he was a little worse for the wear after the weekend. "He may not look like much, but he's a shark. You stick with him and he'll get you where you need to be. Just trust and believe."

With that, Leila gave Everett a tepid smile and a raised brow. "I don't know what to say. Now you've got me wondering if I should sleep with one eye open. Next, you'll have me featured on one of your 'I married a sociopath' shows."

Everett looked at her and laughed. "Hardly. If there's anyone who should watch out, it's our boy here. With your reputation, one would be smart to guard their heart, for fear it will end up broken forever."

Carter coughed which in the scheme of things felt pretty weak by way of interruptions and standing up for one's wife.

Leila gave him a hard look, then smiled, turning Carter's way. "Well, it's a good thing neither of us has to worry about that in this situation."

"So your boss is a little bit of a, um, jerk?" They were at Antoine's, an Italian eatery that had been in the city for longer than either Carter or Leila had been alive. It had been close to closing a few years ago, but thanks to the fact that all that goes around comes around, Antoine's great-great-great-grands were reaping the benefits of the resurgence in quaint down-home cooking. But the fact that it was trendy was purely a plus when it came to wooing clients, as Carter genuinely liked the food and the laid-back ambiance. Not seeing a way out of lunch with his wife after Everett's intrusion and insistence they go to lunch, he'd had Karen get them a quick reservation.

Normally, Carter was used to coming in to Antoine's and making only mild waves, being that he usually entered with an entourage of other network suits. Walking into the restaurant with Leila was another thing entirely. The woman had even left Franco, the maître d', who was seventy if he was a day, stammering as he went to seat them. The poor waiter barely made it through the specials, he was stammering so badly.

"No, he really isn't," Carter said, referring to her "jerk" assessment. "He's quite a brilliant mind. He's brought WBC from nothing to being a top competing network. His innovativeness and success can't be denied." Why he was defending Everett after yes, he was just a jerk was beyond him.

Leila looked at him squarely and picked up her wineglass, she took a long pull. Then she offered no comment for a moment but only studied Carter, to the point where he, though he hated to admit it, got uncomfortable. Finally, she shrugged and spoke. "Well, he's got the right champion in you. He should consider himself lucky to have such a loyal . . ." She paused before speaking again. "Employee."

Carter felt his rancor start to prick at the surface of his skin. "You say this as if it's a bad thing. Tell me what have I done to irritate you? We were fine this morning, when I left your place."

Long moments passed when thankfully the waiter came with their meals. Carter had ordered his usual lunch, grilled salmon over linguini, and Leila had gone for the prawns.

Once the waiter had left their table, Leila gave Carter a dismissive wave of her hand. "It's really not worth talking about. You are here to get a job done, and so am I. We both have our missions. Nothing wrong with that. You have your rules you have to play by, and I can respect that."

With the food before her, it seemed that Leila was ready to forget, at least momentarily, their conversation. She dug right into her dish. She took her first bite and closed her eyes, her lips caressing the fork in the most tantalizing way. In the same moment Carter seemed to lose his appetite, at least for food, and focused on her. This was the woman he'd fallen for, he thought. The woman, this woman right here, the one doing nothing more than enjoying her meal, but with an innate sexual abandon that couldn't be denied, she was the one who could make his career.

But Carter wasn't ready to let it go. The employee comment had more than pricked him. She might be his wife in name only, but she was still his wife. And speaking of his wife, Carter looked around, noticing he wasn't the only one who was focused on her: practically all the male eyes were currently trained on Leila and were watching her eat. Damn. If she could pull them in just like this, why even produce a show? They could do an hour of Leila eating and still make big bucks.

She looked at him and nodded her head. "Why aren't you eating? Are you not one to talk and eat?"

Carter went to say something but found he had no voice. As he reached for his water, his ring clinked against the cool glass. What was he doing here? He was sure he was playing this thing all wrong. He took a bite of his food. The normally sweet, succulent fish soured on his tongue.

"I'm sorry if I upset you back at the office or if Everett did," Carter said, his tone purposefully placating. He decided then and there he'd find the right tone with her if it killed him. He'd get her to see things his way and come on board with *Brentwood,* and long before these six months were over.

They were only on one day, well, a half day, into being publicly out as a couple, and he knew that if there were going to be days full of this much animosity, with him feeling totally off kilter, then he wouldn't last. He had to switch tactics. "It's just that I have so much on my plate with this launch that I was completely in work mode back there. You'll learn that about me," he said softly. "Being a workaholic is my only main fault."

She raised her brow. "Only?" She snorted. "You sure you don't want to add humility to that?"

He laughed. "But really, you can understand it, can't you?" Carter looked her in the eyes. "I know you have this party girl reputation."

"Who says it's just a rep? I enjoy a good party." Leila twined some of her pasta on her fork and shoveled it into her mouth.

"As do I, but I also know a person doesn't get to where you are without a pretty driven work ethic. So you may party hard, but I don't buy it. At least not fully."

"Well, then, I guess that's something we can both agree on, because I don't fully believe this buttoned-up worker bee, loyal errand boy thing you've got going here."

Carter felt his brows draw in tight, and he let out a breath, forcing them to relax.

"What I've got going is not a *thing,* Leila. I'm no actor on a stage."

Leila snorted and took a sip of her wine. "You're full of crap, Carter Bain."

Carter felt his anger rise at the same time he felt the beginning of stirring of desire. "What are you talking about?"

"I can see it in your eyes. I saw it that night, too, back in Jasper's suite. If I were really smart, I probably should have run from it instead of toward it. It's the same thing I see in the mirror. You and I are the same. You know as well as I do that as soon as you step out the front door, you're on-stage." Leila poked her fork toward Carter's plate. "Now, are you going to finish that? If not, can I have a piece?" Without waiting for his reply, Leila reached over and, with a grin, forked herself a large hunk of his fish. He frowned at the exact moment there was the distinct blowback of a flash coming from a camera outside the restaurant's window.

"You bring company?" Carter asked.

"I was hoping not. So far this had been a pretty good day. But you know . . ." Leila shrugged, then looked at him seriously. Suddenly, there was a weariness in her eyes. But just as quickly, she brightened and smiled. "Hey, don't you live close by here? Why don't we blow this place and you show me your apartment? That way we can end the great apartment showdown once and for all."

Carter knew when he was beat and in this round she had him. The work could wait, besides when he was with Leila he was technically still on the company's clock. Might as well make the lady happy and give her what she wants.

CHAPTER 13

"I warn you," Carter began as he put his key in the lock to open his apartment door. "You've already won the apartment bet. There's not much to see here."

This was ridiculous. He'd never before had any type of feelings of trepidation about bringing a woman back to his apartment. Hell, his place was female catnip. Simply but graciously decorated, it spoke to his style and love of the minimalistic and his appreciation of order. The spare but well-appointed rooms, which featured furniture and artwork handpicked by Everett's own decorator, showed his impeccable taste and appreciation for the finer things.

So what was he worried about? It wasn't like he was bringing Leila here for a booty call. No, with their arrangement, there'd be no real chance of that. She'd made it clear, and rightly so, that all their amorous inter-action would be strictly PDA. Though, they both still needed to get the ground rules right on that. For his part, he was having a damn hard time getting his hormones to separate from his head on that matter. Case in point, the sight of her now, looking delicious and delectable, as he stuck his key in the lock on his front door was setting off all sorts of signals and alarms, which under normal circumstances would be welcome, but he knew had to be squelched entirely.

Leila looked up at him and let out a frustrated sigh. "Is there a reason we're still on this side of the door and not the other? One would think you have something in there you want to hide."

Carter gave her a look. "Hardly. Nothing to hide on my part."

And with that, they walked inside. Carter gave a little flourish with his hand as he let Leila enter first into his tiny foyer. She smiled as she looked around and then walked farther into the hallway of his convertible one-bedroom on the West Side. Her smile gave him pause but still caused a small swell of pride. He wondered briefly how she saw his place. Did she see it as he'd wanted her to see it and, therefore, see him? As someone on her level, or at least as someone on a level she'd want to deal with for not just the next six months but beyond that. Someone she could trust to take her to the next level in her career. And who knew? Maybe even further? Carter felt a twinge of hope.

But just then she stopped mid-step and frowned as she looked down, having noticed the red high heels perched under his entryway table. She turned to him with fire and, surprisingly, hurt in her eyes. Leila poked a hard fingernail into his chest. "Good to know my track record still stands, even if this deal was nothing but business. I thought at least someone like you would stand by your word."

Carter stepped back. "First of all, ouch! Again. What's with you and the hands?" Then he said, "I don't know what's with the shoes. I haven't lied to you. Those weren't there when I dropped my bags off this morning. What are you getting all upset about? You could give me a chance to get to the bottom of this."

Leila shook her head and tried to sidestep him in the narrow hallway, the tight quarters bringing her body close to his. So close he could smell the scent of the lavender she used in her hair. Even as he put up his arms to get out of the angry woman's way, Carter inhaled.

"I'm not staying around to listen to whatever lies you quickly try to come up with," Leila said. "My time is too valuable to play games. We can chalk this up in the press to another one of my stunts and move on. There are other shows, other networks."

Carter's temper flared. "Now, wait a minute. Don't be such a hothead. It's just a pair of damned shoes." He paused. "Shoes that shouldn't be in my house." It was then that recognition came to him, and Carter knew whose shoes they probably were. "Oh hell! Maybe you're right. We both should go." Carter put a gentle hand on Leila's upper arm to lead her toward the door.

"Oh, no you don't. Carter Reginald Bain, you may be able to dodge me over the phone, but you can't face-to-face. Get in here and hug your mama before I come over there and whack you!"

Carter let out a low moan as Leila froze and looked wide-eyed at him before they both turned towards the voice in unison. There she was, all 115 petite pounds of her, soaking wet but feisty enough to take on any heavyweight she came up against. Faye Bain was standing in her bare feet, wearing pedal pusher jeans and a black, off-the-shoulder tee that had nothing on it but a bejeweled black power fist. Her wild riot of salt-and-pepper curls bounced around her head as she gave her only son a stern but loving look and a shake of the head. Carter walked forward and took his mother in a warm embrace.

"What are you doing here, Mama? I thought we'd agreed you would call before coming by."

Faye raised a brow. "And I thought we didn't have to agree to something like you not getting married without discussing it with me and your father. So, you know what you can do with that agreement." She looked past Carter and over at Leila and raised a brow. "So," she said, letting the word just sit there.

Leila said nothing. Just stared at Faye, trying, Carter was sure, to square in her mind this woman with the image that Carter had presented. Finally, Leila smiled and started to walk forward, shooting Carter a look as she passed him.

"It would seem your son is at a loss for words. It's so nice to meet you, Mrs. Bain. I can see where Carter gets his good looks and his determination." Leila put out a hand, and to Carter's relief, his mother took it. She was the toughest of critics, so Leila couldn't expect more than that.

"And judging by that fight I heard starting, I can see you've got a little gumption yourself. What is this I heard about a business deal? What kind of unholy mess did you two kids get yourselves into?"

Leila looked at Carter, wide-eyed and silent, as he let out yet another low growl.

Faye Bain gave him a quick slap on his arm. "Boy, if this has anything to do with that dammed Everett Walker and his company, I'm going to have your hide."

Carter let out a low breath as he looked at his mother. "Now, Mama, don't start. You've got to let me explain."

Faye gave him a sharp look and put up a hand, shaking her head. "Let me sit down, because I already know I'm not going to like how this turns out. Talk of deals and shows." She turned to Leila and looked her up and down. "I wanted you to fall in love, settle down with a wife, be happy, have babies, not broker some deal with a girl who is only with you for the come up." At Carter's skeptical expression, Faye waved her hand. "Oh, I know the lingo you kids use. Yes, *the come up*. And, hell, this one here looks like she's never even cooked a proper meal in her life. Like the world's been rolled out for her because of her good looks or whatever."

Leila sucked in a breath, and Carter swallowed. *Damn.* That was low, even for his mother, who he knew wanted only the best for him.

"Now, Ma, I know you're angry, but that's uncalled for." Faye looked at her son with shocked eyes. Never one to talk back, Carter knew she would be upset. "Now, you're right. This isn't a love match, and I'd appreciate it if you kept that between us, but Leila is extremely talented, and most importantly, as of today, right now, she's my wife, so you need to respect that. She's a Bain, which means we all had better act like it."

Carter stared at his mother, knowing if he didn't win this battle here and now, the next six months would be pure hell. His mother had never been one to shy away from giving her opinion, so he needed his mother on their side. Who knew who she would talk to in her anger and let the wrong information slip out? Plus Leila was too high profile to lose, and honestly, he didn't want to see her hurt, especially not by another person he cared for.

Finally, his mother let out a breath. She glanced up at her new in name only daughter-in-law and looked her in the eye before speaking. "I'm sorry. What I said was over the line, and whatever this is doesn't matter. You're connected to my son, which means you're connected to me. We take care of our own, honey. You'll never hear me say a word otherwise."

"Thank you," was Leila's only reply, and it left Carter feeling oddly uneasy.

Faye turned to Carter with a nod, as if to say, "Is that good enough?" And he gave her a nod in return. "Besides, now it's just another person for me to take care of. With that figure of yours, you'll never convince me you're some great cook," Faye declared.

Leila gave his mother a quick up and down and Carter could tell she was weighing her words over in her mind. "No, I'm no great cook, but I am a champion at eating." She paused and stared at Faye, taking her in then from head to toe. "I have to say though, for all your talk about my figure, yours would suggest you're no great cook either. Going by your own standards of course."

Faye looked a Leila carefully then and Carter almost held his breath during the momentary standoff between his wife and his mother. "Well, I guess appearances can be deceiving," his mother finally said before smiling. "Now, good to know there is a bright side to this. I won't just have one child to cook for now. Instead, I'll be cooking for two!" She reached out and took Leila's hand a lot more warmly this time and pulled her into an embrace. When they pulled back, she looked into Leila's eyes. "Now that that is over, tell me, how did it go when you introduced Carter to your family?"

With that, Leila let out a groan similar to the one Carter had given when he realized it was his mother's shoes by his front door.

CHAPTER 14

Leila was standing in famed designer Donetta Feretta's workroom, wearing a one-of-
a-kind couture gown, or what was soon to
be a couture gown, once the final fitting was
done and it was sewn up. But thanks to her
technical husband, Carter Bain, and her —
heaven help her — not all that technical
mother-in-law, she couldn't even enjoy the
process. The mention by Carter's mother,
Faye, of Leila's father had Leila fretting
anew over the inevitable bomb that would
go off when her father finally did meet Carter for the first time. Fake marriage or not,
Carter was married to Leila, and without
her father's giving his blessing or even having met him. That made Carter public
enemy number one.

So far Leila had skated by on twelve
judgment-free marital hours without her
father's disapproval by pretending to be
busy and answering him only with vague,

emoji-filled text messages. She knew this tactic wouldn't last more than twelve more hours, though. She was back in town, and she had to face the music. But first she wanted to get through at least one night with Carter alone. Well, if they could not be alone in the normal sense of the word, then at least they could be alone to hash out how they would proceed.

Though she'd talked with Jasper earlier about playing this carefully, now that the word was out, the formal announcement that had been made to the press was that Leila was indeed "blissfully happy and would appreciate the media respecting their privacy at this time." A bunch of words strung together that meant nothing and kept tongues wagging, hopefully, if she played her cards right in the right direction. Still, Leila was skeptical.

She and Carter had left his mother in his apartment on a better note then when they arrived. Faye had promised to cook enough for the two of them to eat for the week and was seemingly behind their clandestine plan.

Leila and Carter had parted ways on Broadway — he to go back to work, and she to head to a late fitting for the following week's shows — with the promise that he'd return to her place later that evening. But what was she supposed to do with that? Normally, she was used to calling the shots, but for some reason, Carter had taken her out of her depth. His reaction to her surprising him at his office, not to mention that kiss, had let her know she'd have to tread carefully if she wanted to stay on solid ground with him. However, as it were, it didn't feel like she was on solid ground at all. Not by a long shot.

Three times. Three times he'd kissed her, and she'd come out worse for wear each time. Frankly, though his kisses were more than mildly okay, and surprisingly way more than mildly intoxicating, Leila wasn't sure she liked the feelings he left her with. She was used to men swooning over her, not the other way around. And it wasn't as if any part of this deal was meant to make him swoon, but if she were to have any advantage at all when this thing was said and done, she had to be the one left with the upper hand.

She stood chewing on her bottom lip, with her mind so deep in thought that she barely even roused when Donetta finally snapped a heavily bejeweled finger in front of her eyes. Leila blinked and looked at the bleached blonde, with her extra-puffy lips, like she'd grown two heads.

But Donetta was not moved. "I swear, dahling, you are completely out of it today. Where is the spark? The energy?" She punctuated each word with a clap of her hands, putting on quite a show for the bevy of black-clad assistants who were huddled around.

Normally, Leila would have snapped back, annoyed at being called out. But Donetta was right. She was off her game, and this was work. She was being paid handsomely by Donetta to be there and be present. "I'm sorry, Donetta. It was a long weekend of travel, but I should be more together." She straightened her back and stood up taller.

Donetta smiled at this and looked her in the eye. She came closer, so close that Leila could see where her cakey foundation was doing a piss-poor job of hiding her Botox needle marks. But her eyes went soft, then widened slightly as she pulled back. "Poor dahling," she said in a low voice. Her voice became higher once again for her gaggle of geese. "You see, children. You listen to Donna here. Don't waste your time on love. It throws you off every time. You go in, and you have the sex. You bang all those feelings out, and then you're fine to work happily the next day." She said all this with a flour-ish and a wave of her hand, while the assistants nodded, as if she'd just given them the secret to a flawless bias cut jersey dress. "You mark my words. Have the sex. Stay away from the love, and you'll go far." She turned back to Leila and shook her head. "You, dahling, I don't know. Is it love with this husband of yours?"

To that, Leila just smiled. "Now, Donetta, you read the statement. I'm no longer commenting on my personal life."

Donetta stared at her before letting out a bark of laughter. "Okay then. I'll hope not. At least for your sake." She then shrugged. "My sake too. Because I need you on if you're closing my show in this dress."

It was getting late. Well, it was later than she'd expected, though what should she have expected, since Carter had never said what time he'd make it back to her place that evening? It was almost nine 'o clock, and Leila had turned down meeting some friends for dinner that night, thinking she should be there to greet Carter when he arrived. He was her husband and all, and well, it seemed the wifely thing to do.

Leila stood at the kitchen counter. She still had not shopped, and so she considered ordering from the deli downstairs. But should she wait for him? Why was he so rude as not even to call and say that he had decided to back out and wasn't coming by, after all, or that he was running late? Was Donetta right? Why did she even care? If she was falling for her husband, then she was in a world of trouble.

Leila picked up her phone and hit Nia's number. "That's it. He's not coming," she said when Nia picked up. "I think we need to prepare for damage control and another bust."

She heard Nia let out a slow breath. "You know you're interrupting my favorite dating show, don't you? This had better be worth it."

"I'm sorry," Leila said. "But right now my life is quickly turning out to be more drama filled than anything on reality TV."

"Well, you've got a point there. A liar, you're not. So what's gotten you into such a tizzy today, and how do you know he's not coming? Did he tell you?"

"Well, firstly, I met his mom, and she's a right piece of work. I'm not sure if I like her, but I can't say that I don't. But I'll tell you what. It's a good thing that this is not real, because she sure as hell doesn't like me. She made it clear as glass that she wants a good girl for her son. A traditional wife who can cook up the bacon and push out babies while she's doing it."

"Eww," Nia said. "Really?"

"Well, kinda really. She wasn't all that bad, but I sure as hell didn't pass muster. Even though she does not like the fake marriage thing, I think after meeting me, she was relieved by it." Leila paused, thinking of how it all went down. "I will say Carter was nice about coming to my defense. I've never had that happen with a guy before."

"See there?" Nia said. "So now why do you think he's not coming tonight? I'll ask again. Did he tell you? Give you any indication that he wanted to bail?"

"Of course he didn't tell me. Do they ever tell you? No, they just do some crap, like not showing up or stealing your money or screwing some other chick in your bed!"

"Whoa there, Nelly!" Nia said. "You jumping off there to conclusions pretty quick, aren't you?" She paused. "And you want to explain why this matters so much, or at least why you're so passionate about what he's up to at nine p.m.? I get that you're raw, but you get that this thing is in name only, right? Please don't tell me that you're falling. It hasn't been two full days yet."

Leila was silent, and she considered Nia's words.

Finally, Nia chimed in again. "Leila? Come on. Talk to me."

"Well . . . ," Leila began, hating the weak sound of her voice but wanting to get this off her chest. "Besides, he's kissed me three times. Three times and he's never once been moved."

"Moved? What! As in moved down there? Are you two grinding? Has this business arrangement gone there already?" Nia asked, her voice full of shock.

"No, the kisses were just for show and we haven't gotten close enough for any down there action for me to access. It's just that I don't seem to rattle him. We kiss and he moves on. You'd think the kisses meant nothing."

"Shit," her friend said then let out a low breath. "I knew this was a bad idea. I should have never let you and Jasper go through with this awful idea. But he always thinks he's so damned smart. You just hold tight and let me call him. We'll put our heads together and find a way out of this. Obviously, you're not ready for this type of situation. You're coming off the relationship with Miles. This was a bad deal all around. Either you or Carter is going to end up getting hurt here. There is no way you're going to let him off the hook with daring not to fall at your feet, and then, when he does, then what? Where does the bet go from there? You had it right in the beginning. It's time to pull the plug before this thing goes too deep."

Leila suddenly felt her heart start to race with panic. "No! I didn't have it right, and don't call Jasper. I'm fine. I'm obviously reading too much into all of this and probably need more sleep. I'll be fine tomorrow. You're right. I'm overreacting. This will all be fine. You go back to your program, and we'll chat tomorrow." Just then the downstairs intercom chimed, alerting Leila to Carter's arrival. "I've gotta run. See, he's here. I overreacted."

"Wait!" Nia shouted. "I can still come by. I don't think you should be alone with him just yet."

Leila gave her what she hoped was a convincing laugh. "Don't worry. I'll be fine. Why would I not let him up? He's my husband."

"That right there is exactly what I'm afraid of."

CHAPTER 15

You have the sex. You bang all those feelings out. Donetta's crude, but nonetheless insightful, words came back to Leila as she looked through her peephole and prepared to open the apartment door and let Carter in. She tried her best to push down her wild emotions, but she was having the hardest time. It seemed that in that moment, with him standing in her hallway, waiting to gain entry to her apartment, all she could think of was following Donetta's advice and, for lack of a better term, jumping his bones.

"I've got to get it together," she whispered to herself. "But what would be the harm in following Donetta's advice and just going for it?" This final comment she directed at a now perplexed Ollie, who had stopped his barking and was looking at her as if he was trying to say, "Oh, come on. Get on with it and just open the damned door!"

Leila shook her head. "I know, I know. It

would be a disaster all around. Damn it. I hate it when you're right." Ollie's ears perked up as Leila shook her head. She'd been down that road before, and anyway, sex was not a part of this deal, whether she wanted it or not. She knew it would be a mistake.

"Excuse me? Are you by any chance talking to me, or is this a 'you and you' type of conversation?" Carter asked through the door.

Crap! Just how thin was her door, and how good was his hearing?

"I don't know what you're talking about," she yelled. "I'll be just a minute." Already she was kicking herself for calling Nia and playing the part of the hysterical wife. Yeah, she'd have a ton of explaining to do tomorrow about that one. But right now it was showtime.

Leila opened her apartment door with a flourish and a smile. "Welcome home, honey!" She said the words brightly and added a laugh so that it was clear to Carter that she was indeed joking with the honey tag.

The nervous side glance he gave her, while jumping out of the way of a once again barking Ollie, gave her pause and made her wonder if the joke had fallen flat. "Ollie, no!

231

Stop! Go inside and be quiet. You know Carter. He's a friend!" In that moment, Leila really hoped those words were true. She looked back up at Carter. "Too soon?" she asked, referring back to their rather testy afternoon.

He gave Ollie a cautious glance, then looked at her, offering up a small and frankly unconvincing smile. "No, not at all. We're fine." He looked down again as Ollie stood still at his feet between the hall and the doorway and gave him a low growl. "Now I know for sure your building has the best security," Carter said. "I don't think Ollie here likes me. Looks like I'm not getting in anytime soon. He's not hearing you on the friend deal. Maybe I should stay at my place and we ease into this."

Something about his words struck her, or maybe it was the easiness with which he said them. It wouldn't be the first time a man had used her dog as an excuse to bail, either. No, it wasn't the smoothest excuse, but as far as excuses went, it still worked. Not that she blamed him. She was sure his mother had given him a right earful that afternoon on the reasons why he shouldn't continue with their arrangement. And why should she blame him? She'd already proven to be a lunatic hothead who flew off the handle with the slightest provocation. Why would he want to be married to someone like her? Fake or not.

That was okay. She'd play it cool and not show she was bothered. Why let him see she cared? Leila waved a hand. "Listen, I get it. It's not as if this afternoon went well. So if you want out, take your out. Though you could have called me. You didn't have to go out of your way and take a trip all the way down to —"

He stopped her rudely by putting his index finger to her lips. Ollie growled louder, and Carter put his hand back down slowly. "Down, boy." This comment he directed Ollie's way, and the damned dog complied once Leila said, "Shhh," and then added, "Please." As if that made it all right.

Carter looked at her. "You love getting a word in, don't you? I get it. Though you don't know me that well, I, too, like to get a word or two in here or there. Now, would you mind calling off this beast so that I can bring in my bags?"

Leila blinked hard and for the first time noticed the bag handle to the side of the door. "Fine. Well, why didn't you say so first off?" She let out a huff and stepped back out of his way. "Ollie, chill it for a minute. He's coming in."

Leila watched as Ollie got her tone and followed her command, getting over his little power trip as he scurried around and let Carter carry in his small rolling suitcase and a larger garment bag. Over the top of the roller, he also had a large reusable shopping bag from a local city grocery. She swallowed as her heart began to pound. So this was happening. Despite all her relationships, she'd never once had a guy really move in. They had all just sort of crashed. First, they'd bring a toothbrush, and later they might add a tee or two, a pair of jeans, and maybe an errant pair of boxers, but none of them had ever come with a full suitcase. She snorted to herself. How ironic that the one who finally did was her husband, and he was moving his bags into her guest room.

Carter turned her way and handed her the shopping bag. He gave her a cute crooked smile that held a bit of caution. "It's from my mother. After we left, she went a little crazy in my kitchen. Just a few meals to hold us over for a couple of days."

Leila peeked in the bag to see dish after dish in carefully sealed and labeled plasticware. There was enough food in there to keep them stuffed for the better part of a week or more. Did Carter's mother always cook for him like this? She looked back up at him, and as if guessing her thoughts, he said, "No, she doesn't always cook for me."

Leila tilted her head and raised a brow. "Really?"

He suddenly looked embarrassed. "Well, not every week."

Leila gave him a slight grin. "Well, then, thank her for me. Why don't you go and get settled? Did you eat yet? Because I haven't, and I'm sure whatever's in here is better than what I was going to order. You want me to heat you up something?"

Carter gave her a slightly surprised expression, as if he had expected a different response. But he nodded and started on his way to the guest room. "Sure. I mean if you don't mind or I could just do it myself."

Leila gave him a raised brow.

"Thanks. That would be great."

Leila let out a long breath, trying her best to inject some normalcy into this most abnormal moment then headed to the kitchen, telling herself that she'd handled that well, all things considered. Now, if she could just figure out how to get her hormones to stop raging every time he got anywhere near her, she'd be all right. Only five months, give or take twenty-nine days, and the part of a lifetime could be hers.

■ ■ ■ ■

Maybe if he just had sex with her, it would all be all right.

Carter laughed to himself at the ridiculous thought as he laid the garment bag out on the bed, then hoisted up his suitcase. *Yeah, right.* As if that was an option. Number 1) It wasn't like he really had a chance in hell with her. Number 2) He was now officially in business with her and was going by his own rules, and it didn't matter that the business just so happened to be that they were to appear to be in a relationship, to convince the public only. By all rights, Leila was now a colleague, and that took her out of the potential sex lane and landed her firmly in the "keep it clean" work lane, so . . . Number 3) What did it matter? Going back to number 1, it wasn't like he had a chance in hell.

But, Carter thought, as he went over to the tall bureau and carefully placed the few changes of underwear he had brought with him, seeing her in that doorway, once again looking beautiful, fresh faced, and makeup free, he knew this assignment was going to be hard. And in the end, how was he really supposed to win?

That part still got to him. When Jasper had proposed the bet that night, it was late. And who knows? Maybe Carter's mind had been foggy from the taste he'd taken of the horrific blue vodka. But what did he really expect from this little experiment? Sure, he got the part about him choosing a show or her choosing a show, but how was one supposed to bail on the whole marriage thing? What could he possibly do to make her want to bail? Did Jasper really expect him to go about wooing his most high-profile client, then let her down? Carter suddenly paused midway in the act of hanging up his suit in the little closet space she'd given him, noting that she'd shoved quite a few dresses of questionable length to the far end of the closet to accommodate him. He recalled Leila's look of surprise as she fell into him at the airport, her breasts pressing against his body, and the way she had shown up unannounced at his office and had practically dared him to kiss her. *Wait a minute.* Did Jasper expect Leila to seduce him? Rein him in and then somehow send him packing, like she had her other dudes?

Suddenly the hairs on the back of his neck stood at attention. She was rather welcoming tonight, although at the same time she had told him it was okay to walk away. So what was that all about? Carter looked toward the open doorway and Ollie; his smushed dog face and dark eyes almost taunted him in their mockery. "I'm screwed, aren't I?" Carter said to the dog.

For his answer, all he got was Ollie's behind, as the dog gave a surprisingly dignified huff and walked away. Yeah, he was screwed. Even the dog didn't find him worthy of a backward glance. That was all right. Leila and Jasper would soon find out they had picked the wrong mark. He'd worked too hard for an opportunity like Sphere, and there was no way he was letting anyone, no matter how enticing or sexy she may be, jeopardize his chances of making it a success. She'd get through these six months, or at least close to it, with her reputation raised and the potential to be the next star, they both needed to make his *Brentwood* show a success. No, he wasn't going to resort to seducing her, or he wouldn't have to, since by the time this deal was over, she'd be eating out of his hands and begging to be given the lead on the *Brentwood* show.

"This is really delicious. Here. Are you sure you don't want some more?"

Leila put out her hand and waved it in

front of his mouth, offering him a bite of the crusty bread his mother had sent along with the chicken and vegetable stew she'd made. Leila had taken the bread and had sopped up some leftover sauce with it. She'd then taken her last piece of chicken and balanced it on top of the bread. In his seat across the kitchen island, Carter only shook his head as he looked at her, resembling a defiant toddler, and so she shrugged and ate the final bite herself.

She looked at him and smiled. "Wow! You've got to thank your mother for me. It's been so long since I've had a home-cooked meal that I'd forgotten how much I actually missed it." She paused and for the first time noticed how deep Carter's frown went. "I'm sorry," she said. "Am I boring you or keeping you from something?"

He blinked, as if coming back to life. "No. I'm sorry. It's me. I just didn't expect this," he said, waving his hand over the island, at the spread-out mess of used dishes.

She frowned. "What? Eating, dinner, food?"

He leaned back, stretching a bit, while he rubbed his large hand over the back of his neck. Then he looked at her. Those dark eyes, which had seemed to see so much when he first looked at her, now looked at her like she was a stranger. "Yes, all of it. The dinner, the food. Honestly, Leila, I don't know what I expected, but it wasn't this much." He sucked in a breath as she waited.

What should he say? Maybe from him at least she'd find out what it was that had sent so many other men fleeing for greener pastures.

Finally, he finished his thought. "I don't know . . . normalcy."

Leila pulled back. "Normalcy?" She shook her head and picked up her dish, then brought it over to the trash to discard the bones, careful to keep the stray bits from Ollie. Carter got up to help, but Leila snatched the plate from his hand and gave him a tight smile. "I've got it."

Carter gave the plate to her but then took the other dishes to the sink and proceeded to wash them. "I'm sorry. I didn't know the word *normalcy* was so bad," he said by way of apology.

"Well, it is. At least the way you are saying it." Leila came over to his side and attempted to edge him out of the way of the sink. "I've worked too long in this business to be thought of as normal." She pushed a hip against his own. He didn't budge. Just let the dishwater fill in the sink as he added soap.

"I get that, and you've done a great job of it. No one would figure out that you're the type who enjoys chilling at home with a chicken and rice dinner. I'm sure there are fans of yours camped out, waiting at Club Haze or one of the other hot nightspots."

And with that, Leila's hip checked him again. "Shows what you know," she said, though he still wouldn't budge. "I swear, you must live with your nose in the weekly gossip rags." She looked over at him, angry that he would ruin a night that she was trying to make perfectly lovely and, yes, perfectly normal, despite the perfectly abnormal situation they found themselves in. "Now, would you please move? I'd like to rinse these dishes. I don't know why you put in so much soap. I have a dishwasher, you know."

He looked at her dead on, giving her that look of his that, she was starting to realize, meant she'd just said something he thought was totally ridiculous. It gave her the sudden urge to punch him in that smug face of his. "Why would you run the dishwasher and waste so much water when you have so few dirty dishes?" he asked.

Seriously? First, he criticized her for be-

241

ing normal, and now she was abnormal because she wanted to use a dishwasher. Leila looked at the sudsy water, then over at his pristine white collared shirt, still tucked into his perfectly pressed pants. Except for the fact that his cuffs were rolled up, you'd think it was 9:00 a.m., as the man still looked so good, so unruffled. All this did was remind her that she really hadn't thought through the logistics of this "getting hitched" deal. What did she have in common with this man besides business? And even when it came to that, they were at odds. Here he was, standing there, being all perfectly himself, winged tips and all; and here she was in her bare feet, leggings, and a T-shirt, her hair by now, probably a mess about her head, looking more like she'd just rolled out of bed than a woman ready to launch her big acting career. How in the world was she supposed to convince this man to make her the lead in his next hit? Besides, right now he was looking at her like he could barely tolerate her.

It was utterly and completely infuriating. He was in her house, damn it! Without really thinking, or maybe after thinking way too much, Leila reached down into the sink, scooped up a handful of the sudsy water, and sloshed it right in Carter's face.

Carter sputtered and jumped back. "What are you doing?"

Not answering, Leila stepped into his place at the sink and proceeded to rinse the dishes calmly, feeling somehow at ease, while he wiped himself down with a paper towel.

The ease she felt was short lived, though, and she swallowed the sudden lump in her throat when he went to unbutton his now spotted white shirt and was left standing there in just his slacks and a white tank. It was no matter, she told herself. She'd won that round.

Leila placed the dishes in the dishwasher and was about to hit START when Carter came up behind her. Close. Way too close. "Wait. Don't start it yet. You forgot this," he said, handing her a glass. Yes, she'd won that round.

Or had she? The heat from his body was almost measurable as it simmered around her. So he was going for a whole other tactic entirely, she thought as she stood there and slowly took the glass from his hand, their fingers just barely glancing off each other. "Thanks," she said, her voice slightly breathy, and at that point, Leila didn't know if it was intentional or natural. All she knew was that he was close, and he smelled like heaven dipped in just enough hell to make him interesting. *Damn it.* He wasn't supposed to be interesting.

She let out a breath as she watched his Adam's apple bob in his throat, and the overwhelming urge to lean in just a little and stick out her tongue to give it a little taste was almost too much. But she didn't. Instead, she took a step back. And turned away. Put the wayward glass in the dishwater from the most awkward position.

When she turned back around, he was on the other side of the counter taking a seat. He gave her a smile. The devil seemed to have backed down, and once again he was as docile as a lamb. "So," he began. "This is it. Day one together under our belts."

Leila nodded and gave him a halfhearted smile. "It would seem so." She tilted her head. "I guess we did all right, all things considered." She let out a sigh. "Sorry about your shirt."

He shrugged. "It's just a shirt. And I was being a little . . . judgy. It's your place. I get that."

"If you leave it with me, I'll have it cleaned."

Carter shook his head. "Don't worry about it. I have a place near work." He looked at her with soft eyes. Those eyes that

made her wonder if he knew how dangerous they really could be. "But thanks for
the offer."

There was an awkward silence, and his
wistful smile broke her heart a little as she
thought of the compromising that they both
were engaging in. "Uh, do you want to
watch TV? A movie or something?"

He shook his head. "Thanks, but no. I
think I'm going to head to my room and
get a little more work done." He looked at
her with a little more concern on his face.
"That is, if you don't mind. I understand
this is our first real night together." He
grinned wider. "Wifey."

Leila eked out a smile. "No problem,
hubby. It's not like we're doing this for
real." She gave an awkward laugh but hoped
he was convinced of it. "I mean, if we were
doing this for *real* real, I'm sure we'd both
have our minds on things that newly-weds
do." She laughed again and then silently
told herself to zip it. This was getting more
than awkward and becoming downright
weird. Leila let out a cough. "You let me
know if you need anything. I'll be right
across the hall."

Carter gave her a nod. "I'm sure I'll be
fine," he said while stretching his arms
above his head, showing off the width of his

chest. "I'm an early riser. I like to get into work by eight or eight thirty, and before that I work out. I'll try to be quiet, though."

She waved his words off. "It's no problem. I have an early boot camp class with Nia tomorrow. With my appetite, I have to be diligent about my workouts. So I'll be up early."

He got up from his seat by the counter and came her way. "Well, good night." For a second, she thought he might shake her hand. And he actually extended his hand over the top of Ollie's head. The dog was seated on the floor at her feet, taking in the whole awkward exchange.

"Yes, good night," she squeaked out, an unoriginal reply, and suddenly she felt much sadder than she should. She wished he'd just go off to his room and leave her to her emotions. But then he shocked her once again and took her hand, pulled her softly toward him as he took a step forward, gently took her in his arms, and kissed the top of her head tenderly.

"Don't worry, Lei. We'll be all right. We're in this crazy thing together. I still don't see either of us losing here."

Leila took the opportunity to inhale deeply to cement the smell of him and the memory of this moment in her mind. To remember that he wasn't thoroughly evil and there had once been something she liked about him. Finally, Leila pushed against his sides, and he let her go. She smiled, or attempted to. "You say that now. But we've only just begun. Just wait until tomorrow, when the circus is in full swing."

CHAPTER 16

Well, so much for plans. Carter had gone into the kitchen to eat dinner, thinking he'd somehow be able to pull Leila in with his charm and have her eating out of his hands, and what had she done? She'd immediately turned the tables on him. So much so she'd had him stammering and putting his foot in his mouth. And then how had he ended the night? By kissing her on top of her head. On top of her head. *Who does that? Talk about sending mixed signals.* If this didn't put him in the loser column, or better yet, make him the honorary chair of Losers Inc., he didn't know what would.

Frustrated, Carter pulled out his laptop and laid it out on the bed. He sat down and for the first time got a feel for where he'd be sleeping for the greater part of these next six months, if all went as planned. Carter briefly pumped his body up and down, testing the mattress's firmness, and found it adequate, though not as good as his bed at home. It would do. He'd think of this as an extended hotel stay. Sort of like being sent to work abroad.

But just then he heard a shuffle from across the hall, and it was as if the air was sucked from his lungs. Hotel, his ass. This wasn't a hotel, and this wasn't just any old bed. Suddenly, Carter looked down at the nondescript gray duvet, and all he could see in his mind's eye was the image of Leila spread out upon it. Looking beautiful in a simple tee and nothing else but her panties. Bare skin, luminous eyes, and a smile that was meant only for him. He closed his eyes and let out a breath as the fantasy of the woman he'd dreamed of for so long once again captured his imagination. Just then Ollie barked, and Carter's eyes shot open. The gray duvet, empty save his laptop, filled his field of vision. He jumped up as if burned. Too bad there was no running from his now rock-hard erection.

"Nice going, idiot," he mumbled to himself when he heard Leila's tinkling laughter through the bedroom door. *Shit.* Right now she was probably laughing about the stooge she had sleeping in the next room. The one who was willing to gamble his career on childish fantasies.

Carter let out a breath. *A shower.* He'd take a cold shower and somehow get through this night and each night that followed. And in the morning, he'd burn off the rest of his energy with a run. Monks got through life somehow, he thought and then looked at his closed bedroom door. Yeah, but monks didn't push it by living life next to their temptation.

Carter took off his pants and carefully hung them before heading to the bathroom in his boxers and tee. In the bathroom he was once again surprised by Leila's thoughtfulness. She'd put out ample towels for him and even had specialty soap and extra toothbrushes, though he'd brought his own.

Carter leaned in to flip the shower on and was shocked when he got a harsh, sputtering spray of water in his face, chest, just about everywhere else, as the water shot out all over the small bathroom. "What the hell!" he yelled as he quickly went to turn the faucet back off. Could things get any worse? he thought. Well, that was one way to lose an erection right quick.

Carter had just finished that thought when Leila came running into the bathroom. "Are you all right?"

And it was back. He let out a long breath and silently willed himself to maintain control of his body and not embarrass himself. Clearing his throat, Carter did his best "eyes up here" and hoped to high heaven she would do the same, as he explained the mess. But there she was. His earlier fantasy come to life and running to his rescue, her face full of very real concern. She was wearing a cropped white tee that showed that sexy as hell toned belly of hers and, Lord of all that is holy, nothing else but white panties that highlighted the fact she was every bit a woman and in the best way possible.

Right then, in that very moment, Carter wanted nothing more out of his entire life than to drop to his knees and worship her until she screamed out his name and it echoed against the tiled walls. But he couldn't, so he didn't. No, he stood there, wet and hard and silly looking, trying to explain why he had made a mess of her lovely bathroom. "I'm, uh, sorry. I don't know what happened," he began. "I just turned on the shower, and everything went haywire."

Leila slapped a hand on her forehead. "Crap! I'm so sorry. I should have checked that, and I forgot." She looked at him with apologetic eyes. "My brother Greg was supposed to call someone to fix that showerhead while I was on the West Coast. I'm going to kill him."

Carter shook his head. "No, don't do that. Not on my account." He gave her a weak smile. Mostly because he didn't know what else to do. "Just give me a minute. I'll have it cleaned up." He took a now half-wet towel and held it up.

Leila shook her head. "I'll help. This is my fault. You can use my shower until it's fixed. I'll have someone here by tomorrow." She turned to get a towel, and Carter damn near passed out from the beauty of the view and the rush of blood from his brain. But then Leila quickly tuned back his way, her bare feet slipping on the wet floor. Carter caught her by the elbows and pulled her toward him, righting her again. He caught the exact moment she noticed his rock-hard erection and her eyes widened.

He looked away and went to move back. But she moved with him. One would think there would be a chill in the room with the air-conditioning up as high as it was, but no. He was on fire, and judging by the fact that her breathing was now short and stuttered, so was she. He looked at her hard, then gave her a smile. "I don't know if this is a good part of the plan. Us being newly-weds and all."

Leila laughed at that. Her eyes had become soft, and Carter knew she was thinking things over, probably as hard as they both should have the night they'd made that bet. Finally, she spoke. "You know, part of me wishes we had just gone forward and done it that night, instead of making our ridiculous bet. Everything would have been so much easier."

Carter frowned, confused by her words. "What are you talking about?"

She leaned into him and put her head on his shoulder and swayed there, and as if on automatic pilot, his hand came up and stroked her along her spine. He wanted to comfort her. Comfort her almost as much as he wanted to make love to her.

Finally, she let out a breath and spoke. "Had sex."

Carter felt the world stop for a moment, and he had to remind himself to breathe again when she continued to speak.

"Well, if we had, we'd have both gotten what we wanted, and you would have clearly gotten me out of your system. Sex with the fantasy girl." When Carter breathed in, readying his rebuttal, she stopped him by continuing. "No, I may not have had the part I wanted, but at least we'd have known where we both stood. But now, even this early in the game, I'm at a loss. I don't know if sex is the answer, and then moving on, or if getting to know you and us becoming actual friends is. The question is, which will hurt the least? Because both you and I know that in the end one of us is moving on from this."

Carter stood stock-still as the blow from Leila's words hit him worse than if she had taken a bat to his cranium. How was it that while he was over on one side of the apartment, trying to figure out how to start this thing, she already had the end of the affair figured out? It struck him as both genius and utter madness. It also saddened him to no end that she'd been hurt so much that she didn't see any silver lining anywhere in their scenario. He pulled her back and looked her in the eyes.

"You know, it doesn't have to be like you say. Nowhere near as dismal as all that. I told you that first night, I'm not like the other men you've encountered."

Leila smiled, and he could see her switch being turned on. More than anything, he wanted to flip it back. To shut it down, to tell her to stop. Stay in neutral. Tell her that she didn't have to be "on" for him.

"Of course you're not. This is why I decided to make the bet with you. And I'm here to prove I'm not like other women you know. I will convince you that I can handle any role thrown at me. No matter what."

And with that, Leila leaned in and kissed him. Her lips were soft as they caressed his. Her body fit against his perfectly as it sensuously curved into his. He felt himself grow impossibly harder as his hands, now taking an entirely different turn, curved around the perfect swell of her ass. This was bliss. So much so that when her tongue dipped out and touched his crease, he moaned out loud, then captured her tongue with his own. Carter felt like he could feast on her all night and not be satisfied. The fullness of her breasts as she pushed against his chest had his hands itching to move up and caress them. And just when he did, she took a step back and looked at him. She licked at her top lip, then lowered her lashes before looking at him again and then gazing around the bathroom.

"Yeah, I think it's best if we slow this down," she announced. "It won't end well. No matter which way we go. I'll get you some more towels, and I'll call the super about getting a plumber here tomorrow."

Carter cleared his throat as he tried to focus once again on where he was.

Leila looked him up and down. "In the

meantime, if you still want that shower, you're free to use mine."

He gave her a long look, taking in the just kissed fullness of her lips, the glow of her cheeks, then shook his head. "I'll take one in the morning. But you have at it. You may need one, just as much as I do."

Chapter 17

"Are you sure you're all right?" This was the third time Nia had asked Leila if she was all right. The first two times were cute and showed she was concerned, but now the question was frankly starting to get on Leila's nerves.

"I said I'm fine. Could you just drop it?" Leila hissed between short gasps for breath as she did sweat busting burpees on the small patch of grass that called itself a park.

She and Nia were part of an elite group of women — all of them pretty much on their game and solid in their professions — who were torturing themselves in this early morning boot camp. There were a few other models, a couple of lawyers, some top financial whizzes, and a couple of CEOs, with a few high-powered mom magnates mixed in, but there was a moment during each of these sunrise workouts when Leila didn't know if the whole lot of them was insane. And now, as Trap Hines came her way, barking his trademark "Dig deeper!" over her head and eliminating any further opportunity for Nia to meddle, she knew that once again she'd reached that moment.

Thankfully, she'd also reached the end of the workout, having survived one more. She and Trap would live to see another workout. Besides, he was right. Photo-worthy abs might be genetic, but they sure as hell didn't stay that way without work. Breathless and sweaty, she nodded her silent good-byes to the other women in the group before she and Nia started walking back toward her place. Some days she and Nia would head over to the local diner and share a protein-fueled breakfast to celebrate having worked out, but Leila felt the need both to head home and to check to see if Carter got going okay. At the same time, though, she was dreading it. Part of her wanted to be alone with her thoughts, but what good would that do? She'd been alone, tossing and turning, all night, and all it had done was give her plenty of time to replay the scene in her bathroom over and over in her mind.

Jeez, she'd totally screwed that up, but she had to admit that he'd felt and tasted so good, and so she couldn't bring herself to be as upset with herself as she should be.

She knew it was wrong, that she was wrong for laying it all out there. For letting him, for just a moment, see the cards she was holding back. Too much of that, and he'd know exactly how to play her. But, damn, it was all worth it. Besides, how could she resist after seeing him all hard, sexy, and wet?

Just then she got a poke in her side and twisted out of the way. "Hey!" she said, looking at Nia with hard eyes.

Nia gave her a glare right back. "Well, I had to do something to get your attention. This is what I was talking about." Nia's eyes softened. "You're not all here. What happened last night? Are you okay?"

Leila shook her head. "I told you, I'm fine, and nothing much happened."

"Sure," Nia said. "It's just the little word *much* in there that implies so very much."

Leila shook her head. "Just relax. It's all good. I've got a handle on this. Besides, he's probably off to work by now, which is where you should be going. So bye. And I need to get home. I've got to be at the apartment to let the plumber in to fix my pipes."

At that Nia snorted. "Fix your pipes? Is that what you're calling it?"

Leila shot her a look. "Seriously, what are you? Like, twelve?"

Nia laughed and gave her a small shove. "No, thirteen, as of my last birthday." She stuck out her tongue but then hugged her friend. After pulling back, she looked her in the eye. "You're good?"

Leila gave her what she hoped was a totally convincing smile. "I'm perfectly fine. You go and light a fire under Jasper. Make sure he's working hard and bringing that bacon in for me. Tell him I'll be calling later."

Nia gave her a nod as she turned to catch the oncoming uptown bus. "Will do."

As it turned out, though, Leila didn't need Nia to poke at Jasper, after all, since he was waiting for her in her lobby when she walked into her building a few minutes later.

"Hey," she said with a smile and a kiss to his cheek. "What are you doing here at this hour? Don't tell me we have a problem?" Leila said.

Jasper gave her a hug and then waved the paper he had in his hands. "I'd say so, honey, and it has the potential to be a big one if you don't nip it in the bud quickly. I'm looking at some of the worst PR pics ever. We have got to get some spark between you and that husband of yours. I came early to catch both you and your husband at home and find out what's the deal."

"Well, you're not alone in that," said another male voice. Leila froze. That voice, which had come from over her shoulder, had her suddenly wishing the ground would swallow her up. Dammit. Her father was there. Leila almost physically winced when she thought about the fireworks that were about to go off.

But instead, she pushed her shoulders back and pulled herself up to her full height before turning around with a bright smile. "Hello, Dad, Garret, Greg, Ben." She walked forward and kissed each of her brothers on the cheek. Looking for potential allies in their dark gazes. When she got to her father, she reached out, forcing him come forward and pull her into a hug. "I missed you, Daddy."

Leila's father hugged her tight, then pushed her back slightly and looked her in the eyes, searching, Leila knew, for answers she wasn't prepared to give.

She smiled and stalled by saying, "It's good to see the gang's all here. Makes me wonder if you missed me. You guys should have called. I'd have prepared breakfast."

Her father let out a ragged breath that could have been a growl.

"Yeah, right," her brother Greg said. "As

261

if you cook."

Leila gave him a quick glare.

"Stop stalling, Leila, and let's go upstairs. It's bad enough we're here at all under these terrible circumstances. But before I jump to any conclusions and get to breaking legs, I'll hear what's going on from your lips." Her father looked Jasper's way when he mentioned breaking some legs, and Leila saw Jasper plaster on a wobbly smile.

Leila looked at her father steadily. Told herself not to give in. Not to let him have the upper hand. She was an adult, damn it. "You'll do no such thing, but fine. Let's head upstairs."

Leading all the men into the smallish elevator, as if she were trying to load a clown car, was almost laughable, but Leila took the time to say a brief prayer and hoped that Carter was true to his word and had left already. She could almost feel the anger radiating off her father, and though she understood it, she didn't stop it from fueling her own. Why couldn't he just trust her to do what was right for her? She had this under control. Well, sort of. Either way, he needed to lay off.

They were barely off the elevator when her mouth got ahead of her and she started talking. "Daddy, you didn't need to come here." She looked at her brothers, giving them the side eye. "Especially with your little reinforcements. Besides, I'm sure Carter is off to work and what's going on is just like I told you, well, texted you. It's all platonic. Strictly a work thing."

"What?" her oldest brother, Garret, yelled. He turned to Jasper. "What kind of bullshit did you get our sister into now? You're supposed to be watching out for her."

Jasper balked. "And I am. I always do. She's fine. You'll see when you meet him that Carter is totally cool and everything is aboveboard."

Leila turned to Garret and looked between him and her seething father as they stood outside the door to her apartment. "See? It's all aboveboard. Trust me, I'm doing this for a worthwhile end goal, and there are no sparks of romance or anything like that happening."

"Though a little something for the cameras wouldn't hurt our cause," Jasper mumbled under his breath.

Leila gave him a quick elbow jab. "Could you not help?"

He shook his head and shrugged. "I'm just saying."

Leila let out a sigh and put her key in the door. She turned to her father. "Really,

Daddy, everything is fine. And Carter is harmless. He's a corporate suit, and so far from my type, he's not even a blip on my radar."

She swung open her door, and they all walked in, just in time to see Carter exiting her bedroom, naked and glistening, save the towel he had loosely wrapped around his waist and the other he was using to rub his wet head. "Thanks for the shower. It was just what I needed after last night," he called out to the sound of her in the apartment.

Leila's jaw dropped at the same time she heard her father and her brothers growl on either side of her. Carter turned her way just then and looked at them all straight on with openmouthed shock.

The only person, it would seem, who was capable of using their voice was Jasper. He looked from Carter to Leila and grinned. "Yep, that right there. That's the type of spark I'm talking about. More of that, and publicity will be the last of our problems."

Leila's younger brother Benjamin chose then to contribute to the conversation. "So, yeah, that's definitely not a suit he's wearing."

As far as "meeting the in-laws" stories went, Carter had to say that if this were a real marriage, he'd have an epic tale to tell. He would have made a joke and laughed out loud when he set eyes on Leila's family if 1) Leila's brothers weren't so damned big and formidable looking as they stood there, arms folded, and stared him down like he was about to be pummeling practice; 2) a glance at Leila's father didn't have him thinking that with all that anger in his eyes, maybe the older man could take him down; and finally, 3) one look at Leila's shocked and desperate expression had not let him know that these men, in this moment, meant more to her then he'd even guessed. If he screwed up, not only would he hurt her, but he'd also ruin any chance of signing her on for *Brentwood*. Challenge or not.

So he'd better get his shit together and quick.

After throwing aside the smaller towel so that it landed in a heap on his own bed, Carter tightened the towel around his waist with one hand and stuck the other hand out in an automatic greeting, but not before he adjusted his slipping glasses. "Hello. I'm Carter Bain, and really, I'm sorry about" — he looked down at his ridiculous state of undress — "this." He pulled his untouched hand back. "Believe me, it's all perfectly innocent. You see, the guest shower was broken. I'll let Leila explain it further while I dress." Just then he saw Leila shoot a look toward one of her brothers — it must have been Greg — before turning back to him with wide eyes. "Yes, I'll be back in just a moment."

Carter scurried off to his bedroom, holding tight to his towel, and left Leila to handle her brooding lot. No matter that his back was still slightly damp, he pulled the T-shirt down over his torso. *Damn.* Why hadn't Leila prepared him, sent him a text or something? And why had he chosen today, of all days, to oversleep? Any other day he'd be long gone by this time, or at least fully dressed and headed out the door. He let out a breath. The fact that he'd barely gotten any sleep — having finally closed his eyes around 4:00 a.m., after tossing and turning, and playing and then hitting the repeat button on their time in the bathroom more times than he could count — was surely to blame for his oversleeping.

Carter knew he had to get a handle on these intense emotions. If he didn't, inside of a week he'd be walking around like an extra from a zombie movie. Who in their right mind could last six months with a woman like her right across the hall and not lose it? Just the thought of her on a normal day sent his sexual impulses skyrocketing, and then he had had to go and add the temptation of last night and whatever the hell she had tried to pretend was her version of pajamas?

Carter made a mental note to ask Karen where he could shop for things like loose nightgowns and granny panties, but he quickly dismissed it, not ready to take the ridicule that particular query would bring on. He shook his head. *Six months? Six long and extremely hard months.* Something would definitely have to give. Carter picked up his tie and quickly brought it over his collar. If this marriage was in name only, then what would they both do to satisfy their sexual urges during that time? His mind quickly did a scan of his usual dates and late-night callers; all of them, surprisingly, were less appealing to him now than they had been a week before. Yep, he was screwed, and not in any good sense of the word.

As he was finishing up, and steeling himself to go back out to the living area, Carter heard raised male voices and paused at the bedroom door. This was a bit much for so early in the workday. And not what he'd anticipated when he'd taken on the bet. He briefly considered staying in the bedroom until the family feud blew over. It really wasn't his fight to have. Especially since he was attached to Leila only on a technicality. But then he heard it. Her voice, high and determined, as she started to explain, but there was something else there. Something he'd never heard before. A slight tremor, just below the surface.

"I can't believe you're saying this. So what if you don't like him? You should at least love and trust me," Leila said. Her tone pierced Carter's heart in a way it never had been touched before.

He walked out of the bedroom and saw Leila sitting on the couch, looking smaller than he'd ever seen her look, as her father stood over her. Two of her brothers flanked both sides of him, and Jasper and the other brother, Greg, were on one of the other smaller couches, observing.

Carter walked over and stood behind Leila, then put his hands on her shoulders, looking her father in the eye. "I'm sorry I wasn't presentable before," he began. "Like I said, the shower in the guest bedroom was broken, so when Leila was out this morning, I used hers."

Her father gave him a dismissive nod, then spoke. "That's all fine and good. Now would you care to be quiet or better yet, leave? This doesn't concern you."

Jasper shook his head. "I'm sorry about that, too, but I can't be quiet and I'm definitely not leaving, because I think this directly concerns me. Besides, I don't like hearing Leila so upset."

The two brothers flanking their dad got slightly wide eyed and looked at their father with "oh no he didn't" expressions.

"What do you know about my daughter's feelings?" Leila's dad said through clenched teeth.

Carter shrugged. "Frankly, not much. As I'm sure you're well aware. We pretty much entered into a mostly crazy and hopefully genius idea, thought up by Jasper here, and if it works out, it will bring Leila and her career to the next level."

Leila's dad snorted. "And yours, too, I'm guessing. You're not in this for nothing."

Carter felt Leila's shoulders go tight with those words, and he knew he couldn't sidestep this and bullshit his way around it. He looked down at Leila and then back at her father. "You're right. And mine, too. Which is why I don't plan to screw it up by jerking Leila around. We hit it off immediately, and I instantly saw how special she is." He watched as Leila's dad carefully took in his words. "Please believe me. Leila is right now my top priority. I don't plan on doing her wrong or disrespecting her in any way. Like I told her, I'm not like anyone she's dealt with in the past."

It was then that he saw Leila's dad visibly soften and his shoulders relaxed just a little. Her dad moved and sat beside Leila. Carter stepped back and let out a breath as he watched the older man take Leila's hand in his.

"Sweetheart, you don't know how much I wish your mother were here right now. She'd know what to say, what to do." Her dad shook his head. "I can barely handle these hardheaded boys. What do I know about keeping you happy?"

And then, once again, Carter's heart experienced that piercing thing as he watched Leila blink back tears as she laid her head on her father's shoulder. "You know a lot, Daddy. You do just fine. Please just trust me. I'll be all right."

They sat there quietly for a few moments, until finally Jasper cleared his throat. "Are we good now, family?" he said, his voice loud and a little too boisterous for the room. "Because I have some more strategizing to do with my client."

It was then that the largest of Leila's brothers spoke up and took a step toward

Jasper. "I don't know about that, Jasper. Dad may be cool, but know if this thing goes south, we're coming for you."

Jasper gave him a nod back. "Yeah, sure, Garret. You've been coming for me since junior high. See if you can catch me first."

Leila and her father got up, and Leila went over to the coffeemaker to start some brew. Once again Carter found himself face-to-face with the older man. Carter was surprised when he put out his hand for Carter to shake it.

"John Darling," he said. Carter grinned and eagerly took the man's hand, happy to have the hard part done and over with. But then John pulled him in close and spoke in a low tone. "You said my daughter is your priority for now. I'd very much like to know what happens when 'for now' is over."

"Daddy, let him go! Don't go smashing my new husband's hand. He may need to use that hand to sign contracts later."

John let Carter go with a wink and a half smile, which let him know without a doubt that nothing was funny about their current situation.

CHAPTER 18

"Now that the unhappy family hour is done, you think we can get down to business?" Jasper said.

Leila let out a long breath. So far this had been the longest of mornings, she thought, and the day had barely gotten started.

Carter slid Jasper an impatient look. "Can this wait? I need to get going. I've already had Karen postpone one of my morning meetings. I can't move another."

Carter looked Leila's way, his eyes softening. She had to admit he had come through for her this morning after catching her off guard and getting her off balance. She smiled to herself. He had also caught her father and brothers off guard, and that was something that rarely happened. She'd never seen any of her exes stand up to them the way Carter had. And though they weren't technically together, he had stood up for her in a way that she'd always hoped someone in love with her would. That thought left her feeling both hollow and angry over all her time she'd wasted.

She turned to Jasper. "Yes, can it wait? It's been a long morning, and I don't have much time to get ready for my fittings that I have later. Plus, the plumber will be here any minute. And I have my acting workshop."

Her father had offered to stay and fix the shower himself, but she had had enough and had sent him and her brothers off to their respective jobs. No use pushing her luck. Better to end, if not on a high note, at least on a plateau.

Jasper shook his head and waved the paper he'd flailed about on the elevator. "No, this can't wait. It seems our statement about being happy and in love and having no further comment only went so far, and then we have photos like this one." He placed the paper on the counter for both her and Carter to see. "Of you and Mr. Sunshine here looking anything but in love. With this, you make me and my statement a joke. Read the caption."

Leila leaned over the photo and read the caption aloud. "Is the honeymoon over for Darling before it begins?" Her eyes now thoroughly examined the photo, and she let out a sigh. It was of her and Carter and had obviously been taken at lunch yesterday. She was waving her fork at him in a way that looked like she was about to stab him with it, and he was looking at her with that stern expression of his that she'd come to know as nothing more than his resting "nope" face. The man looked at practically everyone like they were getting in the way of something he had to do. With her gesture and his expression, the photo told the story of a couple clearly not in a state of wedded bliss. She looked up at Jasper and shook her head.

He nodded. "See what I mean?"

They both turned to Carter, and he frowned back at them, then shrugged. "So it's not my best photo."

Jasper snorted. "Not your best? Dude, I've seen corpses in more animated shots than this one. If you're going to be in this, then I need you to be in it. You're playing on my team now, and I don't go for half-assing."

Leila watched as Carter's brows drew together and his nostrils flared. "You know me, and I don't half-ass anything."

Jasper pulled his shoulders up and back. Pulled at the cuffs of his snowy white shirt. "Well, then, I'm glad to hear it. Because you made a big show about making Leila a priority with her father, and for your sake, it better be true. Because if you think *he* can be tough, you haven't begun to deal with me. I made it clear before that Leila is my client, as well as my friend, and two things I don't like a person to screw around with are my money and my friends. As to what comes first, you take your pick. They're equally as precious."

Carter took the bait and took a wide step, ending up just about nose to nose with Jasper. "Are you trying to call me out or something? Because I'm not appreciating what you are insinuating about my integrity or intentions. As a matter of fact, I've had enough of it for one morning."

Leila let out a long sigh. They both looked incredibly handsome, all well-groomed and impeccably dressed, but at the same time they were absolutely ridiculous for standing in the middle of her kitchen, going at it as they were. At this point she wouldn't be surprised if one challenged the other to a duel, demanding satisfaction.

She took a step toward them, pried them apart by wedging her hands in between their hard chests, and looked from one to the other. "As cute as this gentlemanly pissing contest is, none of us have time for it. So let's stand down, boys." She was relieved when both men parted, neither really wanting to go at it and both just wanting to do business, and that business was getting the best out of her. Leila looked toward Jasper. "So where do we go from here?"

He nodded. "From here we follow a plan. You two are to go out and are to be seen at only the best places. You keep mum and reserve your comments for when they matter. We set up an interview regarding your Sundance nod, and there they'll ask questions about you two. You will be coy but will say something about Carter being the one you've been waiting for. He'll just so happen to be on set to pick you up, and so he can slip in for a quick Q & A."

He turned to Carter then. "Finally, when you're out with her, you can cool it on the 'resting bastard' face and try to soften it, make it something a bit more mysterious so that when you're with her, people get the idea that this at least looks like something that resembles love. Not sure if you've ever experienced that emotion, but if not, go and watch some old romantic comedies then do your best to wing it. I'll have a guy I know, a photographer who freelances out and about, to counteract any of these awful pics. He'll be taking photos of you all, too."

Carter grumbled, "Do we really need yet

another parasite on our tails?"

Jasper frowned and then let out an impatient snort. "You still don't get it, and if anyone should, it should be you. The media will be there, anyway, so we might as well at least have someone in the trenches we can control."

Carter shook his head, and Leila could tell he was about at the end of his patience for one morning. She reached over and put her hand on top of his closed fist. "Are we good, Hubby?"

He looked at her and gave a half smile. Before he looked back at Jasper, his lips thinned, but still he gave a nod of acceptance. He then turned back to Leila. "Sure, Wifey. We're perfect."

Jasper clapped his hands together loudly. "I'm glad we're all in agreement. You'll have your first road test tonight down at the Everleaf Gallery."

"What and why?" Leila asked.

Jasper gave her an incredulous look. "Because instead of club hopping, this is what you're doing now, and besides, it's trending, so on brand. A hot up-and-coming designer is showing there, and instead of using regular models, he's supposedly showing his clothes in some new and exciting way. I hear it will be the place to be."

Carter looked at Leila. "So then we shall be there." He reached for his jacket and bag and headed for the door. "I'll pick you up here at eight thirty?"

Leila nodded.

"What? No kiss?" Jasper yelled after Carter.

Carter raised a brow. "For that, Jasper, you'd have to at least buy me dinner first."

CHAPTER 19

Leila was ready when Carter got to the apartment. Once again, she looked beautiful, and once again, she was completely transformed. It wasn't lost on him that this chameleon of a woman was the type that a man would probably never grow bored with, since being with her was like enjoying a visual surprise party every day. Tonight she was going for understated sleek. She wore a pair of slim black stretch pants that would look nondescript on anyone else, but on her, they were anything but. She'd paired the pants with a fairly loose black halter top that skimmed over her body perfectly. Her hair was not her usual sexy tousled hair, but it was straightened and parted in the middle. And she wore minimal makeup: her only accent was her full, sexy red lips.

She just about took his breath away when those lips spread wide in a smile, indicating she was happy to see him. "You're right on time. Punctuality," she said. "I like that in a man."

"Good," he replied, stepping into the apartment. "I'm glad to hear it. I brought my car from home and have it in a visitor spot down in your garage. Do you want me to drive, or should we cab it?"

She thought for a moment then looked at him. "How about we just take a cab? It's not far, and parking will be a nightmare." She seemed pensive for a moment. "You know, I didn't think of your car before, but I'll call and take care of it so that you can keep that spot."

She smiled again and held up what she'd been holding all along. At the end of her long, delicate fingers was a set of two keys on a ring, along with a slim card of some sort.

Carter stared at her. "Are you sure?"

Leila nodded. "For now, I am. At least as long as this" — she breathed in deeply and let out a sigh — "partnership lasts, you should be able to go in and out freely. I know it's soon, but I trust you. You were great with my father and brothers today and besides, we're legal. If I can trust you when I sleep across the hall from you, I can trust you if I give you a key."

Carter stared at her. The fact that she was

talking to him about trust, a trust that he didn't think he'd by rights earned, both swelled his heart and made him feel deeply unworthy.

"Leila, you know I didn't earn this. Maybe you should reconsider." He pushed back her hand with the keys. But she shook her hand and placed it against his chest, so that her hand was now over his heart.

"Then do something to earn this."

She looked at him, her wide, deep brown eyes connecting with his, challenging him to step up to the plate and once and for all really take a stand that would cost him something. In all his time, with all he'd accomplished, he'd done it freely and recklessly, because he'd never had anything to lose. Carter was starting to feel different about this deal. Like maybe with this deal, there was so much more on the line.

He cleared his throat and gave her a smile as he gently took the keys from her and placed them in his pocket. "Thank you."

She let out a long breath. "You're welcome."

He laughed. "Now I feel like I've got to give you a set of my keys."

She raised a brow. "Don't think that I won't take you up on that. If it gets too crowded up in here with all my brothers stopping by, like they sometimes do, I may just need a place to escape to. Now let's go."

She grabbed his hand easily and pulled him toward the door, but he pulled her back. "Wait a minute. What do you mean, your brothers stop by here often?"

But Leila just laughed and pulled him out into the hallway.

"What in all the ever-loving hell is this?" Carter asked over the hard-thumping hip-hop that the DJ was mixing in a corner of the Everleaf Gallery. He was holding a glass of champagne and looking at something. What, he didn't rightly know.

Leila blinked by his side and reached into her bag. Although it was nighttime, she pulled out her shades and put them on. She looked at him before saying, "I don't know."

He looked at her seriously. Tried his best not to burst out laughing as her lip quivered. He leaned down toward her ear. "You're laughing behind those shades, aren't you?"

She let out a little snort. "So what if I am? This is a hot mess."

Carter shook his head and pulled back.

Leila pulled him back in again. "And don't get too far from me. I'd rather smell you than anything in here. It stinks to all hell."

He pulled her in toward him and just stopped short of wrapping his suit jacket around her and letting her bury her face there. He would if he could. Surrounding them was, he guessed, a collection of the most god-awful clothes he'd ever seen, and to hammer home the fact that they were terrible, they were being modeled in the most bizarre way imaginable. Each piece was showcased by either a quite interesting nudist or a goat or a sheep straight from a farm in upstate New York. As to what had been imported — the goats, sheep, or nudists — no one knew. Carter had a feeling it was all three.

He and Leila currently had a view of a couple in what had to be their seventies. They were as pale as could be. *Good for them for staying out of the sun,* he thought. The woman was wearing a pink plastic skirt of some kind with matching rain boots and nothing more. As for her companion, he was holding a yellow umbrella over his lady love, he supposed to appear chivalrous. And to prevent his nether regions from getting a chill, he was wearing a bright yellow cod piece, flip-flops, and gym socks, which, Carter got the feeling, were remnants of the man's youth, and that was the extent of his outfit.

Just then Carter got a nudge in his leg and looked down to see he'd been checked by a goat wearing red headphones and a matching tutu, and for the life of him he couldn't get the significance of that one. A waiter walked by, holding a tray, with the perfect expression of seasoned ambivalence on his face, so much so that Carter wanted to applaud him then and there. The waiter took Leila's glass from her and added both their glasses to the tray with a nod.

"You think we've done this dance long enough?" Carter asked.

Leila nodded. "I hope so. At the very least, let's go outside and get some fresh air."

But as they made their way just outside the gallery door and toward the blessed fresh air, they were held up by the arrival of another party.

"Hey, Darlings!" Chloe Caraway giggled as she got her own pun. "Wow, that really works in this case, doesn't it?"

Carter tilted his head and was about to say something but thought better of it. He could feel the tension as it immediately began to radiate off Leila, though looking at her expression, one would never know it.

"Barely," Leila said. "But it's cute. I'll give

you that." She then slipped her hand into Carter's seamlessly and pulled him closer to her side.

Chloe looked at him, then back to Leila. "Well, either way, I congratulate you. And to think you said absolutely nothing about it when I saw you in Vegas." She turned to Carter. "And you, either, when we were chatting the week before." She batted her lashes flirtatiously. "I mean, I didn't even know you two were friends when we were chatting about my role in *Shadowed Dreams.*"

Shit. Carter just looked at Chloe. At the same time he noticed Leila loosen her grip on his hand. Or try to. He held on to her hand a little tighter and smiled Chloe's way. "Well, that was business. I don't talk about my personal life during business dealings."

Chloe smiled and inched closer to the couple. Looked into Carter's eyes. "Oh, come on," she said. "We're friends. You can tell me. I love hearing about true love and all that." She turned to Leila, with a grin covering her face. "And I'm so happy for you, my dear friend. It's great to see you bouncing back after Miles. Carter seems so much more worthy of you. So much more . . ." She put her fingers to her lips and feigned being at a loss for words. "How shall I say it? Your speed."

And just then the photographers outside the club started to yell Chloe's name and demand a photo of the three of them.

Carter looked to Leila, and she gave him a hard glare back before taking into account that they were on. Finally, her lips widened, and she got into the groove of things. She got on the opposite side of Carter and posed with him and Chloe.

Before Chloe turned to walk into the club, she said, "Au revoir and mazel, you two."

Carter let out a long breath as he heard Leila curse under her own.

"Her part? Hag. Throwing around accents for no reason," Leila mumbled before she stormed past the bevy of photographers and headed up the block toward her . . . well, temporarily their apartment.

"Leila, slow down." She heard Carter say it, and she would if she could or if she thought slowing down was a good idea, but she knew it wasn't. Not at that particular time. Because if she stopped walking or slowed down and looked Carter in the eye and let him see just how truly upset she was by that encounter with freaking Chloe Caraway, all would be lost.

"Darling, come on," he said.

Now she paused. The heat was rising so fast, she thought her head might pop off from it. She turned and looked at him. "Don't you do that! Don't you, of all people, dare screw around and play with my name like that."

"I had to do something to make you stop. Short of sprinting after you and really causing a scene. You getting all pissed just because you don't like Chloe and then storming off in front of the paparazzi does nothing for your image or our deal. Look, I'm sorry. No darling. Is sweetheart better?"

She shook her head and felt some of her tension evaporate. "Not by a long shot."

He walked over to her and gently took her hand in his. Her first instinct was to pull her hand back, but he gave her a look and held tight. "Come on," he whispered. "Remember what Jasper said? Who knows? He may even have his guy around as we speak. And you already knew about Chloe and the show."

Leila looked up and down the block, but all she saw were the usual New York pedestrians walking about and the traffic going to and fro. She shrugged. Yeah, she had known about Chloe and the show, but it still irritated the hell out her. "I don't think so. And it looks like the paps stayed back at the gallery to see who else would show. We're not so interesting right now."

He cocked his head to the side and looked her in the eye. "Hey, you never know. We still should give a show just in case." With that, he inched down just a bit and ran his lips gently over hers. They were cool and soft. Soothing her in that moment, just when she needed it. When he pulled back, it was with a sweet smile.

"Thank you," was all Leila said.

Carter frowned. "For what?"

"For going all in for your part. You'd think with a kiss like that, you were the one taking acting lessons."

"Who's acting?" he replied, throwing her off guard and looking more serious than she cared to acknowledge.

They ducked into a small bistro and ordered dinner. Leila was happy to put the horrific gallery thing and Chloe behind her, even though she knew putting Chloe behind her would be a lot harder than a few wrinkly butts and poorly dressed goats.

"So tell me about your class? Are you finding it helpful?" Carter asked, surprising her, after their food had come. He had ordered the steak and fries, and she had got the shrimp risotto.

Leila let out a breath. She was happy to

move on to a new subject. "I am. Shelley Atwood is a genius. And she says she sees real talent in me. She's staging her year-end production, and I think I have a shot at being in it. It's a short run thing, but I'd love to get in on it. It has a stellar reputation, and those who have done it have gone on to do great things. I'm almost ashamed to say how much I really want it." Leila felt a frown come on. Why was she sharing this with him?

Carter smiled at her. His eyes softened, and just for that moment she halfway thought he believed in her. But then she remembered that he didn't really. Sure, he did to a certain extent. The extent to which he believed in her prancing around and looking cute and making them laugh in his little sitcom. But not in the big, deep way. Leila looked down then and dug into her meal.

Carter reached out and took her hand. "What is it? Why did you stop? I want to hear more about the possibility of the play. You were excited, and you're right. It could mean great things. I know about that stage production. It's really hard to get tickets to it. And you shouldn't be ashamed of anything that you want. That's called determination." He smiled at her. "Hey, if you get a part in the show, then maybe I'll have a shot at actually getting a ticket."

Leila smiled at him. He really was convincing. In terms of timing, Atwood's year-end show would butt up against the holidays and the end of their six-month challange. She wondered if they would still be together at that point and if she would even have the opportunity to offer him tickets.

Carter squeezed her hand again. "Leila, stop. You keep thinking that far ahead, you'll never be able to enjoy this moment."

She laughed and looked at him. The laugh that felt hollow and stuck in her throat. "That's funny coming from you. I bet if you had your way, you'd have me sign on the dotted line for your show right now and go running for the hills, contract in hand. Tell me, am I wasting my time? Chloe is talking like she's a done deal."

Carter let her hand go, leaned back, and took a swig of his beer, looking her in the eye, all playfulness gone. The only thing left that she could see was an undercurrent of simmering desire. He shook his head. "And there you go, thinking you're so smart," he said, his voice low and deep. So much so she had to lean in a little closer to hear him. "Nothing is done and I have a feeling that Chloe was putting on a show to push your buttons." His look changed then and took on a simmering heat. "Also you'd lose the sign on the dotted line bet. I'm looking forward to this time together, Ms. Darling. The whole six months. For now my darling. I say bring it on."

Chapter 20

Leila could make this work. At least that was what she told herself. Heck, she'd made it a full week without breaking things off with Carter or jumping his bones, so she was already way ahead of the game. Sure, it probably helped that he had taken to leaving a lot earlier in the morning and coming in a lot later in the evening ever since their night out at the gallery, where Chloe had shown up, and their dinner talk later that night, which had featured his strange and shocking admission. But still no one had quit.

At dinner that night she thought she'd done a good job of sweeping his words under the rug when the waiter came over to ask if everything was okay. Of course, everything was not okay. Carter Bain had essentially just admitted to wanting to be with her these next six months, possibly more than he wanted to get her to star in his T and A sitcom. What the hell was she supposed to do with that bit of info?

Thankfully, the shower had been fixed, so at night and in the morning, all she had to contend with was listening to the water run and imagining the rivulets as they ran over his muscles while he steamed up her guest bathroom and did or did not think about her. It was driving her insane. Well, there was no avoiding him this afternoon. She had her interview down at the station with Kit Michelle from *Fast Pass Hollywood* on the success of *Robot-x* and her supposed balance between acting and modeling. *Yeah, some balance.* It wasn't as if there was a bunch of people knocking down Jasper's door with other movie offers. Though he'd fielded a few calls so far, Carter's offer for that Swoops deal had honestly been the most promising. Everything else was more of the same. It seemed she would never be more than a face and a body to people, so executing her image makeover was that much more important. And thus today's interview.

Carter was supposed to come down and check on her on the set, thereby opening the door to them being questioned together and hopefully moving some of the spotlight off Miles and his awful song.

But as she came on set and looked around, Carter was nowhere in sight. She couldn't help the nerves that settled in. Despite the fact that hers was a supposed fluff show, Kit was no easy interviewer. She could be tough, so Leila knew she had to be on her A game.

"Don't worry," Nia said in her ear. She and Jasper were there, lending moral support.

Leila saw Jasper standing off to the side, punching a few buttons on his cell. She had no doubt he was calling upstairs and looking for Carter. Part of her wanted to tell him not to bother. She had a sinking feeling that Carter had bailed and wasn't coming. She'd barely seen him all week. They had exchanged only a few stilted hellos and good-byes, and some awkward grunts by the fridge if they so happened to have a craving at the same time. So who knew? Maybe he'd decided she just wasn't worth it. Maybe he'd even decided that she wasn't even worth the Swoops' show.

Just as her mind started to get the better of her, Kit walked over her way. A striking older woman, she had tons of big Hollywood hair — she was a brunette — and wore her pink cotton shirt dress with a wide gold belt and the collar turned up. She spoke with a clipped British accent that somehow made whatever she was saying sound extra exclusive, whether she was reporting on the royals' comings and goings or the latest drunken meltdown of some has-been pop star. She held out a heavily bejeweled hand to Leila, who suddenly felt small and underdressed in her simple, elegant jumpsuit compared to the much more petite woman.

"Leila Darling. Look at you. What a beauty. Your photographs don't do you justice." Kit beckoned her to follow her lead, and they headed toward the small box that was the lit set. "Come. Let's chat awhile. I promise, I won't bite." She leaned into Leila and whispered, "Besides, you're a fave of the boss, so can't go messing with family or biting the hand that feeds me, now can I? A girl isn't stupid, you know." She gave a hearty chuckle at her own joke, leaving Leila feeling slightly queasy from that one, but she reserved comment.

Both women sat. Leila was quickly miked, and they got a last-minute makeup touch-up as the crew checked the lighting. And just like that they were on. But where was Carter? Leila let out a breath and willed her heart rate to slow down. When she looked back up, he was there. A shadowed figure on the other side of Nia. She watched as her friend put up both thumbs. Leila smiled as Kit came at her with her questions.

Leila fielded the usual questions about her family, how she got her start in modeling, and what brought her to acting. So far all was going well. It was then that Kit paused, leaned in close, and got a gleam in her eye. Once again Leila's heart began to race.

"Though I hate to bring it up, I wouldn't be doing my job if I didn't, so I must," Kit said, then added a dramatic sigh. "The whole 'Darling Leila' song . . . You have to know it's a huge hit for Miles G. Many are touting it as the song of the summer."

To that, Leila gave Kit what she hoped was a serene smile. "I'm very happy for him."

Kit gave her a look that said she wasn't believing any of it. "Really? How very enlightened of you, being that the song's lyrics speak about a sexually insatiable woman who changes men like outfits, wearing them and then moving on to the next trend."

Leila raised a brow. "How very clever of him. Like I said, I'm happy for him."

Kit gave her a raised brow back. "Tell me, are you just as happy for your costar in *Robot-x*, Wade Shephard and his new romance?"

Leila tried hard not to bristle outwardly wondering who Wade was hooked up with now. It didn't matter, in reality, she wouldn't mind seeing Wade come down with a terminal case of diarrhea, but of course, that wasn't proper TV-viewing dinner conversation. Instead, she smiled some more. She was starting to think her face would freeze this way. "Of course I'm happy for Wade. He was so much fun to work with, and I learned so much about the craft while working with him."

Kit pulled a face. "The craft, huh? Is that what they're calling it? It would seem you two did a lot more than learn about the craft. Weren't you two engaged?"

Leila felt the heat churn in her belly and quickly rise to her chest and then up to her face. She lowered her lashes and then glanced up to look Kit squarely in the eye. "Well, I'd rather not speak on past relationships. Especially when the other party is not around. Just know that Wade is a wonderful guy and a great friend." *And also a total cheating jerk with poor taste in jump-offs, but that is neither here nor there,* she thought.

Kit looked at her for one beat, then two, before she smiled wide again. "Well, it's lucky for me and, more importantly, for our viewers that we just so happen to have on set your secret, but not so secret anymore, mystery man. The past is the past. It looks like someone finally stole your heart once and for all." She then gave the camera a conspiratorial wink and added, "Well, once and for now."

With this comment, Leila felt her anger rise again, and she fought to tamp it down. The nerve of this woman implying that she didn't have sincere intentions when it came to Carter. Never mind that she didn't have sincere intentions when it came to Carter. It wasn't for the likes of Kit Michelle to tell the whole world.

Leila smiled, her teeth practically grinding. "I assure you, my new husband is all I've ever dreamed of."

With that comment, Kit just about lit up like a Christmas tree, clapping her hands and bouncing in her seat. "Well, there you have it, viewers, confirmation once and for all that Leila Darling, or Darling Leila as she's sometimes called —"

Leila interrupted there. "Not by my friends, of course."

"Touché," Kit said to Leila before turning back to the camera. "Well, Leila Darling is officially off the market." She paused before looking around. "Now, I wonder if we can get the other half of this dynamic duo of love on set for a moment so that everyone can meet him?"

Leila shook her head. "I don't know. He's not an entertainer. He's used to being on the other side of things."

Kit gave a wave. "Come on now, Mr. Darling," she said with a laugh, joking. "Won't you join your bride on set?"

It was then that Carter shyly walked into the view of the cameras, then went up to Leila and leaned down toward her. A key person on the crew scurried out and placed a chair beside Leila, and Carter sat down, then leaned in easily to give her a quick kiss on the lips, causing her to lean back as her eyes widened before she kissed him back. Leila tried to play it off by looking shyly at the camera before lowering her lashes.

Kit gave a gushy "Ahh!" for the viewers. "You two are adorable," she said as Carter clasped Leila's hand with his own and brought it briefly to his lips.

Leila straightened and fidgeted a little, surprised by the touch of this man with whom she'd barely communicated in the past week. But she went with it. Forced herself to relax, since she knew the cameras would zoom in on the intimate connection.

"I just adore new love. And the 'Mr. Darling,' you know, was just a tease. You are quite the mogul in your own right," Kit said.

Carter waved her off with a smile. "Hardly. Leila is the bright star of our duo. I'm just the lucky one with a front-row seat to see her shine."

Kit looked suitably pleased by this answer but not put off. "Oh, come on now. Don't be shy. Full disclosure. You are a rising exec in our very own parent company and the soon-to-be head of a new offshoot, that is, if the trade papers are to be believed."

Leila could feel the tension as it subtly started to radiate off Carter. He ran his thumb across her knuckles as he continued to smile. "I'd love to comment, but I can't," he said. "I will just say exciting things are in the works, and with Leila by my side, I feel incredibly blessed." He looked into Leila's eyes, and she into his. She thought she was making a connection but was not sure. Either way, she hoped the viewers were buying it. They could do this.

"That's fabulous," Kit said. "I love your modesty and discretion. And I'm sure your future projects will be a hit, especially with you meeting with Hollywood heavy hitters like Chloe Caraway."

Leila watched as Carter's eyes narrowed and he swallowed. Hers narrowed, too, as she silently asked, "And when did this meeting take place, and how was it that Kit knew about it?"

Leila let out a slow breath and turned to Kit, her smile firmly in place. "Yes, Carter is a force to be reckoned with. He's way too modest to speak about himself, but needless to say, whatever it is he's up to, you can bet it will be worth the wait."

Kit smiled. It was a half-feral sort of smile, and Leila didn't know if there was a gotcha there or if this was just her style of interviewing. "You are clearly proud of him. As you should be. Now, tell me, both of you, was it love at first sight?"

Leila steeled herself, trying her best to put the Chloe comment aside. What could she do about it? This was business first, and no matter what was happening with them, business had to go on. She wondered if Carter would go for the truth and tell the story of being unimpressed with her. Gee, how would that go over? She decided to jump in then.

"I doubt that. I think he was frankly unimpressed with me."

Carter didn't miss a beat and chimed in immediately, patting her hand and shaking his head. "No. You know how men are, trying to be cool when internally they're freaking out. Sure it was love at first sight. Leila has had my attention since I first laid eyes on her."

Leila looked at him, surprised, but tried her best not to let it show on her face.

Kit nodded, then directed her next question to Leila. "And you? Were you instantly smitten?"

Leila gave Carter a quick up and down before turning back to Kit. "Let's just say I was immediately intrigued. I felt a certain amount of stability and passion in him. But I will say I wanted to make him work a little. What girl doesn't like the chase?"

Kit nodded. "I hear that. The chase is the most fun part." She grinned wide. "Now, you two, before I let you go, let's play a quick lightning round of my version of *The Newlywed Game* and see how you two add up. Just say the first answer that pops into your head when I read the question. But the trick is you have to answer as you think your mate would answer. Deal?"

Leila looked at Carter, a certain amount of panic in her eyes, but he gave her a reassuring nod, which made her think they could possibly do this thing. They turned back to Kit and said in unison, "Deal."

Kit began. "Coffee or tea?"

They both chimed in quickly with "Coffee."

"All right! Score one for the Darling-Bains," Kit said. "Cats or dogs?"

"Dogs," Carter said, and Leila nodded.

"Dogs," Leila said, and Carter shook his head.

"Neither. I'm not a pet person," he revealed.

Leila pulled a face. *Poor Ollie.*

Kit raised a brow. "Morning person or night owl?" Kit asked.

"Night owl," Carter said, and Leila shook her head this time.

"Morning person," Leila responded.

Kit gave a skeptical side eye to the camera. "Okay, sweetgums. This is the final one for all the marbles. Left or right side of the bed?"

"Left!" they blurted out at the same time.

Kit let out a long sigh as she shook her head, then smiled. "Leila, meet Carter. Carter, meet your wife, Leila. It's a good thing you two are young and have plenty of time to get to know each other."

Leila laughed as Carter squeezed her hand tighter and gave Kit a nod and a smile. Leila counted backward from one hundred as he let her hand go and she was un-miked, in order to hold back the tears that were threatening to overflow after that disaster of a so-called quiz. Could there possibly be two people more unsuited for each other? If there was, she didn't know. Just like she didn't know why she had agreed to do this interview. All it had done was highlight the fact that she was married to a total and complete stranger, who in six months would be more than ready to see the back of her.

Kit gave her a hug that was anything but warm when she said her good-byes. "You take care, darling. I see what's happening here, and though you've been in the game awhile, know you're in new territory by going from print to film," the older woman whispered in her ear. "Things can be even more brutal on this side of the business, so just watch yourself." Kit pulled back and looked at Leila, giving her the first sincere smile she'd seen from the woman. "I'm rooting for you."

Leila gave her a wobbly smile and a nod before walking over to where Carter was huddled with Jasper and Nia, the three of them looking like they were strategizing for the next Geneva Summit.

"Don't worry," Nia said as she put an arm around Leila as she walked into the fold. "No one pays attention to these things."

Leila gave her a sharp side eye. "If by *nobody,* you mean everybody, then you've got it absolutely right."

"Okay. You're right," Nia said. "But I was just trying to lighten things up a bit."

Leila let out a breath. "Sorry. It's not your fault we're screwed. It's mine. I should have never gone and gotten us into this."

Carter took her hand; she stilled, looking up at him. "What is blaming yourself going to do? We knew it was risky." He leaned in and kissed her hand again. This time the cameras were off, and she could feel the eyes of all the people watching them, especially Jasper and Nia.

"See that right there? That is what we need. More of that Sir Galahad stuff and less of the Mr. Stiff Upper Lip," Jasper said.

Leila pulled her hand out of Carter's grasp, remembering Kit's words and the fact that Carter had been Mr. Stiff or, well, Mr. Invisible for the past week. "I doubt that will do it. No one will go for this, save me announcing a pregnancy within the next week."

She saw Jasper's eyes light up.

"Don't get excited," she warned. "Besides I've got shows, contracts."

"That's right you do," Jasper agreed. "So don't go getting ideas in that direction without consulting me and your work calendar."

Leila shook her head. "You'll be the first I

won't tell. How about that? Now can we go?" She turned to Carter. "And don't you have work to get back to?"

He was looking pensive but snapped to attention quickly. "I do. Let's go."

As they stood by the elevator bank, Leila and her crew waiting for the down elevator while Carter waited for the up one to take him to his floor, Leila could see that Carter was lost in thought. He was probably thinking about his next meeting or maybe the disaster of an interview, she thought.

Suddenly Carter looked at her. "Can you get away for a few days? A long weekend?" He looked at Jasper. "Do you still have your guy, the photographer?"

Jasper nodded. Then raised his brows. "What are you getting at? And if it's what I think it is, I already like it."

"I'm sure this interview didn't do nearly as much damage as we think, but we don't want to give them any more fodder," Carter explained. "I'd much rather get ahead of it, so I'm thinking Leila and I should do a little mini honeymoon getaway and you could let it leak to your guy, have him grab a few candid shots, 'catching' us as we do it. That way, once again, we're leading the narrative on this and not anyone else."

Jasper smiled wide, nodding. He turned

to Leila. "I like this man. You picked a winner this time!"

Leila wanted to kick him but held back. She had nothing much planned. There was a party she'd been invited to by some people she barely liked, so that could be blown off. She had an early shoot on Friday morning, and that was it. She was free after. She looked at Carter and considered the idea of a little one-on-one time with him without the responsibilities of work, and her heart began to speed up with excitement. "Fine," she said. "Let's do it."

"Great," Jasper said. "Nia and I will make the arrangements —"

"No," Carter interrupted as the elevator pinged for up. He got on as they watched. "I'll handle it and let you know where to direct your man."

Jasper and Nia nodded, seeming shocked by Carter's stance, as Leila swallowed back any reply. Instead, she just looked at him and gave a wave as the elevator door closed and he went upstairs to carry out the next phase of their plan.

CHAPTER 21

It was late when Carter walked into the apartment. He was surprised to find Leila still up and not in her bedroom, but rather sitting on the couch with Ollie, who didn't come running to the door to greet him like he'd started to make a habit of doing this past week. Not that Carter was looking for that sort of thing from the dog, but still, it was a rather abrupt change. Did he see the interview?

When he walked into the dim apartment, he was also surprised by the quiet and almost didn't see Leila sitting on the couch, burrowed down deep in the cushions as she was. The TV above the fireplace was on, but the volume was muted. And when he went to turn it off, he got a look at her, scrunched down low, eating what appeared to be some of his mother's leftovers out of the plastic containers while looking at some sort of book, with Ollie at her side.

It was immediately apparent by the glassiness of her beautiful brown eyes that she'd been crying, though the fact that she looked up at him and let out a loud sniffle, then a snort, was another dead giveaway. Carter looked from her to the TV screen and noted the channel.

"You watched the interview, didn't you?" he said.

She snorted again. "Of course I watched the interview. How could you think I wouldn't watch it? Didn't you?" She looked him up and down, her eyes full of silent accusations. Ones that would probably be better served to someone in her past. "From wherever you were," she added.

Carter's gut response was to get immediately angry. She had no right to accuse him of anything, since they were man and wife in name only, but still, he felt awful. He knew when he was staying late and finishing up paperwork that he should have been getting home to her and viewing that Kit Michelle interview with her. He shouldn't have had her watch it alone. And at the very least, he should have hightailed it home earlier than this to see how she'd taken it. Of course she'd be upset. She wasn't a robot, no matter her costars.

"I'm sorry," he said softly, taking of his

suit jacket and placing it over the back of the couch. "I should have gotten home earlier and watched it with you, but I was hung up at the office." He leaned over and nudged her feet so she would scooch over and let him sit. She did, but Ollie responded a little more begrudgingly. Smart as ever, he stayed wedged between the two of them, looking up at Carter with an "And now what?" expression.

Once again Leila was in her stripped-down, clean-face home mode, but tonight there was none of the usual cuteness to it, only a raw vulnerability, which made him want to reach out and hold her. Instead, he reached over to get a look at the plastic tub she was holding.

"What you got there?" he asked.

She handed it over to him. Pushed it into his hand. "Here. I've had enough. But it's good. Your mother makes a dammed good cobbler."

He nodded and took a spoonful of the small amount of apple cobbler she had left. "I won't argue with you there." Then his eyes widened when he heard her sniffle at his side. "Come on. It's not that bad. That was just Kit being Kit. It will blow over with her next story."

"It's not that," she said. "It's the cobbler.

Your mother didn't like me on sight, and she could tell we wouldn't be any good together. She knew I would never live up to the kind of woman she'd want for you. I could never cook a cobbler like that." She waved a hand at the plastic tub. "But you know what? My mother could. I just wish that she were around or that I had paid attention when she was and when she tried to teach me." Her next sniffle was louder and came with a serious snort attached. It pierced him right in his heart.

It was then he noticed that the book she was looking at was a photo album. Carter stifled a groan as he took in the full impact of the scene in front of him. Obviously, he'd walked in on something much deeper than Kit and her stupid interview. Carter put the cobbler back on the coffee table. He reached over to the other side of the couch for his suit jacket and pulled a handkerchief out of his pocket. "Here. Come on. Don't do that to yourself."

She took the handkerchief and looked at it through her glassy eyes and gave her nose a wipe.

Carter picked up Ollie and moved him over to the other side of Leila, then took his own place next to Leila. "Sorry, bud, but you've got to move it."

He put his arm around Leila and pulled her into his chest. She felt so warm and right against him. Like she was made to be there. He pulled the photo album over so it lay between their laps. He looked down at the collection of pictures before him, then flipped the page. There was Leila with her brothers in different stages of her life up until, he figured, about eleven or twelve. And in a few of the photos was a beautiful woman with the same eyes as Leila, clear and bright, with the same hint of mystery. She also had the same wide mouth and lovely shaped lips. He noticed in all the photos that she seemed to smile easily, though in the later ones there was a look of melancholy in her eyes.

"I was right when I told your father that you get your beauty from your mother," Carter said. "She was lovely."

Leila nodded. "Yes, she was. She was also a great cook, and strong as hell. She always told me to follow my dreams. Though I don't know if this here is exactly what she meant. Yeah, your mother had the right of it with me."

Carter pulled her in closer and kissed the top of her head, inhaling the subtly sexy scent of her. But instead of softening, he felt her body tense. "Lei, please stop this.

And don't care about what my mother thinks of you. That doesn't matter to me. What do I care if you can cook or not? I can cook for myself. You don't have to worry about what my mother thinks of you."

Carter moved the photo album. He took the handkerchief from her hand and went to wipe her eyes. "Now, come on. Don't cry. These things don't matter. Don't let them worry you."

Leila snorted and snatched the handkerchief from his hand. She looked at him with fire in her eyes as she wiped her nose before throwing the handkerchief back at him.

Carter recoiled. "Really? Like I want your snot!"

"Oh, please. You think you're so smooth with your linens," she said, exaggerating the word *linens*. "And don't worry about your mother, and it doesn't matter. Why? Because *we* don't matter? Because this is not real? Because I mean nothing more to you than future ratings and money in your pocket?" She shook her head and let out a sigh. Like she was tired. And she'd spent all her energy on that speech. But still she wasn't done. "I don't know why I thought you were any different or I could handle this, whether you were or not. Commitment obviously isn't meant for me, be it real or fake."

He looked at her, speechless. A million words were running through his head, but they were going too fast for him to get them out. She thought commitment wasn't for her, and all these years he'd never considered it an option for himself. At least not anytime soon. He had too many things to do first, so many more deals to make. And she was right, at least in one respect. She was just another deal along the way.

But there was a part of him that wanted her to be so much more. That part that looked at her fiery eyes and lush lips as they trembled with rage and — he could feel it now — pent-up passion. Carter continued to stare at her and finally found his voice. "I told you before, I'm not like those other guys."

Her only answer to this was a derisive snort as she started to push up from the couch. But he stopped her by holding on to her wrist. She looked down at him, the challenge clear in her eyes. "What, husband? Are you ready to prove to me just how much you're not like other guys?"

Carter quickly let her go but stood and looked at her eye to eye. So close he could feel her breath as it whispered against his lips. If he leaned in just a little, her breasts would hit against his chest. "I don't have to prove anything," Carter said. "It's already a fact. None of them are here, are they? But I am. I'm the one you call husband. None of them can say that."

She gave him a sly up and down, then said, "And can you? Really?" With that smirk of hers, it was as if she had crooked a finger at him and said, "I dare you."

Oh, he dared, all right. Carter leaned down, and at the same time he took her mouth with his own, he tightly clasped her ass with one hand and cupped her breasts with the other. Instantly, he was rock hard. Tilting his head, he ran his tongue over the crease of her lips and was rewarded when she opened to him. Her tongue was like a sweet drug, practically making him weak in the knees. But Carter knew he had to hold on. He didn't want to stop. Not tonight. Maybe not ever. He was the one, the only one, to carry the title of Leila Darling's husband. And rather real or not, this night he wanted to cast away all her tears, all her doubt, and all her fears about him once and for all.

But still he pulled back. Not because of the deal. No, not that. He pulled back and looked her in the eye once again. "Tell me this is what you want, Leila. Tell me you want me, because more than anything I want you. The bet, our six month challenge, those things mean nothing at this moment, in this space. This is just us. The two of us without the world watching or critiquing. No matter what happens here tonight, tomorrow we will walk out the door and continue the charade we're putting on for the world. From now on I want it to be real for both of us here, in this space. Whether it works out in my favor or not."

Carter stopped breathing for a moment as he awaited her response. He hoped more than anything she would say yes. He'd just taken the biggest gamble of all, and either he'd have his feelings stomped on or his dream would come true. He couldn't begin to calculate the odds on this bet.

Finally, Leila reached out her hand and gently put it on his chest. "Your heart is beating so hard."

Carter nodded. "Maybe I'm nervous about what you're going to say."

She gave him a half smile. "I didn't think you got nervous."

"When it comes to you, I do it all the time. I don't think I've felt like I've stood on steady ground since the moment I laid eyes on you."

She shook her head. "Please don't flatter me. I don't deserve that."

Carter suddenly felt a boulder where his heart should be. "Is that your way of letting me down easy?"

She looked up at him quickly then. "No, no, it's not." She swallowed, then leaned in, kissed him gently. "I want you. More than I can say."

Carter couldn't help his grin and hoped he didn't look a right fool. "Well, then, wife, what you want, you shall have."

Leila had never seen a man get out of his clothes so fast or want a night to go more slowly. Carter took her hand, and together, they walked toward the bedrooms in the back of the loft. They stood for a moment in the hallway, each uncertain about which way to go. Part of her wanted to go into the guest room with Carter. The last man she'd slept with in her own bed was Miles, and there was Wade before him. She didn't want Carter to be just another in that string of men.

He smiled at her. "Oh, boy," Carter began. "I can see those wheels turning already. Are you thinking of an out? Because really you don't have to come up with an excuse. I won't be happy, but you're in control here. If you say stop, I stop."

His words comforted her, and she shook

her head and led him into her bedroom, vowing to order another mattress ASAP. Once inside her bedroom, though, Carter took full and complete charge. His clothes were quickly discarded. He had no patience for her carefully taking off his shirt, button by button, and kissing each beautiful patch of brown skin she exposed. No, when she nipped at the bit of skin just above his undershirt, he moaned aloud and gently pushed her aside. Then he pulled the under-shirt off so quickly, she heard it tear as he toed his shoes off and went for the buckle of his pants.

She gasped," Your shirt."

"There are other shirts, my darling," he croaked out. "But only one first night with you."

Leila smiled, suddenly never feeling shier with a man than she did now. She wanted to make him happy. Wanted to live up to his every expectation. She moved back and pulled off her stretch pants. After quickly tugging off her T-shirt, she threw it onto the nearby chair. Tousling her hair, she licked her lips and arched her back as she looked at him standing in front of her in only his boxers. "I hope I'm all you hoped for."

He looked at her, suddenly more serious, as he walked up to her and took her face in his hands. He looked her deep in her eyes. "You don't have anything to live up to. You have nothing to prove or disprove. My dreams have long since come true just by having you in my life. Already I know that you're so much more than I ever dreamed of. Leila, you are a constant surprise and a delight to learn more about each and every day." He stepped back and looked her up and down. "All this, well, this is just a bonus. But really it's all right up here." He pointed to her head, then her mouth, and then he put his hand on her heart. She heard a distinct crack as his voice wobbled and he lowered his eyes. "These are the things that make you, you. And I pray I can step up and be a man worthy of giving you my name."

Leila sucked in a breath and blinked quickly. Despite all her engagements, never once had there been any talk about the value of her heart or her mind. "You do have a way with words, Mr. Bain."

He smiled and looked back at her. "I'm glad to hear it, but truly, it's not my only talent." And with that, Carter kissed her. Kissed her as he never had before, laying her down on the bed, taking the kiss deeper, until she didn't know where her tongue began and his ended. She was breathless and at the same time on fire when his kisses trailed lower and he tickled her collarbone as his hand traveled gently down her right side. His hand went to her hip and then curved back up. His thumb teased her nipple through the lace of her bra. She arched her back to fill his hand even more, and then he tilted her over, undid her bra clasp, and she reached up and freed her breasts out of impatience and frustration.

Leila moaned aloud when his tongue laved and then teased her pebbled nipple. Then greedily he latched his mouth on to the darkened areola and suckled. Leila heard herself moan as she felt his free hand gently come up the inside of her thigh.

Easy. It was almost too easy the way her thighs spread open to offer him easy access. Without hesitation, he pushed the cotton aside, and she sighed as she felt his fingers caress her. First sliding gently between her folds and then coming up to circle her hard nub. Once again there was a gasp — she could only assume it was hers — and yes, there might have been a buckle as she reflexively tried to close her legs.

"No, Lei. Not now. Not tonight. I'll have you open. Totally and fully open." He suddenly lifted himself from her and pulled her bra completely out of the way. After the bra went flying to the floor, he stood, leaned over, and clasped either side of her panties with his thumbs and tugged them off. Leila moved up on the bed and lay before him, looking up at him.

"Beautiful." It came from his lips as a hoarse declaration. He looked around and frowned. "Wait a minute, my darling."

Leila smiled. Finally. He was saying her name in the most perfect of ways. She had noticed it when he said it before but hadn't want to let herself really hear it and feel any sort of false hope. She watched as he ran from the room, and then she heard him rummaging across the hall. He came back, waving a box of condoms.

"Ever prepared," Leila said.

Carter snorted. "More like *ever hopeful*."

She laughed and pointed to his boxers. They were cute and so very him. All businesslike with their little uniform stripes. "So you going to let me see what my vows bought me? I mean, it's only fair, seeing how I'm lying here." She lay on her side, looking at him with a grin.

Carter inhaled a long breath, then let it out. "I'm warning you. No supermodel here," he said and tugged down his shorts.

Leila felt her smile grow wider as she took

in the impressive show. "But super, nonetheless."

He grinned and shook his head. "Now who's the smooth talker?" Carter tugged at her ankles, pulling her toward him. "But enough of this. I think I was starting something, and it's time I got to finishing it."

Leila was trying to think of a quick retort, but his kiss made that type of thinking impossible, and when he once again let his tongue trail along her skin, it circled her nipples, dipped in her belly button, making her quiver and shiver from the inside out. Still, he dipped lower, coming to his knees before her and spreading her legs wide.

"Yes, beautiful," he whispered.

And it was there that all talk ceased, as Carter feasted on her. Turned her liquid, every nerve coiling and tightening, practically tripping over one another to get to the spot where his tongue caressed her sensitive skin. He was both relentless and ever intuitive, sensing her urgency intensify, then wane just at the moment when all those nerves got to the point of bursting.

Leila twisted. Her back arched as her hand came down on his shoulder and she let out a strangled, "Please."

He brought one of his hands up to her now painfully aching nipple and squeezed it between his thumb and forefinger at the same time his tongue sped up its unrelenting pace on her nub. She could take no more and cried out, "Bain!" as the evidence of her submission spilled forth on his tongue. Leila gasped for breath as he rose. She looked at him through fairly hazy eyes and watched as he tore open a condom and quickly sheathed himself.

Practically panting, she prepared herself as he positioned himself at the juncture of her legs. Even the tip of him, blunt and full, drove her out of her mind with arousal. But little did she know there was so much more still.

Carter entered her slower than she'd expected. Why so, she didn't know. Maybe he was wanting to let the feeling last, wanting to take in every moment of the feeling for himself. But she wondered, did he know what this slow, deliciously torturous stretching of time was doing to her as moment by moment she was overtaken by him, until she felt him not only in her very core but in her every extremity, too? She tightened her thighs around him and squeezed, enjoying the sound of his intake of breath. Breathing his name, Leila reached up to him.

"Kiss me, Carter. I want to feel you everywhere. I need to be yours. All yours."

Carter leaned down and captured her mouth once more. She could feel the sweat from his chest as it hit her breasts. She kissed him with abandon, holding nothing back, as he pulled her in close. She sucked at his tongue, and his strokes came faster, the bend to his back insuring he hit her in just the right spot. Leila felt the stirring of the quiver again and mentally willed it back. It was too soon. She didn't want the night to end. Didn't want the morning to come.

"Don't do it, darling. Don't hold back from me. I've got you, love. You're safe with me." His words just about did her in, stroking her between her ears just as sensually as he was stroking her between her legs. He was right. He really was good.

Leila let out a sigh and spoke, looking at him, willing him to look at her. "Okay," she said, "but only if you stop holding back, too." She squeezed her inner wall muscles tight around his hardness. The barely there rein on her control about to be lost at any moment. So she just went with it and gave in, moving without care for direction or form. Her only mission both his and her mutual pleasure as she enjoyed the sensual feeling of him filling her both intimately and emotionally.

"My God, Leila, I'm done for. I. Can't."

Carter's words were hoarse and clipped. His hands rested on her hips, clasping her, in unwavering possession of her. "Hold. On." She watched as his eyes squeezed shut and his lips pulled back in a grimace. His body shuddered as hers shook. Throbbing around him, she saw starbursts, which came from her very essence, in the back of her eyes. She felt him as he came, his already impossible fullness seeming to expand even more. The moment, though short, seemed to go on for a small eternity, until finally it was over and all that was left was the two of them, shocked and breathing heavily in the dim light.

They lay in the bed awhile before Leila shivered. Carter got up and lifted her. Then placed her under the duvet after toweling them both off. Leila began to close her eyes but then opened them when she heard a whimper at the door.

"Oh no. I meant to take Ollie out once more," she said.

"Shh," Carter said, kissing her on the top of her head. "You sleep, Wifey. I'll take him. Besides, tomorrow starts our big honeymoon weekend."

Leila closed her eyes and tried to block out his words. Tonight was perfect as it was.

She didn't want to ruin it by thinking about
tomorrow.

CHAPTER 22

Carter was worried about this quickly planned trip. This wasn't going to be the exclusive, extravagant honeymoon a woman like Leila was probably expecting. Nor was it the type of trip she was probably used to going on with a man, given her past relationship history. He knew all about those as every extravagant detail had been splashed on the pages of glossy magazines, ones replete with photos with misleading captions, like "Stars, they're just like us." However, this kind of photo with this kind of caption was apt to show said star shopping for groceries with two bodyguards in some designer organic food mart, pushing a cart in which sat her twenty-thousand-dollar handbag.

No, what he had planned was decidedly a little more laid back, and he was hopeful she wouldn't be disappointed in him. After their disaster with Kit, he very much wanted her to see more of the real him, and he wanted the same when it came to her, so he thought a laid-back getaway might be a better way for them to truly have some alone time and get introduced to each other once and for all. Calling in a favor, he had borrowed Aidan's cabin on the water up in Rhode Island. It was remote, so much so that even the Wi-Fi was spotty. Carter had given Jasper the address to pass on to his guy, the photographer, but he had made Jasper promise that his guy would not intrude on their privacy until the end of their trip. He wanted to be sure they could relax without prying eyes.

"Are you really not going to tell me where we're going?" Leila said as he put her duffel in the trunk of his SUV.

Carter shook his head and gave her a grin, then came over and kissed the top of her head before leaning down and seizing one more opportunity to kiss those beautiful lips before getting on the road. Yep, she was just as sweet and delicious as she'd been the night before. When he woke up that morning, his arm wrapped around her waist, his erection strong and on her curvy backside, Carter had thought he was still dreaming. Especially when she had turned to him and, instead of frowning and panicking from a sense of regret, had smiled and proceeded to kiss him. Her hands strong and sure, she'd guided his erection to the exact place he wanted it to go. No, he hadn't been asleep, and it hadn't been all a dream.

She was there. Leila Darling. And somehow he, Carter Bain, had her in his arms and was taking her away for three blissful days all on his own.

"But will you at least tell me why you have groceries packed? Won't where we're going have room service?" she asked.

Carter shook his head. "Stop trying me, woman," he said playfully.

She leaned in and kissed the shell of his ear. Her tongue dipped out and tickled him just behind it. He groaned and stepped back, swatted her on her stretch jeans–clad behind. "And don't try to distract me into giving it up, either," he said with a laugh. "Into the car with you."

Leila laughed and got in the car and let Carter close the door behind her.

They headed up the highway. The fact that this was their first really long car ride together was apparent to them both. The awkwardness of that first flight from Vegas to New York had since evaporated, but with it had come a new awkwardness to contend with. One made of a new familiarity but also hesitation, as they both seemed to struggle with how much to show of their true forms. It was quiet for a while, so Carter tried to fill the quiet with the radio, turning the dial no less than three times in ten minutes when Miles G kept popping up on multiple stations.

Leila let out a frustrated sigh. "I really should get a cut. He's making money hand over fist off me. And, I swear, he'd still be busy trying to get put on for a sample if it wasn't for me appearing in his first video." She let out another sigh. "Do you have any music on your phone? Because I don't think I can take much more of this."

"Sure." Carter handed his cell to her, rattled off his code, and let her flip to his saved music.

"Wow. You have a lot," she said.

"You sound surprised."

"I am," she said, surprising him by pulling up an old seventies funk track that he'd listen to when he was deep in thought on a project and needed to clear his head and chill.

Leila started to bob her head and groove to the music. "I think if my father saw your playlist, he might start to like you. . . ."

But her voice trailed off at the end of the sentence, and he could tell that once again she was thinking about the end of the relationship and what would happen when their six months were up, instead of the present moment. Carter didn't want to go there. The present, this moment with her, was just too perfect for him to jump ahead to the possibilities of where it could all get screwed up.

He smiled, glancing her way. "Now, that sounds hopeful," he said, surprising himself, as he was not one to use such vague and insecure words as *hopeful.* Turning back to the road, he thought it best to focus, since it was late and the traffic was turning heavy. At the rate they were going, unfortunately, it would be past dark when they got to the house; with it being secluded and down a winding road, that wasn't the best scenario.

So they drove, grooving to the music, each deep in thought, until he'd found himself in silent thought a bit too long and looked over to see that Leila was not sleeping, like he had thought she would be, but had her brows pulled in tight and was deep in thought.

"Hey," he began. "You okay over there? You look like you've got the weight of the world on your shoulders."

Caught off guard, Leila instantly smiled. But then her smile faltered. "I'm just thinking about us having sex last night."

It was Carter's turn to frown. "And that gives you a long face? That doesn't bode too well for our getting closer this weekend."

Leila sighed and then smiled at him. She put her hand on his thigh as Carter braced himself for the letdown to come. Perfect. Here he was, thinking he was the man last night, and now he was about to get the "She's just not that into you" speech.

"No, that's not it," she said. "I just think us being married — and even if we weren't, we'd discuss this — but us being married is an odd part of it." She suddenly seemed shy and at a loss for words as she let out a sigh. "I just think we should talk about our sexual health. I mean, last night we crossed a line that we didn't plan to cross in our arrangement, and, well, now that it's happened, I don't see us turning back, at least not in the immediate future." She swallowed. "Well, I, for one, don't want to turn back."

Leila was quiet then; it even seemed like the music and the traffic had hushed. Carter could practically hear the blood rushing in his ears and his own heartbeat. What was she asking him? He'd had sex talks with women before, but he'd never been married to them. He didn't understand what she was getting at. Still, he spoke like he understood

332

perfectly. "I understand." *Shit.* Why did he say that? Carter shook his head. "No, really I don't understand. What are you trying to say? If you want a health report, I'm clean. I can produce the paperwork if you'd like," he said, speeding up and doing a lane change just because it seemed like a better thing to do than glance her way. "If you want, we can both exchange paperwork."

"Fine," Leila said. "And I'm perfectly clean, too. I'm also on the pill and am as regular as can be, so you don't have to worry on that front."

Carter nodded, keeping his eyes on the road. "That's good." He briefly glanced her way. Then he frowned. "Wait. Is there something else?"

She shook her head. "No, well, just I trust you." She paused. "Well, I am trusting you. Doing this, going there right now. This is a lot for me. I want you to know that."

Carter's frown went deeper as everything in him coiled up inside. He let out a breath. "I know."

Carter drove for a while, and when they were nearing a place he normally liked to stop for a coffee and a bit of pie, he looked over at Leila. This time she was sleeping peacefully beside him. *Trust.* He guessed she trusted him to get her to the house safely, so much so that she closed her eyes and went to sleep. When he stopped for gas, he thought of waking her, but they had so few miles to go that he just let her sleep. He roused her only when he'd finally made the last turn down the twisting road to the secluded land.

"Leila, we're here."

"Hmm."

"Darling, we're here."

Leila opened her eyes and looked into Carter's, her smile instantaneous as she took in him smiling back at her.

"We're here. I hope you like the house. I've been here a only few times with Aidan and some friends, but I think it's great," he said.

Laila turned and looked up at the large Nantucket-style structure with its white trim gleaming in the dark and its peaked roof stretching up to the night sky. She went to get out of the car, but Carter stopped her by running around the front of the car and getting her door. She shook her head. "Really, I can do that."

He kissed her. "Of course you can."

She looked back at the house. It seemed dark, which was odd. "Is this a bed-and-breakfast? How long were we on the road?

Have the proprietors gone to sleep?"

"No, it's not, and we're the only proprietors for this weekend. It's Aidan's place. He got it as a weekend getaway a little while back. I've been here only a handful of times with him and Vin to get in some surfing."

Carter laughed as he watched her jaw drop to her chest. "You do not surf," she said. Leila could believe a lot of things about her new husband: the fact that he had surprisingly eclectic and good taste in music, that he could cook — something she had yet to see — and yes, was supremely skilled in the bedroom. But she drew the line at Mr. Suit and Tie, Mr. Sign on the Dotted Line, being a surfer.

"Close your mouth, darling, before a bug flies in," he said with a satisfied smirk.

She shook her head and followed him as he took a few of the bags out of the car and climbed the stairs to the massive wraparound porch. Suddenly, Leila wished it was still daylight and she could see the house to its full advantage. She could smell the water and could tell it was not far off in the distance, and she hear it as the surf collided with the shore. They couldn't be that far from the beach. She should not have slept in the car, but instead stayed awake to see where she was. Carter pulled a set of keys out and let them in the house. Then he retrieved a piece of paper from his pocket, read the instructions on it, and quickly disarmed a side alarm.

After flipping on a light, she was astonished. They might as well have been in a bed-and-breakfast, as the place was so beautiful. All wood and white walls, with ultrahigh ceilings. She could see that everything was staged to show off the back and the side of the house, which in the daytime must be magnificent, because it was all glass and windows surrounding them. The furniture, all white with touches of tasteful beige and just a bit of blue and orange for pop, completed the look of the house.

"This is gorgeous," she said.

"It really is," Carter agreed. "It wasn't much when he first bought it. The location was the draw. But Eva really brought it all together. She's . . ." Carter got a faraway look on his face for a moment, which had Leila slightly unnerved.

"She's what?" Leila asked.

He shrugged his shoulders. "Well, I guess she's been good for him." He let out a breath. "Let me go and get the rest of the bags and the groceries."

Leila went out to help. She then followed him into the kitchen, where they found they didn't need all the food they had brought, as the fridge had been stocked. Carter shook his head.

"Eva, I'm guessing," Leila said.

Carter nodded. "More than likely, because I can't think of Aidan being so thoughtful as to stock the fridge. Vin, maybe, since he's a chef, but Aidan, no. His mind just doesn't work that way. She probably had the house-keeper do it. She's thoughtful like that."

"So why is it you're surprised she's been good for him?"

Carter paused. "Oh, I don't know. I guess when you're young, you think you and your boys will hang forever, never change, never be held down. That sort of thing is for the other poor suckers. And Eva, she sort of came out of left field, and it was all kind of my fault. I even almost broke them up. For her to do this for me . . . Well, it's really nice. Maybe it means I really am back in her good graces."

Leila smiled and picked up the note that had been left on the kitchen island, along with flowers from a local florist. She chuck-led as she read it aloud.

Enjoy the weekend, you two. I hope to meet you soon, Leila, and, Carter, no

working. Everything is not about business.
E & A

"I think I like her already," Leila observed.

Carter shook his head. "Yeah, she's cool. A bit tough, so I think you two would hit it off."

Leila couldn't help but wonder why that would matter. Why should she be introduced to the significant others of his friends, get to know his family, form any attachments? What would doing all that do? She knew it was easier to make a break when there were no other parties involved. Leila put the note back and turned away from Carter to pull herself together. She looked around at the well-appointed, but still cozy, living and dining area and saw how the cathedral ceilings afforded a view to the rooms above. She picked up her duffel.

"Care to show me where we'll be sleeping tonight?" she asked.

Carter came around and kissed her on her head, then trailed his kisses lower to her ear, ending the trail at her lips. "I'm so glad to have you here with me," he said, his voice full of a sincerity, which she dared not try to hold on to.

Instead, she gave him a nudge. "Come on. Let's get these upstairs, and then you can show me proof of these skills in the kitchen you keep talking about."

Carter picked her up and placed her atop the marble counter with a sly grin. "Are you challenging me? Because my skills are with more than pots and pans." He nuzzled her neck and licked at the shell of her ear. When his hands came up and his thumb grazed her breast, she let out a moan and pushed him back.

"Oh, no you don't. We're not going at it on these nice people's counter. Upstairs with you!"

The upstairs portion of the house was just as impressive as the downstairs. Carter and Leila took a bedroom on the opposite side of the master suite, one that almost mirrored the master. It had a beautiful high double bed with a canopy and a gas fireplace. There was even a balcony, which had Leila sucking in her breath as she walked out and took in the beauty of the ocean lit by the light of the moon.

Carter came up behind her and wrapped her in his arms. The night was warm, but there was a slight chill coming off the water. Even though it was dark, the lack of electric lights on either side of them made her think the house was pretty isolated.

"My God, it's secluded here. How did he

get this spot?" she said.

She felt Carter shrug against her. "Old money goes far."

Leila tilted her head as she turned around to face him and wrapped her arms around his waist. "Well, it's good to have friends."

Carter frowned. "That it is. Honestly, I don't know where I'd be without my friends. Especially Aidan. Sure, I'd be okay. But his friendship, the connections with his family have afforded me a lot."

Leila shook her head. "I'm starting to know you, and I think connections or not, you'd find your way to the top, Mr. Bain. Now who's not giving themselves enough credit?"

Carter shrugged, looking less his usual dynamic self and now slightly vulnerable. It tugged at her. "I don't know," he said. "Coming from where I do, it doesn't just happen with determination."

"And yet here you are. I don't believe it is just fate and connections that got you where you are or will get you where you're going. You have to know that a lot of it is on you."

Carter smiled. "If you say so, Wifey."

"I do, Hubby. Now let's eat." She pointed to the beautiful moonlit scene of the beach and the surf. "We can revisit this later." She walked back into the bedroom. "And this, too."

Carter laughed. "Okay, Miss Talk a Lot."

Leila headed down the stairs, then looked back at him. "Of course, this all is contingent on your so-called mad cooking skills."

"There you go, daring me again."

Leila grinned. "Maybe I like living on the edge."

"Okay, so you've proven yourself, mister," Leila said. "You've got skills. I'm stuffed."

Carter tried to be humble, but he was feeling a little smug right then. He was passing Leila dishes as she washed. He'd told her he'd wash, but she'd said she wouldn't hear of it after he'd cooked. Sure, he didn't have the professional chef skills in the kitchen of Vin, but he could still burn enough to impress a woman. Leila seemed pretty wowed by his simple seared scallops in brown butter sauce, and he had at least three more dinners in his arsenal that he could impress her with, so this weekend should be a rousing success. At least he hoped so.

He was sure Leila had been wined and dined in some of the best restaurants in the world. But that thought didn't quite bring about the kinds of thoughts he wanted to focus on when he was trying to embrace the idea of Leila as his wife, rather than as just his potential business ally. The idea of her sitting across from some slick talker who just wanted to use her was not particularly appealing. Hell, up until the other day, he would have been that slick talker.

"Hello. Earth to Carter." It was Leila's sharp tone that brought Carter blinking back to focus.

"Huh?"

"Where did you go? There I was, gushing over you, and I lost you. Also, how about handing me that pan? Don't tell me you're already losing interest. I thought we'd at least make it to the old seven-week itch." She grinned at him, letting him know she was joking.

He handed her the frying pan with a soft kiss on her cheek. "I can't imagine ever growing tired of you."

She didn't answer, just grew silent and continued washing. Carter came closer and wrapped his arms around her, but he could feel her closing herself off to him. He wanted more than anything in that moment to pull her back, to keep that door open, to insure he had a chance to win her over. As he kissed the side of her neck, a simple act he knew she thoroughly enjoyed, he could tell that she was holding back. That something was keeping her from letting go and giving herself to him fully, from relaxing and freely taking her pleasure. No, she just continued to wash the same pan, which, he was sure, was clean by now.

So Carter took a hand and brought it under her shirt. The feel of her warm skin was so enticing, he fought back a tremble as he ran a finger over her nipple. Her small shudder was his reward. "Please don't hold back, Leila. Not with me."

She dropped the pan. "I'm all wet." she said. *Here's hoping.*

Carter turned her around and looked into her eyes. The doubt was there, just as he'd suspected, and it was warring with her desire. He knew that no amount of talking would convince her. It would take his action in this moment and every day thereafter. The thought filled him with a certain amount of fear but also excitement. Leila was a challenge he was glad to take up. He moved his hand and brought it around to rub along her spine slowly. He enjoyed the moment when those fine muscles started to relax and yield under his caresses.

"Come, darling. It's been a long day. You must be tired," he said after a moment.

She looked up at him with eyes less doubtful and leaning more into the column of desirous. "Tired, yes, though not too tired."

Leila took his hand and guided him to the stairs. He followed her eagerly as she slowly walked upstairs. His excitement had him feeling like a schoolboy. In fact, he was so excited, he almost passed her on the steps. But in the bedroom he took a much-needed breath and slowed down. He had a while. All weekend and then some.

"Do you want a bath?" Carter asked as Leila reached for the hem of her shirt, removed the shirt, and placed it on the bed.

"That sounds like the second best thing I want right now."

Carter smiled. She really was devastating. "Then you shall have it and then some."

She dropped the pen. "I'm all wet," she said.

Here's hoping.

Carter headed to the bathroom and drew her a bath, making use of the fragrant oils that Eva had supplied, and even lit a few candles and placed them around the tub. When he came back out, she was standing in the middle of the room, before the bed, naked and glorious.

Carter inhaled. "You steal my breath."

She smiled. A sweet sort of half smile that drew him in and broke him apart. "Come and bathe with me. That tub looked like it will easily fit the two of us," she said.

"That is truly the most enticing invitation I've ever received."

Carter stepped into the large egg-shaped tub first and then held Leila's hand as she followed him. He reminded himself to breathe as she lowered her body, the dim lighting and the glow of the candles creating the most intriguing shadows, in the dips and hollows. He wanted to lean forward and bury himself in each and every one.

After coming forward and sitting between his legs, on her knees, Leila took the bar of soap and proceeded to massage him along his neck and chest while looking him in the eye. Her movements were slow and deliberate, and she had him relaxing and turning as liquid as the water between them with each stroke. Carter leaned his back on the edge of the tub and closed his eyes, wanting to imprint the feel of this on his memory forever as he let out a moan.

"You're so beautiful," he heard her say breathlessly.

He brought his head up and met her eyes again, looking for any hint of sarcasm or embellishment, and couldn't find it. Carter shook his head. "I don't know how you can say that . . . or that you even have to. I know

I'm ordinary at best, total mediocre when it comes to standing by you. But thank you. You have a way of making a mere mortal feel like a king."

Leila looked at him seriously. "Don't sell yourself short. You *are* beautiful, and you should feel like a king. There's nothing wrong with that." She leaned into him, and Carter wrapped his hands around her waist, then curved his thumbs up to skim across the delicate underside of her full breasts. She arched her back and leaned forward more. Inched up and stroked his hard erection.

Carter sucked in a breath. *Breathe. Just breathe man,* he silently told himself as he came forward and took one of her perfect nipples into his mouth.

Her head went back, and he looked up the long regal column of her neck. Suddenly he wished he had more hands, tongues, so he could feel her and feast on more of her at once. After bringing a hand up and around to the back of her neck, he pulled her forward, and their lips fused together, the hot water seeming to grow steamier around them.

They were almost fully connected, kissing deep and rocking against each other, the water enhancing the stimuli all the more.

She was amazing, so hot and wet, but still he wanted more. He wanted all of her then and there.

"I need you now, Lei. Right now."

Her voice was a hoarse whisper as it escaped her lips. "Then have me, husband. Take all of me."

Carter stilled and looked her in the eye. There were no condoms in the bathroom, though he had them in his bag in the bedroom. "Are you sure?" he asked. "The condoms are in the bedroom."

She looked at him seriously through her passion-filled eyes. "I'm perfectly sure."

Their earlier car conversation came to mind, and he remembered her seriousness then.

"I want you, Carter." She was close to his ear, her breasts pressing firmly against his body. She pulled back and looked him in the eye. "I trust you." The words once again pierced his core, but she hit him deep once again. "The question is, do you trust me?"

Carter swallowed. No woman had ever asked him to go so far as to trust her, so he'd never really taken that type of leap. At this moment, he and Leila were both partners and adversaries. Two people with both the same and opposite goals. Did he trust her? He didn't know. She gave him no reason not to. Did he trust himself? She was asking for so very much. But for sure, he knew he wanted her. He wanted her now, and he couldn't imagine a time when he wouldn't want her. "Yes," was all he said.

Leila rose, and he shifted to meet her at the juncture of her thighs. She eased forward, sliding down onto him slowly, almost tortuously tight, taking him into her warm center, as he pulled her closer and took her mouth again. Their tongues twined together, their breaths becoming one as their heartbeats became synced in time.

The water sloshed over the edge of the tub, and their movements turned more frantic. Before long, she was arching back, her hair spreading out into the water behind her, as she continued to ride him, and he brought his hands down to her center, where his thumb made small circles on that hard bud of hers. When she began to tighten and quiver around him, her thighs locking against his, Carter threw his head back and gave himself permission to run free. As he bucked up, no longer able to hold back, his hands scaled her body, going up to squeeze her breasts. Everything in him surged to his core, then burst through, from him to her as she shuddered and met him. The two of them clashing in sensual ecstasy.

CHAPTER 23

Leila couldn't believe what she was seeing. How could this be real? But then again, how could she have ever guessed back in that Vegas suite that the dapper guy with the overly cocky attitude could let loose and turn out to be a surfer?

"Whoo-hoo! Go! Ride it. You are amazing!" Leila yelled out to a wave-riding Carter from where she was on the shore. She watched, amazed, as he expertly balanced on the surfboard, dipping and weaving against the force of the sea as it rushed him forward toward the shore. Finally, the wave petered out, and Carter gracefully slipped off the board. Leila's heart, for a moment, dipped in fear, until he came up again with a wave, his smile as bright as could be. Though he'd done it many times already that morning, the act had not yet begun to stop thrilling her. *He* had not yet begun to stop thrilling her, and that in itself was a thrill.

Carter had offered to give her, her first lesson in surfing that morning, but Leila had declined. Stated that her runway clients probably wouldn't take too kindly to her breaking a leg and having to bow out of her upcoming show commitments. Still, she was having so much fun. The house, despite all its elegance, had a downstairs play area that was a big kid's paradise. There was a game room, a media room, and then there was a large mudroom off the deck that led out to the portico and the pool area. In the highly decked-out mudroom was where the surfboards were stored. She had to admit, she really had thought that Carter was embellishing when he'd said he surfed.

She watched as he coolly carried his board under his arm and walked toward her. After shoving it hard into the sand on the side of their blanket, he finally knelt down beside her and kissed her, his cool, wet lips a refreshing balm against the warm sun.

"You were fantastic!" Leila said. "I'll admit when I've been bested. I didn't think you were serious. You really got me on that one."

He grinned and kissed her again. "See there, darling, that will teach you about underestimating me."

Leila pulled a serious face. "I've been properly schooled, sir. Lesson well learned."

Carter gave her a sly look as he licked his lips and moved in closer to her. "I don't know. You don't look like a woman who's learned her lesson. I think you could do with a little more teaching. Perhaps some extra tutoring."

Leila gave him a sly half smile and batted her eyes. "Oh, really, now? Perhaps you're right. I can maybe do with an extra lesson or two." She pushed at his chest, and he fell onto his back on the blanket. She straddled him, then ran her hands up his bare chest while moving her hips seductively in her bikini. "You know, surfing looks to me to be all about balance, and that seems terribly difficult when the sea get all rocky and unpredictable."

Carter smiled as his hands went around her hips and lovingly caressed the round globes of her behind. He rocked up to meet her and bucked against her every thrust. "You seem to have an innate ability, darling. I dare say, you're a natural."

Leila grinned before she leaned down and licked at his lips and then nipped at his bottom lip, causing him to jerk back.

Carter laughed and gave her a playful pat

on her hip before he came up to meet her and quickly flipped her around so that their positions were reversed and she was now the one flat on her back. He felt delicious, all hot from the sun and cool from the sea, as he towered above her, strong and glorious. His head came down, and her arms went up to meet him as her legs wrapped around him, seemingly of their own accord.

"You seemed to forget the unpredictable part, darling."

Leila could not help the giggle that bubbled up in her throat as his lips feasted on her collarbone and the swell at the top of her breasts. "Forget? I'm counting on it, Mr. Bain."

Carter grinned, then leaned forward to kiss her. It was the kind of kiss she was quickly becoming addicted to and could see herself becoming attached to. She ran her hands up his back, loving the sinewy feel of the corded muscles there, then let her hands go farther to the waistband of his trunks, where she trailed her thumb along the edge while her tongue suckled with his.

Rewarded by his deep moan, she smiled. "We're about to get sand in places where it will be very difficult to remove."

Carter pulled back and looked around briefly. "Come, darling," he said, rising up on his knees. "Though we have this section of beach to ourselves, I think we should head in. As you said, sand can be a bitch to get out."

Leila pulled a face. "Not to mention it's the devil on friction."

He laughed and got up, then reached a hand out to help her up. Leila looked around. "You don't think anyone saw us, do you?" she asked.

Carter did a quick scan of the beach; she did, as well. They did seem to be alone on their little stretch, the house being perfectly situated between two rock formations. It was kind of an oasis of dreams.

"No, I think we're good. This is all still just for us, darling, and I'm the happier for it. Besides, Jasper's dude is not scheduled to surface until tomorrow, when we're due to take impromptu walks in town. Dinner and ice cream, or some such thing, looking quaint and cute." He pulled her in and kissed her solidly. "So while I still have you to myself, how about I take you back to the house to continue your lessons?" He ran a hand down her spine, then let it slowly ease around to her behind.

Leila looked at him, losing herself in his eyes. She tilted her head and kissed at his chin. Let her hands explore him freely.

"Let's go. I think there are a few things I might teach you, too, Mr. Smarty-Pants."

Carter knew Leila didn't want to go out, and in truth, he didn't, either. Why would he? Going out would bring the real world into their little slice of paradise. It would bring tomorrow down upon them, and it would also make the bubble of what they shared all the more fragile. Too bad he didn't calculate just how fragile it was.

"Seriously. I think you may be a little overdressed for a casual dinner, Bain," Leila said as they got into his car and headed into town. When he just raised a brow and she shook her head, he couldn't help but laugh.

"There is nothing wrong with my outfit. I've got on a shirt and a pair of pants. Nothing wrong with that. And I've got a beautiful woman on my arm. That's a lot to live up to. A man has to dress to impress."

She slid him a quick side eye, checking out his casual khakis and oxford shirt. He was plenty casual, being that he'd gone and put on soft deck shoes.

"A guy's got to be prepared. You never know who you're going to meet," he added.

For her part, she was more laid back in a flirty cotton skirt with a white tee that skimmed her body perfectly. On her feet she wore casual white slip-on sneakers. Her hair was tousled and sexy as it flowed around her shoulders, and she looked every bit a vision of summer. Carter had to admit they made quite the odd couple. Feeling suddenly self-conscious, he wondered if he had overdressed and if the supposed candid photos would only further the belief that they did not suit each other.

"Stop worrying, hubby. I'm only teasing. I don't care what you wear. Although, the fewer garments in your case, the better, in my opinion."

Carter's snort was swift. "Now who's the sweet talker? Let's go and eat."

Dinner was good — and, thankfully, uneventful — at a local Mexican restaurant. The quaint townspeople, though impressed with the likes of Leila, left them to eat their meal in peace, with only minimal gawking and a few exclamations of "Is that her?" And then, after they were done, they got ice cream at a local shop, where, recognized by some teens, Leila took a few selfies with the kids. On the way home they passed a small fair, and Carter couldn't help but be mesmerized by the way her eyes brightened at the sight of it.

They stopped and played some games. Carter spent too much money on the ring toss and that one where you tried to get balls in a basket that was tilted perfectly so that they would never land in a basket. But all was not lost when Leila bested him in the water balloon game and won her own teddy bear.

"In your face!" she told him.

Carter pulled her down onto his lap while he sat, defeated, on the stool. "You'll pay for this, Wifey," he said, then kissed her playfully.

"Promises, promises," she teased, then pulled him toward the Ferris wheel.

If Jasper's guy was anywhere nearby, taking candid photos of them, he'd hidden himself well, because neither Carter nor Leila could find him. By the time they got back to the house, they were full and happy and had only enough energy left to satisfy each other and fall asleep in each other's arms.

By the time they were heading back to New York, the original purpose of the trip no longer mattered. All that mattered was that they'd taken it together. And made it through.

CHAPTER 24

"I can think of so many more things I'd rather be doing than going to this dinner tonight," Leila said.

"I know, darling. Me too," Carter responded as he put his arm around her and kissed her on the side of her neck. She smiled at him in the bedroom mirror.

The past week had been so lovely that she'd almost let herself forget that first and foremost, they were together as a business arrangement. But this summoning to Everett Walker's place for their supposed wedding celebration dinner just brought home the fact that they were business partners and adversaries. They'd successfully gotten over the disastrous interview with Kit. It seemed that Jasper's guy had been up there in Rhode Island, taking pics of them from somewhere during their weekend away, and he'd caught them dining in town and even frolicking at the fair. He'd snapped some nice candid shots, which "just so happened" to get picked up by all the gossip columns, debunking the narrative of those naysayers who were speculating about the authenticity of their relationship.

When coming home from their blissful weekend, she and Carter had picked up Ollie on the way and had entered the apartment almost like a new family of three. Ollie had even seemed genuinely happy to see Carter. No doubt this newfound love was being fueled by the expensive treats that Carter had picked up for him, but, hey, he was making an effort. And though Carter still kept his things in the guest bedroom, he found his way to her bed every night and woke up with her every morning. The guest bedroom had become a glorified dressing room. Which worked out well, since it was turning out that they had very different tastes when it came to personal space. She was more on the "live and let live" side of things, and he was more of an "every object has its place" kind of guy.

She had thought he would just about pass out when he got his first real glimpse of her bathroom and vanity, with its dizzying array of beauty products strewn about. Not to mention the half-closed drawers of hair extensions and wigs, multicolored pieces that inched out to tease his legs as he walked by. It made her laugh, as well as scared her, when she thought of all they had left to learn and figure out how to deal with if they rode this thing out. But so far they were hanging in.

But tonight would be a big test. It would be his boss and the boss's wife hosting. Plus, Carter's friends Aidan and Eva, Aidan's wife, and also his other friend Vin and Vin's wife, Lily. Carter's parents had been invited, as had Leila's father, Jasper, and Nia. And who else, she didn't even know. She hadn't agreed to the guest list but had found that it was already set in stone when they returned from their long weekend getaway. Everett Walker's heavy hand spread long and wide.

She handed Carter her necklace for him to clasp for her. "This will be a disaster, won't it?" she asked as he wrapped the tiny circle of diamonds around her neck. He finished and turned her around. She hoped the simple white chiffon dress was elegant enough and sent the right signal. Carter had said she looked beautiful, but she wanted to make a good impression on Everett tonight and show a different side of herself than the sexy sidekick she knew he and the other execs saw her as. Her hair was put in as loose chignon, with only a few tendrils loose around her face. She looked into Carter's eyes for reassurance.

He smiled. "I have to admit, darling, it really has the potential to be. Though through no fault of our own. For the life of me, I don't know why Everett would go and invite the parents, too. I wish he hadn't gone and done that. At least he could have consulted with me first. Our families go back, but only because of the friendship between me and Aidan. And he and my parents have never gotten along. My parents always loved Aidan, and I think in a way they resented Everett's and my closeness. They blamed him for me going all corporate capitalist, as my dad calls it."

Leila frowned, then smiled. "Now I'm more intrigued than ever to meet your father."

Carter shook his head. "I'm not, darling. He's going to love you. But don't let him sweet-talk you. Or sway you. He's quite the bullshit artist and ladies' man."

Leila laughed and leaned up to kiss him teasingly. "Is he? Now, why am I not surprised by this?"

They arrived at the Walkers' Park Avenue apartment only a fashionable half hour late, and already there were raised voices.

"Oh, hell," Carter mumbled as he made out the sound of Everett Walker and his father in a heated debate even from where they stood still in the foyer. He looked at the Walkers' longtime butler, Monroe, and raised a brow. "Really?" he asked.

Monroe shook his head, raised a bushy brow back, and gave a sigh. "I'm afraid so."

Carter let out a breath, then turned toward Leila, forcing a smile. He would not get rattled, not yet. The night was still young. "Monroe, may I introduce you to my beautiful wife, Leila Darling?"

Monroe gave an elegant bow and took Leila's hand in his gloved one. "It's so nice to meet you, and may I offer congratulations?"

Carter laughed. "Laying the elegance on a little thick there, aren't you, man?" he asked the older gentleman.

Monroe chuckled. "Have you seen your wife, Mr. Carter? No doubt she deserves that and then some."

Leila laughed. "It's so nice to meet you, Monroe." She then frowned when another voice was added to the argument. "Oh no." She looked at Monroe. "Is my father here, too?"

"Yes, he is, ma'am."

Leila sucked in a breath and turned to Carter. "Guess it's time we joined the fun."

Carter took her hand and led her into Everett's grand salon. He had always loved this room. When he first saw it as a kid of fourteen, he was awed by it. By the fact that one family in New York could have a room of this size just for entertaining, a room that wasn't a public hall. Part of it still boggled his mind. At that time he remembered thinking that his family's apartment could fit in this wood-paneled room three times over. And here Aidan Walker just walked through it like it was nothing on his way to the kitchen for snacks.

As they stood in the entrance to the room, it took a moment for the little ruckus to quiet down. From what Carter could gather that ruckus had something to do with rent stabilization and gentrification, one of his father's favorite fights, and the gleam in his eye told Carter he was having a high time. Carter looked around the room and saw that beyond the assorted family and friends, there were quite a few high-profile clients and would-be investors, including two of the Hills. He felt his ire amp up. How could Everett invite all these people without consulting him? He hated walking into a potential situation unprepared. Just then he felt Leila squeeze his hand.

"You all right, Hubby?" He turned and looked into her bright, shining eyes. "Don't go tensing up on me now," she whispered. "We have to tackle this as a team."

He smiled at her use of the word *team*. The thought of teaming up with her gave him the boost he needed. He leaned over and kissed her softly on the cheek.

"Ahh, there they are! Our guests of honor!" It was Diane Walker, Everett's wife and Aidan's mother. She looked her usual beautiful and timelessly elegant self in her beaded lace cocktail dress, with her hair in its signature bob cut. While she was older, her face was still beautiful and lacked telltale evidence of plastic surgery and fillers, which so many of her peers had made fashionable. Carter took note as she headed their way that she looked relieved to see them both. She clasped both of Carter's hands and pulled him in to kiss him on both cheeks. "It's been too long, Carter. I guess Everett has been keeping you to himself in that damned office, and now that Aidan is all grown up, you've forgotten me."

Carter shook his head. "Never, Mrs. Walker."

She waved a hand and shook her head, then turned Leila's way with a smile. "It's all right, my dear. I've grown quite used to it by now. All my men have deserted me." She gave Leila a wink. "But as they say, life goes on, and I see you've done beautifully." She leaned in and kissed Leila's cheeks. "Come in, darling." Diana giggled at her own joke. She looked back at Leila. "You must get that all the time."

Leila gave her a professional smile. "You'd be surprised."

Everett Walker came their way, both fathers fast on his heels, seemingly jockeying for position as they vied to get to the couple first. Carter saw Leila's eyes widen. He laughed.

"This should be good," he said.

"Well, hello there, newlyweds. Glad you could make it," Everett commented.

Not taking the bait, Leila countered with only a gracious smile and said, "Thank you so much for hosting us. This is wonderful." She turned to her father and grinned wide, happy for his solid presence there. "Daddy."

"Hey, baby girl," John Darling said, bringing his daughter in for a hug. Carter could see Leila melt into the comfort of her father's arms, and in that moment he forgot about the awkwardness of the situation and was just happy that she had the comfort of her family around her.

When she pulled back, Carter cleared his throat. "Leila, I'd like you to meet my father, Malcolm Bain."

Leila turned to his father, whom many called an older version of Carter, only about a million times cooler. The man was Carter's height and was still relatively fit. He had the same brown complexion, deep-set dark eyes, strong nose, and angular jaw, but that was about where the similarities ended. Whereas Carter's skin was smooth and mostly free of hair, his father wore his salt-and-pepper beard with pride. Whereas Carter kept his hair cropped low, his father wore his dreaded and in a long ponytail down his back. The fact that tonight his father was in his version of a suit — matching slacks and a blazer with a Resist Capitalism tee underneath — was a testament to the gravity of the occasion and probably a direct shot at Everett Walker.

Carter watched as his father gave Leila a long up-and-down assessing look and then broke out into a wide smile. "Lord, girl, if I had two lifetimes, I don't think I'd be able to capture the beauty of you on my canvas."

Carter let out a low growl, while Everett Walker snorted beside him. Carter saw a couple of Leila's brothers heading their way. "Seriously?" he said to his father. "You meet your new daughter-in-law and you're putting on the moves? Also nice shirt."

"Thanks, I like it." His father grinned. "And I was just giving her a compliment. Is she not beautiful? Do you not have eyes, or are you so brainwashed by this one that you see only numbers and dollar signs? Besides, I'm a happily married man. And, hell, if I were putting on the moves, you'd be out one wife."

"I'm sure he would be," Leila began, stepping in. "It's wonderful to meet you, Mr. Bain. I can see where Carter gets his good looks and, I dare say, his charm." She looked around the room. "I think Carter and I have some mingling to do. You guys, play nice." Leila pulled Carter by the hand away from the potentially volatile group. "All right," she said, her tone low. "Seven minutes in and we're already up inching up to the near boil point. I think we'd better pace ourselves, or it's going to be the longest night ever."

Carter leaned down and kissed her again. "Thank you."

Leila looked up at him with confusion. "For what?"

"For being you."

They made their way to Greyson and Waymon Hill and their wives.

"Carter," Greyson said. "Look at you, boy." Carter bristled at the slight put-down but let it slide, considering the potential deal on the table. But it still niggled at him, especially since it was said in Leila's presence. "How sly of you to keep something like this under wraps," he said, indicating Leila.

"Something?" Leila said smoothly.

Grayson chuckled. "And she's got fire." He looked Leila's way. "I really like that."

"You always do, my dear. How about you put a lid on it, though, before you embarrass yourself?" Carter raised a brow as the pretty older woman took control. She reached out a hand to Leila. "Clare Hill. So nice to meet you, and this is my husband, Greyson. Excuse him. My brother-in-law Waymon, and his wife, Bonnie. Congratulations. It's so nice to see a young couple starting out. When you get to where we are, you forget the nuances of young love."

Leila shook Clare Hill's hand. "There is nothing to excuse. It's so nice to meet you. This is my" — she looked up at Carter and smiled — "husband, Carter. I have to say that is still fresh and odd for me to say."

Clare gave a laugh. "I'm sure. Well, you enjoy it. I'm sure you'll have plenty of new things on the horizon. But you are young, so take it slow and enjoy it. I'm sure your mother gave you that same advice."

Carter watched Leila's eyes gloss over, and he instinctively rubbed at the small of her back.

Clare got a look of concern. "I'm sorry, dear. Have I put my foot in it?"

Leila shook her head at the woman. "No, you didn't. I lost my mother quite a few years back. It was cancer. They say time heals. They just don't say how much." She smiled as Clare reached out and took her hand.

"Oh, I really am sorry, and there I go, telling Grayson to shut it."

Leila gave the woman a squeeze. "No, you are fine. As a matter of fact, better than fine. I know about your company but more so about your philanthropic pursuits. My late mother was treated in a hospital with a beautiful chemo space with the most wonderful chairs and well-stocked library. For all its sadness and despair, there was a lot done to make it comfortable. I'll never forget the plaque on the door that said 'Wing made possible by Hillibrand Inc.' So thank you from the bottom of my heart. I'm so grateful." She looked at each of the Hills. "Thank you all. I would very much like to get involved if I can in some way. I think now I may be strong enough, and anything I can do to help, I'd be happy to."

Both Clare and Bonnie pulled Leila into a hug.

"We'd love to have you help out in any way possible," Clare said, "Most of our pursuits are done quietly, but if you could help bring in more high-profile names, maybe that could help with donations."

"Yes," Bonnie chimed in. "Getting young people involved could be a wonderful idea, dear."

Carter had not noticed, but his mother had walked up and had caught the exchange. She gave him a small smile and a pat on his arm.

Carter looked at his wife with nothing but pride and joy, but when his gaze shifted, there was Grayson Hill, not taking in the exchange, but giving Everett a knowing look. Carter got a knot in his chest as the original plan came once again to the forefront of his mind. What would Leila think when she found out that the whole impetus for getting her for the *Brentwood* project was to lure in financing from the Hills? The tangled web was turning into a right knotted mess.

As Carter had guessed she would, Leila got along with both Lily and Eva. He watched as she stood in a small triad. The two women were laughing about something, and then their eyes shifted for a moment over to where Leila was. Leila laughed even harder, and for a moment he thought it would be best if he went over to break up the evil little trinity in the making. What must Eva and Lily be telling her? he wondered. They each had their own unflattering stories, but when Leila slipped him a brief soft smile, his momentary fears were squelched. That was until a hand came and clasped him hard by his shoulder.

"Watch out with those moon eyes, C. Someone might get the impression that you actually love your wife." It was Vin.

Carter turned around slowly and gave his old friend a hard glare as he handed him a beer. Aidan was by his side and chimed in.

"Yeah, you definitely wouldn't want anything like that happening. What if the truth got out? You might lose your leverage or something."

"Oh, shut up," Carter said. "As if both of you completely and totally whipped suckers should have anything to say about me. Besides, Leila and I are under no illusion as to what our relationship is about. We are . . ." Carter's voice trailed off as he looked at Leila once more. She was so beautiful in her white dress. Clearly the most beautiful woman in the room and possibly the world, if you asked him. The image of her that morning, as she slept peacefully, came to his mind. She'd rested like an angel on the pillow next to him, the softness of the morning sun turning her face into something glowing and ethereal, almost other worldly in its beauty.

Aidan snapped a finger in front of Carter's eyes. "You were saying something about us being whipped and then . . ."

His friends laughed, and Carter shot Aidan a look, clearing his throat.

"What I was saying is, we are finding this arrangement to be mutually agreeable."

Both Aidan and Vin looked at him with wide eyes and nodded. They clinked beer bottles as Aidan shook his head.

"Never heard it described as 'mutually agreeable,' but here you go. And you can thank me for the use of my house later," he said.

"How's about I kick your ass later?" Carter retorted. "When are you going to grow up?"

Aidan chuckled. "When you admit you're in love with your wife."

Carter sucked in a breath. The enormity of Aidan's words had hit him like a punch in the gut. "Who said anything about love? I mean, well, there are strong feelings, sure. But nobody said anything about love. Besides, I don't even know what she thinks about me. Not really. She likes me, sure. Tolerates me, yes. But, well, further than that, I don't know."

It was Vin who spoke up next. "Well, judging by the way she's looking from you to the entrance and Chloe Caraway, I don't think she's liking anyone all that much."

Carter's eyes shifted to Leila, and he instantly saw her temper flare. His gaze shifted to the vision of Chloe Caraway greeting Everett Walker and Greyson Hill with an easy familiarity that said way too much. "Oh, shit," he said to his friends. "I'm screwed now."

"And not in a 'happy ending' kind of way, either," Vin noted.

"Shut up and drink your beer," Carter growled.

Chapter 25

Freaking Chloe Caraway. Leila woke the next morning with a monkey on her back about the size of a scene-stealing Chloe Caraway, and it was weighing her down. Weighing her down and throwing her off her game. The way the woman kept showing up in her orbit made her feel like she was Chloe magnetized or something. The fact that she'd been invited to the Walkers' dinner party in their honor was just about the last straw, though. It had taken just about all the cool reserve she had stored up for the next ten years not to take the wench into the beautifully appointed powder room and attempt to flush her ass down the toilet.

Chloe had glided into the party last night like it had been organized for her. She'd greeted Everett Walker and Carter with a familiarity that let Leila know they had had many meetings before last night. Leila had immediately felt her *Shadowed Dreams* hopes slipping away, and any hopes of winning the challenge had faded, too. *The challenge.* She had surprised herself by not really thinking about it for a few days, and this night, this shame of a night, had brought it all back. Who was she fooling by playing house with Carter like she was? She had looked around the room last night and had seen her father deep in conversation with Carter's parents and had felt very real pangs of regret. It was even worse that she'd pulled them into this. Though they knew the truth, there would still be some disappointment when it all ended. She'd looked at Chloe, who was chatting easily with the Hills, looking cool and composed. As if she belonged and was born into the Park Avenue world. Yes, it would end. If not soon, when the six months were up, for sure.

"God, I can't stand her," her sister-in-law, Trish, had said as she stood by Leila's side. Trish was Greg's wife, and Leila loved her like crazy.

"Me neither," her new friend Eva had said, steadily climbing the ranks to BFF status.

"Who does she think she's fooling with that act of hers? Nobody with a lick of sense . . . ," Lily said, chiming in.

Leila smiled. That was it. Would it be rude

if she kissed these women? Got them all matching pins? "You know, you all are the best," she said.

Eva shrugged. "We're just making observations."

"Yep," Trish said. "As is that woman, Clare, over there. And if Miss Chloe doesn't watch the flirty hands, and if the Hill man doesn't watch the eyes, they're both going to have a problem."

Leila grinned now as she thought back to their kindness at the party the evening before. As far as squads went, hers was shaping up quite nicely. But still she felt off as she made her way into improv class. Shelley picked up on it right away in her workshop. When you were with Shelley, it was showtime, and for her, the show must go on regardless. She did not care a fig about anything personal going on in anyone's life, and she wasn't about to hear anything about the likes of a little thing like Chloe. Hell, it was well documented that the woman went onstage and performed her most famous one-woman comedic play flawlessly the night she found out her father died. There were no excuses in Shelley's world. You took an adversity and you used it to your advantage.

So that was what she would do. They were

currently doing an improv, four-person skit, so Leila decided to take on the persona of an over-entitled, over-indulged millennial who was new to her gentrified neighborhood and who couldn't wrap her head around the fact that the bodega on the corner didn't carry Brie for her favorite grilled cheese.

Leila was sure her fellow cast members thought she was crazy, but she had fun with it. Though, that fun was short lived when Shelley called her aside and asked her to stay a few minutes at the end of class.

Openmouthed, Leila looked at the woman, all thoughts of Chloe flittering away on a cloud of her dreams coming true. "Me? Really?" Leila said. "You want me?"

Shelley smiled. "Of course I do," she said in all seriousness, but her eyes were soft. "As I know many others will, but I'm no fool. I want to say I was one of the first to see your greatness. There is a unique talent in you. And not only do you have the talent, but you also have the fire. You'll make me proud." Shelley paused. "That is, if you'll do it. It will take a lot out of your schedule for those weeks and the weeks before with rehearsals."

"Do it?" Leila looked at the woman as if she'd gone mad. "Of course I'll do it. I'll make it work. Whatever it takes. I want this."

Shelley smiled. "I'm glad. What I'm considering will showcase your innate comic ability and will also bring forth your dramatic talents."

Leila felt tears prick at the backs of her eyes, and Shelley pulled her into a hug. "Oh, honey, don't you cry now." She pushed her back and looked at her.

Leila sniffled. "It's okay. I promise the only tears you'll see from now on will be at your direction. Just let me enjoy these a moment longer."

She left Shelley's studio, bursting to tell her father and Jasper, and feeling a deep pang that she couldn't share this with her mother, but more than anything, she couldn't wait for Carter to get home that night so that she could share the news with him.

Carter was near seething as he sat in Everett's office. He should be thanking him for the lovely party he'd thrown for him and Leila the night before, but instead, he couldn't help the rage he felt over being blindsided by having the Hills and Chloe at the party.

Though he tried his best to temper his words, he couldn't help that they came out with clipped annoyance, exposing his anger simmering just below the surface. And more than anything, he didn't want to give Everett the upper hand by letting him know just how angry he truly was. But the fact remained that he was. Though it might have seemed like a good business maneuver in Everett's eyes, it was a slap in the face to Leila.

Carter let out a breath as he crossed and uncrossed his legs slowly while sitting opposite the older man. "I really would have appreciated it if you'd have run it by me. Though, we are grateful for the party and the 'official' couple coming-out, as it were." He waved a hand over the press pieces filled with tidbits about the party that had made it into the papers. "I could have used a heads-up on the Hills being there. They are integral to the success of Sphere, and that's my baby."

Everett nodded. "It very well may be, but you have to remember this whole company is under my jurisdiction, and there are more things to consider besides your little offshoot. Much more advertising to get. Besides, from what I see, things seem to be getting quite complicated where you and Leila are concerned."

Carter frowned. "And you thought inviting someone like Chloe Caraway to our party would help things? Sir, my wife is a lot of things, many of them amazing, but be assured, stupid is nowhere on the list. Your inviting Chloe was a direct insult. And now that the gossips have picked it up, that makes it even worse. She knows that Chloe is her direct competition for *Shadowed Dreams.*"

Everett looked at Carter seriously. "And you should make it clear to her that she's not in contention for *Shadowed Dreams.* We've tapped Chloe for that. We want Leila for *Brentwood.* She's not in competition for anything."

Carter let out a low breath, then looked back at Everett. "I'm not so sure that's the right decision now."

Everett raised his brow. "Is it you or your dick that's not sure?"

Carter's hands seemed to tighten into fists on their own. He told himself to breathe and to remember that the older man was his boss, his mentor. He steadied his voice before speaking. "You know I respect you and always have, but I'd appreciate the same type of respect from you when speaking to me." Carter rose, wanting nothing more than to get out of the older man's presence. "Now, you hired me to do a job, and that was to position Sphere to be a powerhouse primetime network, and I have not forgotten that."

Everett rose, too, then leaned forward across his desk and looked Carter in his eye. "I also hired you to get me the right talent in the right positions, and that includes Leila Darling in the lead role for *Brentwood.* So you damned well better make it happen. I'd like you not to forget how much I've done for you over the years, Carter."

Suddenly, Carter wanted to laugh and call Aidan to apologize for brushing him off when he'd griped about dealing with his father. He smiled at Everett. "And I'd appreciate you doing the same, sir. Now, if you'll excuse me, I have work to do." He turned on his wing tips and headed out the door, hoping more than anything that he hadn't overplayed his hand. He knew both Everett and the Hills still wanted Chloe, and part of him still thought Chloe might be best, but his gut just wouldn't let that decision lie. Was Everett right? Could Carter be thinking with a part of his anatomy that was a lot farther south than his head? Maybe it wasn't his head at all that was leading the way in this endeavor.

Chapter 26

Fashion Week was exhausting, but Leila wasn't jaded enough to be over the thrill and the exhilaration of it all. She and Carter were back on track or as on track as they could be after the Walker party. She had sent a box of cigars to Everett Walker and flowers to his wife as a thank-you. She'd gotten a surprise invitation to lunch from Lily and Eva, which pleased her, but she had to admit it also filled her with a certain amount of trepidation. She couldn't shake the feeling that a shoe was about to drop and she needed to be in position to catch it. Leila had accepted the women's invitation but had put the lunch off until after Fashion Week. She was constantly on the go and barely had time to come up for air.

Thankfully, she also barely had time to let it register that she and Carter were back on slightly unstable ground, where they were trying to be normal but both knew that there was something bubbling just below the surface, that could break though at any moment and burst it all apart. Carter was back to working late hours, though with her getting ready for Fashion Week, it wasn't like she should really notice. She had noticed. As had Ollie, who'd taken to waiting by the door even when she was home.

"Don't you go getting too attached. This deal is still purely probationary," Leila had said the other night, while enjoying a dish from the latest round of meals Carter's mother had dropped off. That night she'd feasted on a paella that was out of this world. The woman could really make a mint on home delivery. If she and Carter didn't work out, she was going to probably miss his mother the most.

Leila had tried to wait up that night, but she'd been exhausted and had had an early call, so her only contact with him that night had been when he came to her bed, warm and solid, and pulled her body in close to his. She'd turned and molded into him easily and wordlessly, and when his mouth had come down on hers softly, she had sleepily, but happily, opened herself to him and taken what he offered. And given as good as she got, afraid these moments were numbered and the countdown clock had begun ticking.

But in this moment now, with the buzz of the backstage frenzy, Leila pushed those thoughts aside and let herself get swept up in the moment. The magic of turning forty models into radiant beings for a mere fifteen minutes — an endeavor that had the potential to change the direction of fashion trends for the next year or more — had always amazed her.

So far it had been a whirlwind week. She'd been running from show to show, but the schedule was finally winding down for her with Donetta's show. Her finale dress was a showstopper, and in the final fitting, it fit her like a dream. She had only two changes in this show, at the opening and the closing.

During the walk-through with the music, she felt like some sort of a rock and roll, rebel angel in the bejeweled confection that was her dress. It was so light that she felt she could almost float away in it and fly to another land. She was even more excited since Carter had promised to make it to this show, her final one of the week. He had seemed truly happy for her when she told him about getting into Shelley's showcase, and for the first time, for a moment, she had dared to think she had someone besides

Jasper, Nia, and her friends and family to share her joyful news with.

"You looked gorgeous." It was Carter.

She turned where she stood, awaiting her place in line, but was careful not to ruin the lines of the outfit she was wearing for the opening of the show. She smiled but still admonished him, saying, "You are supposed to be out there. I didn't want you to see me yet."

"Don't worry. I'm hardly looking," he said with a smile. "I just wanted you to know I'm here."

Leila smiled wider, happier than she thought she could be. "You're here."

Carter leaned in to kiss her but then paused just short. "Your lipstick."

Leila leaned forward the rest of the way. "Fixable. This is all fixable." She kissed him hard before watching him walk away to take his seat out front by Jasper.

Now she was truly ready. But as the houselights flickered, there was a bit of a commotion as she heard the distinct sound of camera shutters going off. Donetta looked out front through her side view. She then stepped back with a wide smile.

"We are ready. Showtime, all! Look alive," she announced. She looked at Leila and gave her a wink as the music cued up.

Leila stomped out to the hard-pounding music and felt alive. She hit her mark and looked toward the seat she knew was Carter's, fully expecting him to have all eyes on her. And there he was, only he seemed to be seething, the anger nearly radiating off him, and his attention was directed elsewhere. She hit the final mark, posed for the photographers, and then trained her eye on Carter, wondering what had gotten him in such a state. Finally, she focused. Miles. There he was, leaning back in his chair, with a girl on either side of him. It wasn't lost on her that they practically looked like literal clones of her. Miles was wearing shades and flashed Leila his dark smile and gave a nod, leaving no one to question his reason for being there.

Leila fought to keep her expression expressionless. *What a jerk.* He'd never shown any interest in fashion, and she knew he could not have come to this show without the express invitation of Donetta. Once again, she felt used. She didn't know how she did it, but she made her way backstage again and nearly ripped her outfit off her body even before her dresser could.

"You were perfect, darling. Now into the chiffon," Donetta said, as if Leila had not seen what she just saw.

Leila looked at the woman like she was crazy. "What is Miles doing here?" she said.

"I don't understand. This is a fabulous turnout. You should be thrilled so many celebrities are here. We are turning them away at the door. You should see who is not here and is trying to get in." She looked down at the dresser. "Please hurry with her. We don't have long." She looked at Leila. "Darling, come on. There is no time to discuss this. We have a show to do."

Leila watched as Donetta hurried more models as she was zipped into her dress. Her makeup was touched up, and her hair was teased higher. Suddenly, she was back under the hot lights, to the applause of the crowd. Then, the music changed and the crowd went wild as the distinctive beats of "Darling Leila" came on. Everyone started to cheer. The screen behind her flashed, and more than anything, Leila wanted to turn and run backstage. Rip the dress off and be done with it. But she was on. She had to take this walk. Taking a breath, she marched. Told herself the woman in that song was no one. Just a made-up character. Someone they wanted her to be, not the woman she ever was or would ever be. She looked at Carter and saw not anger now but deadly rage in his eyes.

What now? It was she more than anyone who was being humiliated up there, and if she could get through this, then, damn it, so should he. But when she got to the end of the runway, turned, and glimpsed her first image on the screen, she saw it. It wasn't just that the song was playing. Miles had put "Darling Leila" in video form and had simulated sex with one Leila look-alike after another to the track of his wacky-ass song. She could barely move another step as the photographers caught her every grief-stricken moment. Finally, she did move and turned to Carter, her dress no longer float-ing around her but dragging her down with its heavy weight. He stepped forward onto the stage as she mouthed over the noise of the music, "I'm sorry."

After taking her hand in his, he kissed it. "You don't have anything to be sorry for," he told her. It was then that Carter looked Miles' way. Miles was standing, grooving to the music. Lip-synching the words in time to the beat. "He, on the other hand, is another story."

Leila wasn't fast enough, and she didn't know if she really wanted to be. But Carter was off the stage and on Miles before she could stop him. The fight was short and swift, both men barely getting off any punches, but from what she saw, Carter's agility got the best of Miles. Donetta's rantings of her show being ruined fell on deaf ears after her stunt. She quieted down quickly when Jasper brought up the possibility of her being sued for exploiting Leila in such a way. Using Leila had worked out smashingly for her. Donetta was getting the most press at this year's Fashion Week.

Leila was a ball of tangled nerves. How could she not have seen this coming? She should have known there would be something else. Other shoes always dropped in her world. Though Miles wasn't going to press charges against Carter, spouting some code about snitches, Leila figured he would probably try to sue Carter, since money was always his endgame. At the least, he'd come out with some weak social media dis to save his cool image.

How could she have dared to think it would be easy for someone like her to make a fresh start? Leila wondered. In that moment, it was as if Operation Image Makeover had failed miserably.

Maybe she could order Carter a T-shirt with the message I WENT TO VEGAS, AND ALL I GOT IS A HOT-MESS WIFE.

CHAPTER 27

"Come on, girl. It's time for you to saddle up and get back on the horse," Nia said, delivering one of her motivational speeches.

They were at Leila's place, each enjoying a pint of chocolate ice cream as therapy, but Nia was ready to call an end to the pity party. "Come on, hon. Enough of this. So you had a little blip."

Leila dropped her spoon in her pint and looked at Nia. "I swear, woman, your talent for downplaying astounds me. A blip? Tripping on the runway is a blip. A major one, but a blip. But having your ex premiere his smash video, in which he simulates multiple sex acts involving women who are made up to look like you on a screen, while you're walking the runway? Well, that's more than a freaking blip. That is an 'off the Richter scale' earthquake."

Nia sighed. "Okay. I'll admit it's a bit of a quake. But not one you can't recover from.

Miles showed his ass. Royally. Donetta too. And now they are both pariahs in their field for it."

"And what about me? What will people think of me now? I was supposed to be making my image better, not worse. Not to mention Carter's reputation. With this disaster, I'll be lucky if they don't take that stupid comedy off the table."

"Well, has he said anything about taking it off the table?"

Leila frowned. "No, but he's not that type. I don't think he would say it. At least not yet. Not now while I'm down. But still, I can tell he's disappointed."

Nia shook her head. "He's probably just pissed." Leila groaned, and Nia reached out to take her hand. "It's not like that. It's that he's probably so pissed at Miles. I don't know what's really going on with the two of you, but I know it's getting serious. He feels for you, and it's not just business. He was seriously wanting to pummel that guy, and not for embarrassing him, but for hurting you."

That realization stopped Leila cold. Could what Nia was saying be true? She knew she wanted to kick Miles's ass for so many reasons, for embarrassing her, for potentially derailing her plan, but mostly, she knew that when she saw the hurt and anger on Carter's face, she wanted to kick Miles in his ass for putting that pain there. When she had taken those vows on a bet or whatever, she had still become Mrs. Carter Bain, and that meant something. That came with a certain amount of responsibility to live up to her and his name.

Suddenly, Leila felt like she had to redeem herself. But how, she didn't know. She looked at Nia. "Time to get back to work, you say. What type of bookings have been coming in?"

Nia smiled. "Well, for one, we need to respond to Shelley and her winter play contract calls."

Leila's jaw dropped as tears came to her eyes. "You mean to tell me she didn't pull it off the table after this mess?"

"Of course she didn't. She wanted us to tell you she still wants you and believes in you."

Leila smiled brightly, feeling it down to her heart for the first time. "That's amazing. Now what else?"

Nia grinned. "Oh, honey. We're about to have a good time, and the best is Jasper is going to have to give me a raise because of this one."

Leila gave her a high five. "I'll be sure he does."

Carter was shocked to find Leila up and smiling and in the kitchen when he got home. After the fiasco at the show, she'd dramatically taken to her bed for a while. He hadn't blamed her. The whole scene had been so embarrassing, and he wished more than anything that he'd gotten a few more blows in with that ass Miles. He could take a lot, but seeing the pain in Leila's eyes as she stood on that runway had just about done him in. Miles had had the nerve to try some shit about suing him, but he had gotten lawyers to squelch that right quick. Carter had threatened to countersue him for damaging his reputation and for slandering his wife, and he'd warned that Leila stood to take a piece of the profits, if not all, from "Darling Leila."

When he'd told Leila all of that, it hadn't raised her spirits much. He'd been trying all his best moves to bring her out of her depressed mood. Then, finally, after a blessed visit from Nia, she had seemed to bounce back, if not to her normal self, then to a version of herself. A woman driven and on a mission. Suddenly, it was as if their roles were reversed, with her spending long hours working with Shelley Atwood on her upcoming winter production or doing the rare print campaign.

Carter was excited for her and the show. He could see she enjoyed acting and it gave her an energy that her other work didn't. Though, he could admit to himself a certain sense of dread over the upcoming show, because with it would also come the end of their six months. And decisions had to be made. Hard decisions. He'd had a lot of blowback at work over his altercation with Miles G. His only saving grace had been Aidan, who had brought home to Everett how Leila had come out with even more fans than ever due to this altercation, and how they would look terrible as a company if they didn't stand by her and Carter during this time.

Tonight, as Carter sidestepped Ollie and looked at his pretty wifey, he sniffed the air. "Hey, darling. Did my mom stop by with a care package?"

Leila gave him a cheeky grin. "No, she did not, though I did consult her."

Carter raised a brow and looked from left to right, making an exaggerated face. "You didn't?"

She nodded playfully. "Oh yes, I did."

He dropped his bag on the couch, then

ran into the kitchen, past her, and lifted the lids on the pots on the stove. There was his favorite — seared steak with mushrooms and wild rice. He closed the lids and took Leila in his arms. "What did you do all this for? You know you don't have to cook for me."

She shrugged, looking up at him, those brown eyes going to his very soul. "I didn't cook for you. I cooked for us. Now, go wash your hands and let's eat."

Carter felt like an idiot for feeling so happy over this small act of domesticity. For a moment, he questioned himself. He didn't want to be one of those guys, but damn it, he liked it and couldn't deny it. He liked seeing her when he got home, going to sleep with her in his arms at night, and waking with her in the morning. As he rinsed his hands, he looked at himself in the bathroom mirror, half expecting to see someone else looking back at him. But no, it was still him. It was just the inside that had changed.

As Leila lay back on the couch, full and supremely relieved that her dinner had turned out well, Carter rubbed her feet and she considered how easily she could get used to this. Her husband really did have very talented hands. He rubbed gently but deeply, hitting all the right spots, and when he hit one, the sensation went clear from her foot up her leg to her very core. She arched her back and moaned.

"I swear, Mr. Bain, you keep that up and you're going to have me screaming your name."

He grinned and looked at her with a devil-ish glint in his dark eyes. "Well, then, let me continue for sure. If I knew this was all it took, I wouldn't have been working so hard in the bedroom."

She kicked her foot out at him playfully. "Don't you dare. No need to go messing with perfection."

Carter grinned wide. "Perfection, you say?"

Leila's eyes went wide as she shook her head. "Wait a minute. I don't think I said *perfection*. I think the word I was looking for was *adequacy*."

"Oh, I know what I heard, Wifey." Carter tickled her foot, causing her to giggle and kick and Ollie to start to jump and bark. Carter crawled on top of her, tickling her sides while kissing on her neck. She laughed even harder when Ollie jumped on his back to nip at his ear.

"Oww! Ollie, no. I'm not hurting her! I love her!"

Both Leila and Ollie froze. Eyes going wide. Leila stared at Carter, her heart beating so hard she thought he might feel it. She pushed at his chest. "Move please. I can't breathe."

He pushed back, got off her, and sat back on his side of the couch.

She looked at him. "Why would you go and say that?"

Carter shook his head. "I don't know, Leila. I've never said it before. Is telling a woman you love her something you plan? Something you have to have a reason for?"

She jumped up, her anger simmering. "Yes. I want a reason, damn it. Why?"

Carter got up and started to pace. "God, woman, you are crazy. Who needs a reason when they say 'I love you'? You either love someone or you don't, and I said, 'I love you.' You want a reason? Fine. It's all your fault. You cooked the damn steak. Why did you go and do that?"

Leila's mouth dropped open. "The *steak*? You love me because I cooked the steak?"

"Well, you asked for a reason. That one is as good as any, isn't it?"

Leila threw her hands up, willing her unshed tears not to fall. "Well, you can better believe that's the last damn steak I cook for you, mister!"

Carter let out a low groan. Then a slow breath. "So why did you do it?"

"Do what?" she asked.

"Cook tonight."

Leila folded her arms then and sat back on the couch. "You know what? This is a stupid fight. Let's just forget it even started." She started to get up to go to the bedroom and just forget it all, but he pulled her to him, forcing her to look him in the eye.

"No, no, we're not going to just forget this. You can just forget that I told you I love you? Now, why did you make the damn dinner? Tell me!"

"Because . . ." She felt her lip start to tremble and willed it to just stay the hell still. "I thought if we made it to Thanksgiving, it would be nice if I could make you something, so that it's not just your mother doing all the cooking. I had this stupid fantasy about all of us together for the holiday. I haven't contributed to a Thanksgiving meal since my mother died. Usually, we went out, and since my brothers are married, we now do Thanksgiving at their homes." She felt herself choking on her words and hated how ridiculous she sounded. "It was stupid. I know it now."

"Shh," Carter said, pulling her in tight. "It is not."

She tried to pull away. "But it is. Our challenge portion of the bet will be over, and you'll be free to go whatever way you want, and so will I."

He looked down at her. "Well, I just told you I loved you, so I don't see myself running for the hills anytime soon. Now, I'm not asking you to tell me you love me back. Just you thinking about spending a potential holiday with me, my darling, is enough for me right now."

Leila let out a breath as he kissed the top of her head, and she leaned into his chest. Let his solid warmth soothe her. Finally, her breathing slowed, and she took him by the hand. "Can we just go to bed?"

"Darling, where you go, I go."

Leila smiled at his easygoing words, which were meant to soothe her in her distress. Carter always seemed to know the right words to say. While his tactfulness used to make her distrust him, now, for the most part, it soothed her, though it did cause a small part of her to be scared to death.

"Besides, I still owe you an ending to that massage," he added.

When they made love that night, all the jokes and the pretense were gone. Carter could barely breathe as he kissed along every curve of her body, worshipping her as the woman he'd now fully admitted to loving. He still couldn't believe he'd let that slip. Not that he'd thought about it. Much. He'd like to blame Aidan and Vin. Ever since the dinner party and all their ribbing about the way he'd looked at Leila and all their talk of love, he couldn't get the word *love* out of his head. And then he'd gone and driven the idea home by losing his cool with Miles at Donetta's show, but honestly, he hadn't been able to help himself. Just the thought of her being exposed like that and hurt by that ass's actions had made him want to punish someone bad.

But Carter couldn't hide what his admission had done to Leila. She wasn't ready to accept his love or to admit that she might love him back. Who knew? Maybe she never would be. Not fully. And with the way negotiations were going at work with Sphere and the shows, she might good and well walk away from the idea of loving him forever.

Everett was now, for some reason, fully committed to the idea of Chloe for *Shadowed Dreams,* even without having her take a test. Carter had hoped to at least get Leila in for a test, but it wasn't working out. He had a feeling that Grayson Hill was behind this push for Chloe, since he'd heard rumors about Chloe finding her way to Tennessee and Grayson taking work trips to both New York and LA. He was sunk. How had it got to this point? Carter had never been in a business predicament that he couldn't think or negotiate his way out of.

He felt Leila tap him on his shoulder. "Where did you go?"

"Nowhere, darling," he said, loving looking at her beautiful eyes in the moonlight as she wrapped her long legs around his waist. "Nowhere. I'm right here with you."

Carter angled his body and placed himself at her center. He kissed her deeper, entered her in one long, swift stroke. As he suckled on her tongue, he matched each tongue stroke with a long stroke down below, until she was worked into a frenzy, as he was, and he felt the beginnings of her telltale quiver.

"Let go with me, darling. Don't hold back. Please let go," he whispered close in her ear.

Leila tightened around him even more, causing him to burst forth unexpectedly, while she breathed out a yes, which he imprinted on his heart as a promise of having her heart forever.

CHAPTER 28

Leila was so nervous, she thought she might throw up. But as she sat at her tiny dressing-room table at the Sixtieth Street Playhouse, she worked hard to will herself not to. She could do this. She would do this. She chanted her little mantra to herself one last time before getting up to go out and peek at the house through the side of the curtains.

It was full, though why she was surprised by this discovery, she didn't know. She knew tonight's opening performance was already a sellout. Hell, she had sold a quarter of the tickets herself, and what she hadn't sold, she had a feeling her father had to all the guys working security for him. She smiled at that. At the very least, she could expect applause by intimidation. Joey and Rocko were not going to let anyone get out without a standing ovation, forced or not.

With one last glance out at the house, though, she let out a small hiss. "Shit."

"What is it now?" Nia said from over her shoulder. "You can't be cursing and getting all pissed. You're about to go on and be all magical. What's got your undies in a bunch?"

Leila crossed her arms and tilted her head. "Chloe mother freaking Caraway is here."

Nia pulled a face. "That bad penny? Okay, it's getting damned near desperate with her. Well, you pay her no mind. Because from what I hear, she's on her last leg and is about near out of options. Turns out Daddy isn't funding her lifestyle anymore, so she's on the lookout for a benefactor. I'd pay her no mind. Tonight is your night. Your chance to meet your destiny."

Leila smiled. Nia was right. This was her night, and there was no way she was letting a pseudo-wannabe ruin it. Tonight she was playing the part of Leslie Hunter, a role that Shelley had written with her in mind. Leslie was a single mother who ran a last-stop bar, and two men who frequented the bar were in love with her, but she was broken and didn't have room in her heart for either of them. It was a role that demanded lots and left no room for the likes of Chloe and her brand of bullshit. She gave Nia a hug. "Thanks, friend. You're right."

Nia gave her an incredulous look. "I know it."

Leila snorted. "And humble, too. Now, go out and enjoy the show." She looked out at the house once more. "Oh, and keep an eye on Jasper. I don't trust him to not be out there dealing my next two years away."

Nia nodded. "I'm on it."

With a last glance, Leila saw Carter and smiled. The warmth of his love filled her with energy, as well as fear. She'd try her best to use it all. He was with his parents and was now helping his mother to her seat. He'd come backstage earlier with flowers, but she'd shooed him away, citing her need to concentrate. And she did need to do exactly that. She didn't need him clouding her thoughts. Tonight was too important. If she failed, she'd never be considered a serious actress. Suddenly, the warning houselights flickered, and Leila considered for a moment making a run for it. Instead, she gave herself a last once-over and then took her mark.

"You were amazing!"

"Bravo!"

"A star is born, darling!"

Leila accepted her congratulations with pride and a bit of disbelief. Did she really just get through that? Part of her didn't believe it, but the adrenaline of the night was wearing off, turning to tiredness, and she was about ready to go home to replay it in her mind from the comfort of her bed and the security of Carter's arms.

Leila posed and took pictures with her cast mates in the restaurant where they awaited the reviews and celebrated the first show. There was a loud cheer when the reviews finally came in, and Leila's heart was near bursting when Carter took her into his arms and spun her around.

She and Shelley posed for a few final photos, and though Leila was wired, now exhaustion was sinking in. After the photos, she looked around and noticed Carter was gone. She thought about texting him but decided he was probably out at the coat check, getting her wrap so they could go home.

"I'll just head him off at the pass, and we can slip out," she mumbled to herself as she headed toward the restaurant's coat check. If she wasn't so tired and hadn't consequently lost her sense of direction, she probably wouldn't have even seen them, but she was and she did.

There was Carter, not at the coat check, but in another little alcove entirely, and he was huddled close with none other than Chloe Caraway. So close that upon first glance, Leila thought they were about to kiss, but then, no, out of the shadows stepped Everett Walker, and she heard the words plain as day as he wrapped his arm around Chloe's shoulder.

"I look forward to having you on board with *Shadowed Dreams.* I know you'll make it a hit."

Shoes. They kept dropping.

Leila stepped forward. "Well, I'm glad that's settled and we don't have to pretend anymore."

Carter's shocked expression let her know she was the last person he wanted to see in that moment. His mouth fell open, but no sound came out. He just looked at her, then turned back to Everett with sharp eyes.

"What, Carter? No perfect words now? Let me help you out." Leila looked at her watch. "We still have a few minutes left on our part of the bet, so guess what? I'll bow out. You win." She looked at Chloe. "Congratulations. I'm sure you'll be . . . more than adequate."

With that, Leila left the party, forgetting about her wrap and heading out into the coolness of the curb. Warmed by her anger and the energy of the still busy New York street, she tried to hail a cab going south on Ninth Avenue. Impatient and too angry to fight for a cab, Leila started walking. She walked and walked, and finally made it to her apartment, where she kicked off her heels as Ollie barked and jumped at her legs.

"I am an idiot for walking in those damned shoes, Ollie. Sorry, it's late, sweetie, and I just can't love on you tonight," she said tiredly.

"What about me?" came a reply from deeper inside the apartment. "I'm an idiot, too."

"What about you?" Leila let out a snort. "I think you know the answer to that. You won and bested me, so you've shown you're not an idiot. You'll be just fine on top with Chloe. She'll do you well for a while. Besides, she's used to picking up after me," Leila said, heading farther into the apartment and over to where Carter was in the kitchen. She put her hands on the counter to steady herself. "So what are you doing here, anyway? You heard me back at the restaurant. I'm out, and you won. So cheers to you. There was no reason for you to come here and gloat."

Carter looked at her straight on. "What if I don't accept you bowing out? What if I don't want this win from you?"

Leila let out a sigh. "That's not for you to say. Besides, why would you not? Chloe is who you wanted from the beginning."

Carter shook his head and groaned. "I don't know. Maybe you *are* an idiot, and it has nothing to do with your choice of tight shoes."

Leila balked. "Screw you, Carter Bain! Do not insult me or my footwear," she yelled, coming over to poke him in the chest.

He took her pokes with barely a flinch. "This is what I'm talking about. You just insulted your shoes yourself, but I can't? And why are we talking about stupid shoes? Don't you get the fact that I could give a rat's ass about Chloe Caraway? You are always who I wanted. For the show and for my life."

"Well, what if what you want doesn't fit in with what I want?" she challenged.

"Then I guess what I want has to shift, because I'm not losing you. No way, no how." He paused for a moment. "If you want a chance at *Shadowed Dreams,* then take it. It's yours. I've made it clear to Everett that you should have a shot at that show. I've also made it clear that you don't want to work with the Swoops. Though, they have agreed to consult with you to talk about *Brentwood* and the direction. You are in the driver's seat for both shows. You've more than proven yourself with your acting chops tonight."

Leila looked at him skeptically. "Wait. Why is that? This doesn't fit in with what Everett Walker wants for the shows."

"Well, it's a good thing that Everett still listens to the public, their opinions, and the way Chloe played with our independent polling was not what he expected. He and his associates also listen to the opinions of their wives, and I'll just say that Chloe took a few work-related trips with Mr. Hill, and his wife didn't appreciate it. So now Everett is willing to look at other options. And even if he wasn't, I made it clear that *I* was. At other networks."

Leila looked at him, shocked. Not by the Chloe revelations. She already knew that the woman was a user and that she would play out. No, she was shocked by the fact that Carter would put his beloved job on the line for her. "You really said that? For me?"

"Of course, I'd do that and then more. If these shows come between us, then I pick us. There will be other jobs, but no other you." He grinned. "Though, I will say. I'm glad Mrs. Walker was there to vouch for me. Seems the visit I had with her the week before reminded her that I was like a son, so she reminded Everett that family watches out for family."

Leila shook her head. She didn't know what to do or how to process tonight. It seemed like she was possibly getting all she wanted in this deal, but still there was the matter of their six months being up. The fact remained that they were still married and had some decisions to make.

"Darling, you know I can see those wheels turning in that beautiful head of yours." He reached into his breast pocket and pulled out a deck of cards. "Come on. One more hand. Double or nothing. I win, I get six more months. You win . . ." He paused, thinking of the right words to say. "You get six more months."

Leila shook her head. "Carter, that's ridiculous. What you just said has you getting six more months either way."

He grinned and took her in his arms. "Haven't you figured me out yet, darling? Though I always stand by my word, I don't play fair. When I make a bet, I can just about guarantee I'm gonna come out the winner. But lucky me, it's a win-win when it comes to you."

Leila smiled and leaned in to kiss him, almost. "No, a win-win is you loving me completely and me giving you all that love right back. Loving you is me finally winning. And I do love you, Carter Bain."

"Wifey, that's all I need to hear."

She kissed him then and was instantly taken back to that first kiss in that Vegas hotel room all those months ago, when sparks went off, letting her in on the secret of what married kissing was all about.

ABOUT THE AUTHOR

A former fashion designer, **K.M. Jackson** won a New Jersey Romance Writers' Golden Leaf Award for her novel *Bounce.* A long-time member of Romance Writers of America, she received the New York Chapter's 2014 Golden Apple Award for Author of the Year. Currently she resides in the suburbs with her husband, twins, and her precocious terrier named Jack — who always keeps her on her toes. More about her work can be found on her website at KMJackson.com, or follow her on Twitter @kwanawrites.